A
Desolate
Splendor

A
Desolate
Splendor

a novel

JOHN
JANTUNEN

ECW PRESS

Published by ECW Press
665 Gerrard Street East
Toronto, Ontario, Canada, M4M 1Y2
416-694-3348 / info@ecwpress.com

Cover design: Michel Vrana
Cover image: Leander Nardin/Stocksy
Author photo: Jeremy Luke Hill

This is a work of fiction. Names, characters, places, and incidents either are the product of the author's imagination or are used fictitiously, and any resemblance to actual persons, living or dead, business establishments, events, or locales is entirely coincidental.

Library and Archives Canada
Cataloguing in Publication

Jantunen, John, 1971–, author
A desolate splendor : a novel / John Jantunen.

Issued in print and electronic formats.
ISBN 978-1-77041-204-0 (paperback)
Also issued as: 978-1-77090-900-7 (pdf)
978-1-77090-899-4 (epub)

I. Title.

PS8619.A6783D47 2016   C813'.6
C2016-902374-5   C2016-902375-3

The publication of *A Desolate Splendor* has been generously supported by the Canada Council for the Arts, which last year invested $153 million to bring the arts to Canadians throughout the country, and by the Government of Canada through the Canada Book Fund. *Nous remercions le Conseil des arts du Canada de son soutien. L'an dernier, le Conseil a investi 153 millions de dollars pour mettre de l'art dans la vie des Canadiennes et des Canadiens de tout le pays. Ce livre est financé en partie par le gouvernement du Canada.* We also acknowledge the support of the Ontario Arts Council (OAC), an agency of the Government of Ontario, which last year funded 1,737 individual artists and 1,095 organizations in 223 communities across Ontario for a total of $52.1 million, and the contribution of the Government of Ontario through the Ontario Book Publishing Tax Credit and the Ontario Media Development Corporation.

Ontario
Ontario Media Development
Corporation

ONTARIO ARTS COUNCIL
CONSEIL DES ARTS DE L'ONTARIO
an Ontario government agency
un organisme du gouvernement de l'Ontario

Canada Council
for the Arts

Conseil des Arts
du Canada

Canadä

PRINTED AND BOUND IN CANADA

PRINTING: MARQUIS   5 4 3 2 1

RECYCLED
Paper made from
recycled material
FSC
www.fsc.org   FSC® C103567

For Tanja

We, while the stars from heaven shall fall,
And mountains are on mountains hurl'd,
Shall stand unmoved amidst them all,
And smile to see a burning world.

—

Charles Wesley
"The Great Archangel's
Trump Shall Sound"

They came into the glade under a full moon, their shadows tilting against the silvered sheen of the poplars at their backs, their eyes fixed as one on the dark outlines of a house and a barn. It had been written that a child shall lead them and so it was. He carried in his hand a lighted torch and as he led his two younger brothers away from The Twelve, its flicker radiated over their shorn heads and the fine lines of the skeletal imprints graven on their faces. The littlest one cast furtive glances back as if gaining courage from his fathers, the men's faces likewise marked though they also wore bones pierced through their flesh in cryptic patterns like the runes of some ancient and savage race. Among the three boys prowled four dogs, also adorned with bones woven into the thick mat of their fur so that they rattled when they walked, the clatter of them moving in tandem through the tall grass chasing at the whine of crickets and cicadas. Shortly, even this was drowned out by a dull thrumming as The Twelve raised their voices to the wind. Each was a human scapula or a hollowed-out femur tied to a piece of twisted sinew and as they swung them above their heads, the many voices became one, growing into a thunderous roar.

A light winked on in the house's upstairs window, lingered a moment then faded, reappearing a moment later in the window below and disappearing again, now emerging onto the porch so that all could see that it was a lantern held aloft by a man, a woman trailing behind, clutching at his hand. From the stark fright painted on their faces, it was clear they'd heard whisperspeak of stories, too terrible to believe, of daemons who came in the night to harvest the souls of the living: dread reapers whom some named Echoes, for all that was known of them was the sound of their voice.

A voice even now fading as the man pulled his wife into a fearful embrace.

Silence once again fell over the field and the eldest boy lifted his torch to lay bare the truth of this night.

Why they's jus children, the woman said.

I

The dogs had been restless all morning.

He could hear them whimpering at the barn door while he milked the she-goats and when he came out with the filled pail, they swirled around him, snarling and fighting, their teeth drawn and bloodlust ripe in their red-rimmed eyes. He yelled at them to shoo and when that didn't put an end to their foolishness, he lashed out at them with the willow switch he kept hitched to his belt. They scurried from his reach and slunk after him, keeping well clear from the maraud of his foot-leathers on their way back to the house, penitent, their heads hung low, almost dragging on the ground. When he slowed at the porch steps, they knocked up against his legs.

Damn near drivin me half-mad, he grumbled as his wife set his breakfast on the table in front of him.

They's always like this when Belle's in heat, she reminded him.

The dirty little buggers. And not a one of em more'n three years out of that ol bitch.

He shook his head and dipped a corner of his cornbread into an egg yolk.

What's bitch? his son asked from under the table.

He was lying beside Blue, the patriarch of their brood of hound dogs and the only one they allowed inside, excepting of course Belle, who was in the barn to keep her from dripping blood all over the floors. The boy was five and without any siblings of his own had taken to acting like he'd been sired by Blue along with the six others that, even now, the man could hear pacing around the porch, growling and snapping, every one more a nuisance than the last.

Git up here and eat yer eggs, he said.

No.

The man looked over his fork at his wife.

Honey, she prodded. It's time to eat.

No. Then after a moment: What's bitch?

It's a girl dog, his mother said. You know that.

Belle's the only bitch we got.

She is.

Pa drownt the rest.

He did.

Why'n he do that?

You'll have to ask him.

Why'n ya drown them other bitches, Pa?

The man cut around the perimeter of his egg white, trimming the edge, yellowed and crisp from the pan. He wrapped the golden frill around his fork and fed it into his mouth.

Weren't no other choice, he said.

Scooping the rest of the egg onto his bread, he stuffed the lot into his mouth then reached for his mug. Bits of charcoal floated on top of the boiled water strained through chicory. He teased one towards the edge with a fingernail, easing it up the side of the tin cup then pressing his thumb pad onto it and holding it up, studying the black dot.

If Ma has a girl, ya goin drown her too?

Tha's not hardly the same thing.

Why?

The man squished the mote between his thumb and his forefinger and looked to his wife again.

Yer ma ain't likely to birth a dog.

She birthed me. And I'ma dog.

The man covered his frown by licking his thumb. He took up the mug of chicory and drank it all at once. It was bitter and the heat of it burned his throat. He then stood and picked up his switch from the table and walked to the door. His straw hat hung from a hook beside it. He lifted it off, set it on his head and reached for the door's latch with a languor that suggested he'd rather be plodding up the stairs towards bed. As he stepped onto the porch there was a sudden clattering as the dogs scurried to get out of reach of his switch.

I'll be in the shop, he said. Send the boy out when he's done.

W hen the boy came out of the house, the six dogs lay bunched in front of the workshop's door, panting against the heat and casting wary glances at the sun's advance upon their haven of shade.

Sky, he called from the porch.

The youngest hound didn't so much as lift his head from his paws.

On the porch's hewn cedar post, there was a thermometer made from a flat circle of wood cut from the thick end of a birch tree. Numbers lined its perimeter around a tightly coiled strip of metal. A nail was soldered to it and its tip was inching past 30 though the sun had barely risen above the treeline. The boy pried the nail back with his finger, as if he could trick the heat into retreat, and let go. The coil pinged and he strode down the steps. The angry stomp of his foot-leathers would have seemed funny to his mother, though he'd never been more serious.

Goddamnit, Sky, he bellowed in pale imitation of his father, don't make me whip ya.

As he crossed the yard he could hear faint strains of music. It was coming, he knew, from his father's gramophone, which he always listened to when he was working in his shop, tinkering, his mother called it in her more generous moods. Drums rolled like thunder and then out of them rose a harmony of strings that reminded him of the first sprinkle of rain before a deluge — violins, the boy thought — and then a deeper sound. A cello maybe.

As he passed into the shade, Sky averted his eyes and then whimpered when the boy grabbed him by the scruff of his neck and tried to drag him to his feet. He was as heavy as a bag of sand.

Well you ain no fun, the boy said and kicked dirt at him.

That you out there, boy? his father called through the open door. Come on in here. I'll let ya drill one of the holes.

The boy wound through the maze of paws and lolling tongues and stopped at the small door set inside a larger one, the latter big enough to drive a bull moose through. The former was open a crack and he peered in at his father, hunched over at his workbench, fitting a length of dowelled wood into one of the holes he'd drilled along the frame of what was to become a crib.

Whadya waitin on? the man said without looking up.

Ma says I'ma pick slugs.

Tha what she said?

Yeah.

Then best git at it.

His mother's garden ran kitty-corner to their pasture. It was a quarter acre fenced in by cedar rails and ringed by orange and yellow marigolds, withered from the heat, and crushed eggshells and hair trimmings, but nothing his mother could do would keep the slugs from coming in at night.

The boy herded their chickens into the patch. He stood a moment, watching as they stalked among the sun-wilted plants plucking bugs from the leaves, then stepped to the row of cucumbers. He duck-waddled from one to the next, peering underneath, their leaves pocked with ragged holes and some no more than frames with tattered flaps of green at the fringes. When he found a slug he pried it off with his pocket knife and put it in a small wooden box. Before he'd been born, it'd had pictures of tomatoes on it, bright and red, but was now marked with only a few faded smudges of orange. Smears of black from past slugs stained the bottom. He extracted a half-dozen and made a run at the squash but his legs were tired by then and he told himself that it was best to let the chickens have their fill anyhow.

He walked along the row until he came to the garden's eastern perimeter where his father had planted his tobacco and aniseed. There was a cherry tree on the far side of the fence. He set the box on the ground within its shade and cut himself a stalk of aniseed with his pocket knife. While he chewed on the liquorice weed he watched the slugs in the box, betting on which would make it to the lip first. He gave odds to one that had tiger stripes but in the end it was a smaller speckled that took the race. He flipped it back with his knife and picked up the box, pressed it through the cedar rails and climbed the fence after it.

In the northwest corner of the pasture, their troop of goats milled around their mule, Spook, the kids gathered in a tight circle amongst their elders. One of them had caught sight of the boy. It took a few steps forward and stopped and watched him with desultory interest while the boy took up the length of string he'd fastened to one of the fence posts. He pulled on it, springing it free from the pasture's scrub, and picked up his box again. Tucking it against his side with one hand, he crimped the string in his other, keeping it loose, letting it draw him along through veins of thistle and milkweed, queen's lace and goldenrod. Grasshoppers battered his legs as he followed the line to a stick he'd driven into the ground to mark a three-foot mound of sand some fifty paces from the fence. Its crest was fringed with grass as if it had simply risen from the earth and a thousand tiny black ants swarmed in and around the holes punctured along its slope. The boy dumped the box upside down and shook the slugs onto the mound's plateau. The ants swarmed over them, paying them no heed as they went about their business. The slugs writhed though, same as if they'd been on fire. He watched and waited for a sign that it was the ants that were tormenting them so but, as far as he could tell, they couldn't have cared less about the gift he'd bestowed upon them.

Taking his magnifying scope from his pocket, he found the sun in its lens and concentrated it on the speckled slug. After a moment it skewed about like a worm on a hook. A tuft of smoke erupted from its back. One of the goats let out a yowl and it startled the boy into a flutter of contrition, same as if it had been his mother hollering at him for committing such a brazen act of cruelty. He tucked the glass disc back into his pocket and tracked the goats, chasing the mule towards the farmyard's gate.

Now what the hell's spooked them?

Then he saw it: a blur of black and tan shag — an animal as big as a bear loping across the field, bounding after the herd. It pounced and he heard a startled bleat and called out, Pa! — a sudden involuntary gasp sprung from his mouth like a frog startled into water. The creature turned towards him and he saw that it was a dog, its ears two devil's horns risen from its crown. It growled and the boy felt its terrible intent in a cold trickle like water down his spine. It charged at him and again he screamed, Pa! as if a word could rend this moment from the next. Pa! But still the grass parted in front of the beast's paws as surely as the seas had for Moses. Pa! Shrieking now. Pa! Pa! The dog so close he could see its ears flattening against its mantle, its black-beaded eyes quivering and the white of its teeth gleaming with an other-worldly sheen: angels calling the boy home.

The dog leapt at him and in that instant of flight Sky crashed into its side, toppling both dogs into the anthill. Sand blew in a fountain. The air filled with grit and the boy turned away. When he looked back, the black and tan was on top with its teeth at the hound's throat.

The boy reached for his pocket and felt the bump of his knife. Then Mo and Billy were on it, tackling it to the ground, and Dempsey was there too, tearing at the dog's groin. There was a clipped yelp and Jazz and Spark pounced, ripping into its belly. Red flashed on the pasture's green, and then only viscous snarls as the pack rung the life out of the thing.

Sky nuzzled the boy's hand. He looked down and the serious-ness of the moment was lost to the hound's goofy grin. Then an arm was wrapping itself around his waist, lifting him, his father gathering him to his breast and turning towards the house at a hard run. Sky raced after them, barking at his master's heels, as if he might have already forgotten who'd saved his son. The boy could hear his mother calling, calling, calling out his name but the sound of her voice seemed so far away, lost as he was to the vision of his other self, lying beside the anthill, splayed open on the ground.

She set her cast-iron pot on the stove, stoked the fire and put another log on top of the coals. When she turned back to the kitchen, the boy was gone. Her breath caught in her throat and she drew in hard, trying to still the thumping in her chest. Her son's voice whispered from the parlour and the thought pressed upon her that she'd be doing the same thing now — brewing a pot of camomile to calm her nerves and hearing echoes from distant corners — if the Good Lord hadn't been watching over her son like He had.

Blue looked up at her from under the table, whimpering. She walked to him and kneeled and rubbed him behind the ears.

It's a'right, she told him. It's a'right.

The dog licked at her fingers and she flopped one of his ears over his eyes, surprising herself with a laugh when he shook it off. She stood again. The bible that her mother had given her before she had died sat open at her place at the table. She was in the habit of reading from it after breakfast, taking a few moments of peace for herself while she drank her chicory, and that's what she'd been doing when she'd heard her son screaming, Pa! Pa! The memory of how she'd felt coming out onto the porch, turning towards the pasture and seeing that unholy beast in mid-flight as it leapt at him was almost more than she could bear. To distract herself from the thought that even now threatened to swallow her into its pit she flipped through the pages until she found the Gospel According to Matthew. She scanned the columns looking for one passage in particular. When she found it she ran the pad of her index finger over the lines as she read them in a fragile whisper.

Look at the birds of the air, she recited, for they neither sow nor reap nor gather into barns; yet your heavenly father feeds them. Are you not of more value than they?

And though she had read it many times before, she saw a

truth hidden in there that she had never seen before and was comforted by its simple message of hope. She read on to the end of the section.

Yes, she thought taking up the purple lace attached to the spine as a page marker, we'll let tomorrow worry about itself.

She set the lace into the bible's crease, smoothed it flat with her finger and closed the book. Then, setting her hand on it, she whispered a prayer of thanks and trailed her fingers along the cover's worn leather as she walked towards the stairs leading to the second floor. Beyond them lay the parlour and she leaned against its door frame, watching her son lead Sky on a tour.

This here'ns Pops, he said stopping in front of the grandfather clock presiding over the room like an old man forgotten in the corner. Sky shook his whole body over, unable to contain his glee. He daubed his nose on the clock's glass door and barked at the tick-tock of its pendulum, vacillating his gaze between it and the boy as if he'd never imagined anything so wondrous.

And these here'n are books. Ma says they ain good for nothin cept collectin dust. This here'ns one of my fav'rits. I'll read ya some of the pictures.

He pried it loose from the shelf beside Pops. Another fell. Sky sniffed at it and the boy picked up the errant book, set it back in place and led the dog to his father's chair. He patted the patchwork quilt hiding the coils poking through its threadbare seat and the hound looked to the boy as if such a thing was beyond him.

It's a'right, Pa won't mind.

He patted the chair again. The dog tested the quilt with his paw and clambered up. He circled the seat twice and sat with his legs jackknifing from beneath him, his back straight and proper, his head held high, proud as a king. The boy squeezed in beside him with the book propped open in his lap.

His mother heard the kitchen door open and she held her

breath, listening to her husband's feet clomping tired over the floor. She felt his hand worming between the door frame and her waist, coming to rest on the bump hanging low in her belly. He leaned in and kissed her shoulder. She exhaled slowly and rubbed her cheek against his brow. He felt tears wet his skin.

How's he doin?

He's fine. Fine. The Good Lord made sure of that.

It was damn lucky a'right.

Whadya reckin it was?

Looked to be a shepherd . . . crossed with a bear. From what was left of it.

Was it alone?

Wun't bet the devil on it.

Ya think it might'n been . . . sick?

Can ya magine . . . Christ.

The clock chimed the hour and the boy looked expectantly at his father.

Thanks Pops, the man said.

The boy smiled. Then to Sky: He always says that.

Whadya goin do? the woman asked when the boy had gone back to his book.

I guess I ought'n burn it.

I mean about the dogs.

The man rubbed at the stubble on his chin.

They wun't start showin fer a few weeks.

They both looked to the chair. Blood darkened the fur at the cuff of the hound's neck and a red smear highlighted the angle of the boy's chin. Sky leaned over and licked at it, washing the smudge clean. The boy scrunched his shoulder to ward him off.

Y'ain't even listenin, he said as his father approached, his fingers wrestling with a piece of loose string in his pants' pockets.

Howya doin, son?

The boy looked up, reticent, as if he'd been caught in a lie. Sky craned forward, begging for a touch.

I tol him ya wouldna mind him settin in yer chair. Jus this once.

Don't mind at all, the man said. Sky, ya can set there arytime you please.

He ran his fingernails over the skin loose against the dog's skull and down the folds clumped along his neck, stopping only when he felt the sticky-damp. Drawing his hand back, he held his crimson-stained fingertips up to the light as if it might reveal some foul presence within.

First I need him to come outside. So we can get him warsht.

Jus one more picture, okay?

Okay, he said, stroking the boy's hair, blond like his mother's and as fine as gossamer.

Pa.

Yeah.

I'ma tryin ta read.

Sorry.

He stepped back and listened to his son describing what he saw in the simple ink drawing on the page.

He got shipwrecked on this island, see? Weren't nobody else there. It was just him and his dog.

The dog in the picture was black and had sad eyes. It was carrying a bird in its maw, a grouse maybe, or a pheasant. A man was bending to it, stroking its wing, telling the dog how much he appreciated the gift. In his other hand there was a musket. He leant stooped over it, looking old and weary, done for the world, if not for the dog, who'd given him hope when there was none.

The dog hunted for him. Brought him food. If it weren't for him, the man'd never have survived. Ain that right, Pa?

Tha's right, son. He most surely woulda perished.

And then he couldn't help himself.

He reached out and set his hand on the boy's head again.

He's gittin blood all over yer mother's quilt, he said. Best git him warsht up.

A'right. Come on, Sky.

The boy slid off the chair. Sky traipsed after him, shaking the stiffness out of his hinds and brushing his master's leg as he passed. The book sat open on the seat and in the drawing of the castaway the man saw more of himself than he would have liked. He looked to his rifle, propped against the fireplace, and to the little tin box on the mantel, trying to recall how many rounds were in there the last time he'd checked, the day he'd buried his father, the old man's dying words practically a plea to guard the bullets at any cost for he would never see another.

There were eight, he thought, or maybe nine.

There'd just be enough.

H e sent Blue to corral the goats while he stood at the barn-yard's gate. Crows circled the pasture, heckling the dead thing below. He watched them spiralling in drastic arcs and then settled his gaze upon the field, trying to take it in all at once as if there was something in there that had escaped him. All of a sudden it seemed flimsy, this scene — the grass tenuous, the breeze sweeping through them transitory, the pine trees on the other side a mirage. He tried to follow the thought through to its end but there was nothing there but a feeling that the world before him was a piece of fabric, worn thin, so that it wouldn't have taken more than the gentlest touch to poke a hole right through it.

Spook had reached the gate and brayed at him. He batted at her muzzle with an open palm and she ducked the blow, shaking her head and snorting at him in protest or perhaps accusation.

I know, I know, he told her as she trod into the barnyard, turning away from him and following the fenceline, picking at whatever grass straggled between the cedar rails.

The goats streamed after, bustling against the man's legs. He let his hand drop among them. His fingers bumped against the steel plates of their foreheads and rode the waxen curve of their horns and trailed over their spines, ridged and knotty, catching whisperspeak of their tails and the flick of their tongues as they passed beneath him.

When they were all through, the man took up his rifle, propped against a fence post. He pulled the gate shut behind him and threaded through the skittering mass bleating at the barn door.

Hold yer horses, he scolded, popping open the latch.

He felt himself momentarily carried along with the rush of them all flowing in at once and grabbed at the door frame to steady himself. Blue gave out a perfunctory yelp and he turned to the hound, his ears pried back and the flap of his tongue dancing beneath his chin.

Easy for you to say, he said.

He motioned to close the door, stopped and looked back at the dog.

Ya comin or not?

Blue leapt past him. His tail thwacked his master's knee and sent a sharp pain up his leg. The man swatted the air after him and whistled to Spook. Her head was tilted to the ground, pushing for a dandelion just out of reach of her tongue. If she heard him, she made no sign.

Suit yerself, the man said, pulling the door shut behind him.

The goats were already settled in their pen, the younger ones nuzzling their elders and the older ones chewing bits of straw and staring with empty eyes at the man as he slid the four cedar rails into the brackets of their gate. One of their tabby cats rubbed its ear against the top of his foot. He ignored it and walked between the stalls, four on either side, all of them vacant except for the last in the row. Blue was crouched in front of it, straining his snout through the wooden bars withholding his mate. Chaff rained about him in a perpetual shower from the hayloft above. When the man reached the end stall, Belle was clawing at the slats. She let out an anguished yowl. He bent to one knee, pressed his cheek to the gate and let her lick it. Her tongue was like wet plaster against the rough of his beard. He fed his hand through the gap and rubbed her behind the ears. The pungency of her oestrum fermented the air.

Ya don't know how much trouble you've caused, ol girl, he said.

As he stood, Belle pounced at the walls of her prison, barking her indignation at him. He walked to the door and opened it, Blue following him out with the utmost reluctance.

The other five dogs skulked around his legs as he secured the latch.

Shoo, he said, his hand reaching for his switch but he didn't have the resolve to draw it out.

All of them bore traces of the dog they'd killed — sparks of red on their jowls and flakes of it drying on their haunches, one of Mo's ears shredded and one of Billy's toenails ripped clean off, leaving a frayed stump so that he sat apart from the rest, licking at it as his master turned towards the house.

The boy and his mother were kneeling on the porch on either side of Sky. The woman dipped a rag into a steel basin and squeezed it over the dog's neck, letting the medicine drain into his wounds.

I'ma take the dogs down to the river, the man called over to them. Ya comin?

The boy looked to his mother, unwilling, it seemed, to leave her.

We'll all go, she answered, easing to her feet, her hand pressed against the hump of her belly as if she was afraid something might fall out.

S he'd made a picnic lunch and the day's drama was soon dulled by boiled eggs and cornbread sweetened with handfuls of cherries. While they ate they watched the boy splashing at the dogs in a little cove in the river where sand had washed into a beach overtop the granite. The dogs barked at him, pouncing in the shallow water, and he chased them into the deep, slapping spray after them and shouting, Cowards!

His father grew weary from the sun and lay on his back. He pulled his hat down over his face and drifted, he hoped, towards sleep listening to his son frolicking in the river.

A moment later, his wife groaned and he sat up again. He righted the hat on his head and when he turned to her she was leaning on one arm, propped against the rock, her hand on her belly, her face scrunched like she was trying to pass a stone.

Y'okay? he asked.

Somethin ain right.

Ya had quite a scare.

It's not that.

It's just nerves.

It's like . . . before.

Cain't be.

It is.

Yer hardly showin.

I was hardly showin then.

Yer maginin things.

Easy fer you to say.

The man swatted at the air with his hat and turned back to

the river. Sky was swimming five feet from the shoal and barking. The boy ran at him and leapt, plunging into the dark depths. His mother gasping and his father driven to his feet watched him surface, clutching at Sky's tail, spitting water and laughing.

You be careful now, his mother called, but the boy would hardly have heard it if it had been a rifle shot, so lost was he in his delight — holding fast to Sky's tail and kicking out then letting go and swimming by himself in imitation of the hound's frenzied strokes.

The man stood and fetched his rifle from the stone terrace and slung it onto his back.

Where you offta? his wife asked, her hand visored against the sun and her lips crimped as if she was expecting a lie.

I'ma take a wander, the man replied. Won be long. Come on, boy.

Blue sluiced from the water, shaking himself off in the cove and bounding up onto the hump of granite with the gait of a much younger dog. He fell in line beside his master and the two of them set off downriver. They kept as close to the shore as the vegetation allowed, scouring amongst the densely festooned forest floor for any signs or smells. It was at a deer crossing that they found the tracks — three paws imprinted in the mud among the sharp hoof points. Blue snarled at them and his master bent and measured the distance from claw to heel between his thumb and forefinger. They were the same size as the ones he'd found at the farm.

They tracked them along the deer path, meandering after the fashion of a creature vexed by overhanging vines and the tatter of woodpeckers and scared of its own shadow. After a time they came to a meadow — a small pool of light amidst the gloom. The deer path wove through the clearing and made a maze among the ferns and snake grass but Blue bypassed it, tracking the dog's scent deeper into the forest. The man retrieved his compass from his pocket and took a bearing. The tracks were leading in a straight line towards home.

When they arrived back at the cove, his wife was packing what was left of the cornbread and the eggs into her leather satchel and the boy was stuffing his mouth with handfuls of cherries. The dogs lay sprawled on the rock, water steaming off their backs.

Ya find arythin? the woman asked.

The man shook his head.

It was a rogue, near as I can tell.

The woman nodded and slung her bag onto her shoulder.

Gawd, yer a mess, she told the boy.

The boy giggled and stuffed the last of the cherries into his mouth. Red streamed down his chin same as if he'd been chewing on glass. His father, now stripped to his naturals, scooped him up on the run. He took three strides, leapt off the hump of granite and they disappeared into the river. The dogs, alert to the boy's sudden shriek and the splash that came after, looked down at the water. When father and son came up a moment later, the both of them laughing, they laid their heads back down on their paws.

Five more minutes, the woman called to them.

But the man had dived down again. He was grabbing the boy by the leg, pulling him under, and her voice was drowned out by the river.

O n their way home, the boy ran ahead, chasing the dogs and shooting endless rounds at invisible foes from a stick he'd found that looked like a rifle. When they came out of the corridor of perfectly spaced Jack pines leading into the pasture, the dogs steered away from the barn, taking a line towards the anthill. The man whistled and all the hounds but Sky wheeled round and cantered back to him.

The boy set his hand on the youngest hound's head as he watched his mother passing a few urgent words with his father. Finally, he nodded and kissed her lightly on the cheek and she turned, herding the dogs to the west. As the man walked towards his son, his arms swung loose and he whistled a tune that immediately made the boy think of spring mornings, before the sun had turned hot.

The song trailed off as he came to Sky. Bending, the man grabbed the dog by the loose flap of his jowl and stared him straight in the eye.

Ya don't listen to yer master no more.

He'll only listen to me, the boy said.

That so?

He told me. He said I'ma his master now.

The man released the dog and looked to his wife corralling the other dogs through the gate.

I'ma need Sky to keep away from ya for a few weeks, he said, turning back to his son.

But he saved me.

I know.

Tain't fair.

I know.

He pushed past him and the boy ran to catch up. The sky was clear all the way to the horizon and as they walked on under the utter quiet of the afternoon's heat, the man scanned over it from under the brim of his hat.

Hard to believe the winter rains are due next moon, he said when they came to the anthill. He quickened a glance at the sky behind, as if it were playing a trick on him, then turned to the depression of trampled grass stained red by the fallen dog. There was nothing left of the creature now but a few tufts of black hair catering to the wind from atop a thistle's head.

Somethin's drug it off, he said, toeing the anthill, causing avalanches to cascade down the slope and over his foot-leather. Damn it all. I knew I shoulda burned it.

He scanned the field to the line of trees but there was nothing but the breeze teasing the grass.

Pa?

Yeah.

I promised Sky I'd show him ma room.

Son—

I promised.

How bout this, his father said, swatting at a deer fly with his hat. I'll make ya a deal. Ya show him yer room then it's right outside. And ya stay away from him until I say.

His father stuck out his hand and the boy studied it, trying to think of a way around shaking.

Son, there ain't no way around it, his father said. Y'ain't never seen a dog had the sickness, I know. So it's hard to magine.

Have you?

His father nodded.

Wun't much older than you. It was one of my pa's hounds. Figured he must have kilt a coon had it.

Howdya know it was sick?

Other dogs wun't go near him. He wun't eat nor even drink. Then he gone strange. Barkin at shadows, droolin foam. Bleedin at the mouth. That's how yer gramps could tell. He'd bit off his own tongue.

Whadya do?

Yer gramps took him out to that tree yonder. He pointed at the oak in the middle of the field where the animals took shelter from the sun. Tied him up. Gave me his rifle. Said when the time come I was to shoot him.

Whyn'tya jus shoot him right away?

I ast him the same question. He told me, he wanted me to see. So I sat and watched that dog all day. By supper it was like the devil'd got a holda him. Eyes were red like the sun at dusk. He'd damn near chewed off his tail. It hung on him like a rat's got caught in a trap. Dinner come and he was pullin so hard on the rope, tryin to git at me, I thought it was goin snap.

So ya shot him?

Weren't no choice. Now ya think if that was Sky.

The boy looked to the dog and his face darkened.

We got a deal?

His father stuck out his hand again. This time the boy reached out and shook it.

Atta boy.

S he watched him from the kitchen window, inching across the field. Sky trotted ahead, looking back every few steps as if, like she was, he was trying to figure out what he was doing. He was holding something between his hands, that she could tell. It looked like a stick, held out in front of him like a dowsing rod.

But why'n his pa ave taught him that? she wondered, when the water in the well is nigh at the rim and ya couldna pump fast enough to drain even an inch from it.

As he came closer, she could see he was winding something around the stick. She watched him until he disappeared behind the cherry tree and then went back to slicing onions for the stew. When she looked up again he was at the edge of the garden. Sky bound after him, nipping at his hands as he darted past, and the boy chased him over the span of marigolds. The dog kept a hand or two out of his reach until he'd made the yard, then looped back and hunkered down, his jowls submerged in the grass and his rump aloft, his tail pointing to his namesake. He growled as the boy came at him with what she could now see were two sticks tied together with kite string. He held one in each hand. He swung the one in his right at the dog and it dodged backwards then quickly snapped forward again. He latched his teeth onto one of the sticks, wrenching it from the boy's grip, and took off at a run. The other stick jerked away from the boy too and bobbed behind the hound, unspooling the string over the ground.

While the boy raced after it, his mother scraped the onions off her board and into the pot on the stove. Fat from the cubes of goat hissed and popped against the heat. Basil hung from the windowsill, drying. She crumbled a handful of it, dosed the stew and looked out the window again but the boy was nowhere to be seen. She heard his feet clomping on the porch. The door thudded open and he came in holding one of the sticks, Sky trailing behind him holding the other, the string dragging on the floor between them.

Wheredya think yer goin? she asked.

Pa said I could show Sky ma room.

He did, did he?

Uh huh.

Well ya can do it after yer chores.

But Ma—

Yer room'll still be there when yer done.

The boy stared over at the stairs, as if maybe thinking she was lying, before turning back to the porch.

Tell yer pa I need a couple of carrots, she called after him. And some garlic.

I thought ya goin have a spek with him.

The man stood at the bottom of the stairs, polishing the path's dirt with his foot-leathers. His wife's frame filled the doorway and the smell coming from the kitchen behind her was like heaven.

I did.

Din't much look it.

I made him a deal.

What kin'a deal?

He told her.

Yer lettin him play ya.

Maybe.

I don't want the boy around em right now.

The dog, he said then stopped.

What?

Nothin.

It weren't nothin when ya started.

It weren't sick.

Howdya know?

The way it come at him.

But y'ain't sure.

No.

Where're ma carrots and garlic?

The man settled his gaze on his wife. Her lips were pulled tight into greyish-blue strips and she was holding a wooden spoon in her hand like she meant to use it. He wheeled around and started for the garden.

You keep those dogs away from him.

E vening found them in the parlour — he in his chair reading a book — she at the upright piano, her eyes closed, her fingers so light on the keys that she seemed to be drawing the music from the room itself. The spiritual she played was meant to be uplifting but tonight the notes sounded brittle. She did not sing, as she sometimes did. Only a transient humming disturbed the flow — a few bars before she caught herself and sealed her lips so as to better concentrate on the weave of her fingers along the ivories.

From upstairs she could hear the scrape of Sky's nails on the floor of her son's room. She looked to her husband, lost in the web of his fantasy, and struck the last key with fierce resolve. The note hovered in the room, solemn and grave. Just as it was fading, a new sound arose — a lone howl that created waxen statues out of both of them. The man looking up from the book, his forefinger cuffed between pages in anticipation of the next. The woman with anxious eyes, her expression wrapped in a superstitious dread as if she was to blame for this sudden dissonance.

Blue, stretched before the stone-rimmed fireplace, growled and it broke the spell. The man shot up from his chair and strode to the window, open wide so that the house could drink at the night air. The howl was fading to the tranquility of cricketsong.

Is it one of ours? his wife asked, now at his side, forcing her hand into his, her worry come to something less tangible.

The man shook his head.

There was a moment of quiet, the peace at the edge of the tumult, and then the howl received its reply: another agonized cry. This one spoke to the man like a flash of lightning upon the horizon, hurrying him from the room, through the kitchen, and bursting onto the porch, racing against the rumble of thunder that was to come so that he could feel its tremble unencumbered. Standing there — his back rigid, his head tilted so as to elevate his good ear, his arm buttressed against the post — he listened as the mad howling wrenched the stillness from the air, turning the calm of this windless night into a gale.

Blue snarled. His fur was bristled in a line along his spine and tension rippled the muscles along his haunches. The man reached for his scruff but he was already gone, bounding down the steps.

Blue! he cried.

He could hear the other dogs yapping at Blue's heels as he bolted past the barn.

Snatching the rifle propped against the post, the man hurtled after them.

Wait! his wife called.

He'll git em all killed, he yelled back, chasing his alarm into the dark and screaming, Blue! Ya son of a bitch. Git back here. Blue. Blue!

Wha's goin on, Ma?

The boy was at the bottom of the kitchen stairs, Sky beside him.

Three rifle shots sounded in reply. Each sent a shock wave through the boy's mother, leaving their mark in a jitter to her hands as she slammed the door, now rushing to the window above the sink, closing it too and turning to her son.

Ma?

Two more shots, one right after the other.

It'll be a'right, she said but her voice wavered and it was clear to the boy that she didn't believe it.

Only when the silence had become unbearable did they venture onto the porch, she holding a lantern aloft in her hand as if the candle inside could pry loose the mantle of dark.

Above them, the cloudless sky harboured a thousand eyes and the moon was but a sliver. The only sounds they could hear were Sky whining and scratching at the door behind them, and further off, Belle barking against her captivity.

A short while later, there arose the swish of footsteps and the man appeared as a shadow from among the drape of the other shadows encasing the barn and the pasture and everything beyond. He was carrying a dog, they couldn't tell which. The boy made to run to him but his mother's hand was locked in his. Together they watched the man stumble towards the porch. Just outside of the lantern's illume, he sagged to his knees and set the dog on the bare earth in front of the steps.

Fetch Belle, he said, his voice cracking against the strain.

His wife let her son's hand go and she prodded the boy's shoulder, hastening him down the steps. When he came breathless to the barn, he turned back and saw his mother bending to his father, the light of her candle framing his face in orange flickers.

Yer hurt, he could just hear her say as he opened the barn's door.

Goats bleated their worry and Belle yipped at him. The boy groped in the dark for her stall and found the wooden slats penning her in. He slid the top one away and then the next. When he reached for the last he felt her wind brush past him. Her paws clamoured on the dirt floor and he heard the door bang open as she pushed through it. He raced after her and into the yard, following the flame of his mother's lantern to the steps where Belle was nosing at the other dog's neck, trying to rouse him. In the light he could see that it was Blue and also that he was dead. His father was kneeling beside him, his face still lit by the candle's glow. Two scratches beaded blood down his cheek.

How many were there? his wife asked, her voice infused with a tone the boy had never heard before: hysteria or possibly madness.

I don't know, his father replied, his own voice steady and tired like he'd been repeating himself for hours. I shot two of em. Another jumped me. I kilt it with my knife. The rest ran off. Five maybe six. I don't know. It was dark.

So they're gone.

For now.

Ya think—

Goddamnit, woman, quit fussin! I told ya it's only a scratch.

His wife's hand startled away from his cheek and the man turned his back on her light, striding towards the pasture.

Whereya goin? she called after him.

To bury ma dogs.

H e built a pyre out of the trimmings from the winter's wood, dragging the branches from behind the shed to the middle of the field. He piled them on top of each other until it was storeyed above him and kindled it with handfuls of timothy grass. Lighting it with his tinderbox, he stood back to watch the flame pulsating in the heart of it. The fire spread to the pyre's many-forked body and the glow it cast penetrated the dark deep into the field.

The man walked within its halo, searching out the dogs, the eight of them scattered in a wide arc within the scrub. His own all had their throats ripped out and, in turn, he knelt beside each, setting his hand upon their blood-slicked coats and intoning a silent prayer before digging waist-deep holes with his spade and rolling them in. The others he carried to the pyre and pitched on top, watching as the flame melted their fur and drew the skin back from their maws, exposing the sharp prongs of their teeth. In the last, he found his knife still bedded to the haft in its throat.

He pulled the blade out and wiped it on the dog's coat. Death had not softened its menace and he pondered on that, wondering what could have happened in the world beyond his to warrant the creation of such a pack of unholy beasts.

First light found him stoking the embers of the fire, pushing about the remains of the three dogs, their charred bones clung to one another by blackened strands of sinew. He took up the shovel and hacked at them, severing heads from spines and crushing skulls with the flat of the blade, shattering ribs. The marrow inside the bones hissed and bubbled. He gathered the shards to the edge of the pit and dug another hole. After he'd pushed them in and covered them up, he heaped dirt onto the wreckage of charcoal then circled it, looking for any cinders that had strayed, flipping them on top and chasing them with a splash of soil.

He found his rifle within a thatch of burrs. It looked to him like it had been abandoned ages ago: a relic from a past life. He thought of leaving it there, for all the good it had done him, but weeded it out anyway. He expelled the bullets into his cupped palm. There were three — the last of the store his father had left him. Loading them into the rifle again, he slung it over his shoulder and trudged back to the house.

He came at it through the garden, giving it a wide berth, angling towards the well. Stripping off his shirt, he primed the pump's lever. He soaked the coarse linen under the spout, scrubbed himself with it and then rinsed off with handfuls of the cold, clear water. Their rooster crowed and he looked to his bedroom window. He waited for the drapes to part, for her to appear. When she didn't, he rung out his shirt and walked to the porch.

Belle lay in vigil beside Blue at the foot of the steps. He knelt to her and patted her side, whispering, Good girl. She licked at the gashes on his face, her tongue stinging like lashes from a whip. The door opened and he heard a dog prancing down the steps. He gave his other cheek up to Sky and looked to the door where the boy stood, staring down at him as if he were a ghost.

Where's yer ma?

Upstairs.

Run and fetch her.

She won come down.

And whyn's that?

She said yer leavin.

Leavin?

And she don't want no part of it.

Tha's what she said?

The boy nodded.

Said yerra hunt them dogs got away.

How's she figure that?

I don't know. Are ya?

I guess I am. She say arythin else?

The boy shook his head and just then caught sight of what Sky was doing to Belle behind his father's back. Hollering, No Sky! he rushed down the steps. He was about to have at the dog with both hands when his father caught him by the arm.

It's okay, he said.

But she's his ma!

I know.

The man turned to the two dogs. Sky was mounted behind Belle, the thin shaft of his sex pink and raw as he pumped at her.

It ain right, his son said.

Necessity breeds the devil. Then letting the boy go: Now how's about ya help me git ol Blue out of the sun?

They buried him in the orchard.

He was the only damn dog I ever knew et apples, the man said as he set a piece of the fruit on the flat stone he'd placed at the head of the grave. Et himself sick if you'da let him.

He stood and picked three more apples from a low branch. He stuffed two in his pants' pockets and bit into the third.

Whoever hearda dog et apples?

He joined his son standing in quiet reverence a few feet away and together they walked back to the house. Sky was sitting on the porch, licking his male parts. Belle lay on the footpath panting in the sun.

The man stopped at the foot of the steps and looked up at his bedroom window. The day was already hot and he could feel the heat draining what little energy he'd held in store from the night's labour.

You really fixin to leave? the boy asked.

I told ya I was.

Well yer shore takin yer sweet-Mary-time bout it.

Ya wan me to go?

No.

Then quit yer bellyachin.

The man batted at the boy's head. The boy ducked and his father bent and pried a pebble loose from the ground with his fingernail. He rolled it about in the palm of his hand and cocked his arm back, making as if to throw it.

Corn's due this moon, the boy said.

Moon ain't yet but a sliver. Then lowering a weary gaze upon his son: Yer ma say to tell me that?

No.

Yer lyin.

I ain't.

You tell her, I shun't be gone but a few days. A week at the most.

Tell her yerself.

I've haffa mind to do just that.

Why don't ya.

Maybe I will.

He looked up at the empty window again and flung the pebble. It winged off the frame and fell onto the porch's roof. He heard it rattling over the sheet metal and waited for it to roll down but it got hung up and he searched about the ground for another.

I need to ask a favour of ya, he said to the boy.

What?

Sky.

Ya cain't. He's mine.

And he'll still be yers when I git back.

Tain't fair.

Ya have a spek with him, a'right.

He reached out for his son and the boy glared back at him through pitted eyes. The man pocketed his hands and strolled past him, pointing his feet at his workshop. When he came out of it a few minutes later, he was carrying three freshly greased fox traps. The boy was sitting on the porch holding up the flap of Sky's ear and whispering into it. His father hung the traps on the pasture gate alongside his rifle and walked to the smoke-shack. He gathered up all the strips of goat he had curing on the rack there and two trout smoked whole. He put them into his satchel and walked over to the garden. He raided it for a dozen carrots and a handful of aniseed then chewed on a yellow tomato while he thought of what else he could take with him.

A cloud had swallowed the sun and he watched its shadow rove over the yard. He'd never felt so tired.

Ary them hardboileds left? he asked the boy as he neared the porch again.

Ma made a fresh batch lass night.

That so?

She said— he started then stopped, thinking of the excuse she'd given him and now measuring it against the truth. I'll fetch em for ya.

I'da preciate it.

The boy walked to the door. Just inside the threshold, he turned back.

I ain't leaving without them eggs, his father said, if'n tha's what yer thinkin.

The boy nodded and went into the kitchen.

As the man waited for him to return the sun reappeared and he fanned his hat against the trickle of sweat wetting his neck. The boy came back with the eggs hammocked in his shirt. His father stowed all of them in his satchel but one, which he rolled against his leg, crumbling the shell, all the while staring up at his bedroom window. Working his thumb under the shell's skin he peeled it, letting the delicate mesh fall to the ground. He clipped the tip off the egg with his teeth and spat it out, something he always did though God hisself couldn't have told him why.

I talked to Sky, his son said.

What he'd say?

He'll go. But only so ya don't git yer-damn-fool-self kilt.

The man pressed the egg into his mouth and chewed it to mush thinking about how much the boy looked like his mother just then.

Y'ought'n say yer goodbye.

His son kneeled. He draped his arms around Sky's head and rubbed noses. His father thought the boy would cry but he didn't.

Come on, Sky.

Sky shrugged off the boy and fell in line beside his master, now turning towards the pasture. The man pulled out the gate's rails and Sky pranced past him, ran a few paces ahead, then stopped and looked back as the man slid the rails into their brackets. The boy wished that Sky would look his way too but he only had eyes for his father, now collecting the rifle and the traps and trudging after him with a tired gait so that from a distance he appeared an old man. The dog scuttled into the tall grass and the boy watched the bob of his father's straw hat as it traversed the field. Shortly, the corridor leading through the pines stole even that and he returned to the kitchen.

His mother sat at the table, her hands clasped on the bible in front of her as if she was praying though her eyes were open.

He's gone, the boy said.

She opened her mouth, closed it again and bit her lip.

He said to tell ya he won't be more'n a few days.

She nodded and looked down at her hands.

He had to go, the boy said, didn't he, Ma? There weren't no choice, right?

She looked up at him and forced a smile.

Whadya fancy for breakfast? she said.

Hardboileds.

I could make griddlecakes. With blueberries. And cream.

I want hardboileds!

He ate the two eggs he'd saved sitting in his mother's cedar-rail chair on the porch. Belle had moved out of the sun and was sitting in a wedge of shadow on the near side of the well. Flies buzzed around her head and she snapped at them idly. From the kitchen he could hear his mother whisper-singing one of the songs from her hymnal.

When he was done eating, he stood and called out to Belle, Come on, y'ol bitch.

The dog lumbered off the ground. She shook herself all over and jogged to meet the boy coming down the steps.

It's jus you and me t'day.

They walked to the pasture gate. The boy climbed onto the third rail and peered into the field. He could see the charred black patch thirty or forty paces from the fence. It was half-covered in dirt and streamers of smoke rose from within. He climbed over the gate and pulled out the bottom rail. Belle slunk through, her nose to the ground, and the boy followed her to a patch of fresh-dug ground just this side of the firepit. She sniffed at it as the boy bent to the grave's marker. Two letters were scratched onto the flat rock.

M-O, he spelled out. M-Mo.

Belle's ears perked at the name and she bore a puzzled look. Seeing her like that, the boy was overwhelmed by tears.

Ya don't even know, do ya? he said, sobbing. He's yer first-born and ya don't even know.

Belle licked at his cheeks. He held her around the neck and cried into her fur. After a time he stood and wiped the tears from his cheek on the sleeve of his shirt.

I'ma miss you, Mo, he said then circled the firepit until he came to another grave. Its marker read S-P-A-R-K. He lowered his head and said, I'ma miss you too, Spark.

In this way he visited all five of the graves and said his goodbyes. Gravity then drew him to the pyre. It was still warm. Blackened bone shards were scattered amongst the dirt and the charred ends of branches. A speck of white gleamed from within the cinders, just out of arm's reach, and the boy tested the soot with his foot. The heat didn't penetrate the leather. He took another step, plucked the tooth from the ash and skipped backwards onto the scorched grass. He jostled the prize in his palm and held it up between his thumb and forefinger. It was better than an inch long and as curved and pale as a crescent moon, though its root was yellowed and blackened from the fire.

He heard his mother calling and he turned to the gate. She was striding through, hollering his name.

I don't want ya leavin the yard, she scolded as he neared.

Belle as with me, he said.

Yer not to leave the yard.

She gave him a hard slap on the rear, hastening him towards the gate. When they got there, his hand found the tooth in his pocket. Joy in his discovery trumped the sting of her hand.

I found a tooth, he said.

A tooth?

It's from one of them dogs kilt Blue and the others.

Let me see it.

The boy held it up.

It's one of its big'uns.

A canine.

Yeah. It's sharp too.

Y'ought'n be touchin dead things.

It was in the fire.

Tain't safe.

She reached for it and the boy skipped away from her grasping hand.

Y'ain goin to take it, he said. You ain't!

He spun round and charged across the yard. She watched him disappear behind the house. Belle rubbed the wet of her nose against her hand and she bent to the dog, cradling her arms around her neck. The hound's fur was damp against her chin.

Ain't no sense in them, is there? she said. No damn sense at all.

For the rest of the morning he hid from his mother, first behind the willow that his father cut his switches from, then, when he was certain she wasn't coming after him, he ventured out and crept to the woodshed. He snuck inside and peered at the house through a knothole in the wall. He watched the kitchen window and waited, his hand rarely out of the pocket where he kept his prize, measuring it against the memory of the teeth on the one that had come after him and thinking of his father tracking the others.

When the night come down it'd be Pa and Sky all alone against them, he thought, all with teeth like this'n or worse.

He rubbed the tooth and prayed for his father, sending him all the hope that he had but it didn't seem near enough.

He thought of Sky coming out of nowhere when his doom had been certain, and of the hounds tearing at the beast, and tried to imagine what his father had looked like in the pasture, facing off against the pack.

How many shots was it? bangbangbang. Then two more. bangbang.

Five in all. Two of the unholy beasts dead. And maybe another two or three wounded. (And they'd be nothing against Pa. When it came down to that, a wounded dog'd be about as much trouble as a blind pup). And then it was just Pa and his knife — that's what he'd said weren't it? One of them had jumped him and he'd kilt it with his knife. His father on the ground, the dog snapping at his throat, clawing at his face. He'd seen the marks, beaded with blood, on his cheek. It had gone for his eyes. His father had fought it back and he'd buried his knife in the dog's neck. The boy could see it clearly now, his father rolling the dead thing off of him, standing, his hand dipped in blood from the tips of his fingers to his cuff. Hollering at the beasts, Come and git me, you sons of bitches. Come and git me. The beasts had heard death in his voice and had fled, leaving the bodies of three of their kin devastated in the field alongside the six hounds.

He saw his father stumbling from one sunken form to the next, weeping and holding each, not a single breath between them. Finally stopping at Blue and seeing that there was still a little life left in him. Picking him up and struggling against the dark. Coming round the barn and spying the light on the porch. All thoughts on Belle now, keeping the dog alive with whispers of his beloved. She ain goin to forgive ya, Blue, ya pass without sayin yer goodbyes. Ya just hold on, Belle'll be with ya right soon. Ya just keep on doin what yer doin. And think of Belle.

Then coming into the light and seeing the boy up there on the porch, stayed by his mother's hand, such a look on his face that he'd hoped he'd never have to see on his son. The words choked out of his mouth, Fetch Belle.

He'd set off, the boy remembered, like there was wind in his legs. He'd brought her back just in time. The light hadn't quite gone from Blue's eyes — he'd seen it — and the dogs had had their goodbye.

The boy wept at the thought of Blue's passing but he bore no sadness for it, seeing it now as he did.

He prayed again. This time hope spilled out of him and he knew that no harm would come to his father, so long as he had the tooth.

F ive days later he was in the barnyard barebacking their mule Spook, shouting orders to the goats, marshalling them from one side of the pen to the other. The older ones soon wised to his game and bunched up in one corner, refusing to move, leaving the kids at the mercy of the young tyrant's switch. His father's old hat flopped, lopsided, against his brow. Its weave was darkened with sweat and the crown was caved in, the straw frayed and torn.

When the first wave of cacklers swept in low, just above the pines on the western edge of the field, he leant his head back and the hat fell to the ground. Spook snatched it up and chewed on it but the act was lost to the boy, marvelling as he was at this flurry of coal-black birds. A second wave soon overwhelmed the stragglers chasing the first. It was followed by a third and a fourth, and on and on until their passings were beyond measure — thousands of birds moving in gusts like the wind given form.

The thresh of their wings was soon lost to a shrill chatter. Such a noise the boy had never heard before. He could feel it in his teeth. A piercing whine absorbing every other sound that dared protest against it — the nervous bleating of the goats and Spook's fearful braying and his own thoughts, shrieking against the abomination. The hair hackled on his arms and his mother's voice pierced the din.

The corn! she cried. She was flailing through the gate, Belle by her side. They's afta the corn!

In one hand she wielded her large kitchen knife and it scissored ahead of her stride, reaping at the goldenrod that had overcome the field with its brazen hue.

The boy slid off the mule. He squeezed between the pen's cedar rails and chased after her. She had already made the path leading through the Jack pines yet was standing there still when the boy caught up with her. Birds were perched along the branches on either side of the path, as plentiful as leaves. The cackling here was so loud that it forced the boy's hands to his ears. Through the gap, the cornfield was a seething mass of utter dark. Nothing could be seen beyond it.

Grabbing the boy's arm, his mother pulled him along the

path behind her. The boy stumbled along the hardened valleys wagon wheels had made on either side, gazing up at the hordes around him. He could see now that not all of them were black. Some had red crowns and others deep blue collars and there were starlings too, and sparrows and chickadees. When the smaller birds landed, the larger ones pecked at them and beat their wings, and the smaller birds flitted away. Everywhere the boy looked he found the same so that it appeared to him one vast struggle: the small against the large, the light against the dark, the weak against the strong.

The forest path broke then upon the field and the boy felt his mother's hand slip from his.

Stay here! she yelled, wading towards the corn patch, swinging the blade in her hand as a scythe, Belle charging ahead of her.

The birds at the edge of the corn rows scattered with the billow of ashes windswept from a fire as his mother hacked at the stalks, slicing them at their base with blow upon blow until a dozen lay felled. Even these the birds assaulted. She cleaved at them, catching one in midflight and severing its wing. It flopped on the ground and she bent to the harvested stalks, bundling them together and dragging them towards the boy, Belle trailing after her, snapping at her winged pursuers.

When she dropped the cornstalks at her son's feet, the dog turned tail and stood guard while her mistress scavenged the treeline. She wrenched a fallen branch from among the bracken. She broke it in two over her knee then strode back to the boy with the thicker piece and pressed it into his hand. It was near as long as he was tall and there were three prongs at its end. The bark was scaled and loose. It crumbled under his grip.

Ya gotta protect the seed, she said.

The boy nodded and she turned, storming back into the fray.

Birds, five or six of them, swooped past the boy's shoulder.

They landed on the pile of seed corn — little brown swallows dodging among the larger blacks. The boy swung his club. A prong caught one of the blue-collared birds in its breast, making it stick. He knocked it off against the ground, swung again and hit another, startling it to flight before it realized that it was already dead. It dropped like a stone.

He swung again and again and again until he was ringed by their mangled, twitching forms.

He tried to raise his club to strike once more but his arms were as rope and it drooped. His throat was too parched to swallow. He ran his tongue over his lips and watched his mother labouring back from the field, towing another load. Beneath the delirious frizz of her hair, blood from a dozen cuts and scrapes painted her cheeks and dribbled in trails down her neck. When she reached her son, she heaved the bundle on top of the others, the birds ravaging the seed taking flight then settling again as she turned back to the rows. The flock there had become as a waterfall, black and foul, pouring from the trees and flooding the cornfield, its mist coal-speckled against the clear blue sky, the clamour of their feast foaming against the roar of their chatter.

Such was the world beyond where his mother stood, her arms limp at her side, her hair as wild as thorn bushes. She craned her neck and looked back at her son, her eyes wide, astonished and fearful. He watched the knife slip from her hand and stick into the sun-parched earth.

Ma! he called out.

Her legs buckled. She teetered sideways and slumped to the ground. He dropped his stick and ran to her screaming, Ma! Ma! When he reached her, he knelt and wiped away the hair lathered to her cheeks with sweat and blood. She lifted her hand towards his face but it faded. The boy clutched at it and she smiled, wan and desperate. A tremor coursed through her and she screamed, jerking her hand away and clutching it tight to her belly. Her eyelids pressed into seamless pits and her teeth mashed against her lips. Then all at a sudden the tension fled her and she went limp against the ground. The boy took her hand again and pressed the back of it against his cheek, its fingers twitching like the legs of some dying thing.

He heard Belle bark and turned. There was a crow pecking at the eyes of the bird he'd impaled with his stick. Belle pounced at it. It took flight and the boy watched it striving for the forest before it was lost to the sun's harsh glare. He felt for his father's hat to guard against the bright but it was gone, he couldn't remember where. Cursing himself for losing it, he looked to his mother's crumpled form. The hem of her skirt was mired in blood, the shadow at her back as thin as a wheat stalk, the air around her miasmic. The cackling seemed to be coming from the other side of the world, its rabid shrill dulled by his exhaustion, and he heard his father's voice raging against its fury.

Git her out of the heat, boy, it said. It'll kill her.

He circled to her front and bent to her ear.

Ma, he said. Ya gotta git out of the heat. Ma!

She groaned and her eyelids shuddered. He waited for her to rouse. When she would not he wrapped an errant strand of her hair around his finger and gave it a sharp jerk, snapping it off at the root. Still she did not stir and he stood and tried to think of what his father'd do in his stead. He saw him lifting her from the ground and turning towards the path. In his mind it didn't take him more than a half-dozen strides to get her through the pines and not a single step more before he made it to the pasture gate.

He scanned the forest, following its line until it gave way to the beaver dam on the far side of the field, then looked back to his mother and saw her knife stuck upright in the dirt. Its handle was made from a piece of maple worn smooth and its blade of a grey metal that reflected only a world cast in shadow. He pried it loose from the soil and skulked along the treeline until he came to a lone cedar among the pines. He hacked at a low branch. After the third swipe it fell to his feet. He hacked at another and severed it in two. Laying one on top of the other, he dragged them back to his mother. He draped the webbed bough of one over her face and then softened a hole in the soil with the knife. He used his hand to dig it down to the depth of his elbow and took up the other bough. He trimmed the infant branches from the stem of it and stuck it in the hole, leaning it over his mother's face and packing its base with dirt.

The shade fell where he'd wanted it but the sun still punctured the gaps, alighting islands on her cheeks and forehead. He dug another hole behind the first and stuck the other bough in, tweaking it until her face was covered by its shade. Returning to the cedar, he harvested another six of its branches, the last as thick as his leg and taking ten swipes to hack loose. He trundled them back in two trips and hedged them between his mother and the sun.

When he was done he was dizzy and had a terrible urge to lie down beside her but was saved from this by his thirst.

Belle had since retreated to within the hedge's cover. When the boy turned towards the path leading into the forest, she stood on wobbled legs and barked feebly at him.

I'ma fetch us some water, the boy said. You stay with Ma.

The dog sat on her haunches and watched the boy set off, dubious it seemed of his slow plod and the way he stumbled over the wagon trail's scored ridges.

The trees were all but emptied along the path. Only a few of the lesser birds skittered amongst the branches. A crow cawed at him from behind, hastening him through the breech and into the pasture. Meadowlarks twittered and dragonflies flitted. Thistles stung his legs and the tall grass tangled his feet. He tripped and fell then rose and drove his legs forward in a staggered line towards the barn.

Spook was at the yard's fence, shaking her head and braying mercilessly. He marched past her, sneaking between the cedar rails and hurrying to the well. He pumped the lever and drank from the flow then pumped again and dunked his head under, wetting his hair.

A splash of cold water like that'd shore do Ma a world a good, he thought, wiping the wet off his face.

As he strode towards the house he tried to think of how he could get more than a potful out to the corn patch.

If ya could carry it, there's that ol milk cask in the shed.

He thought of his father's wheelbarrow, how it was too heavy for him to lift even empty. And of Spook, only a few weeks ago harnessed to a tree felled for winter wood, his father lashing her backside into ribbons to get her to lug it across the pasture. And then he recalled how two summers' past his father had harnessed three of the hounds to an old wagon and had cheered them on as they pulled the boy around the yard. His mother had watched, shaking her head against the foolishness of such a thing, her scorn suddenly turned to horror when one of the wheels had struck a rock hidden in the grass, toppling the wagon and driving the boy into the ground. By the time she'd reached him there was a lump as big as a fist swelling his forehead. While she carried him back to the house, he'd watched his father catch up to the dogs and untether them from the wagon, born into bits from the abuse.

44

So that's that, the boy told himself, hurrying up the steps and onto the porch.

The kitchen door was open. He charged through it, ran to the stove and snatched up his mother's cast-iron pot. Water sloshed in the bottom and he heard the thin knock of eggs against its metal. He pried off the lid — there were three hardboileds in it. He refit the lid and turned for the door thinking he was forgetting something.

It came to him when he'd reached the porch.

A cup, he thought.

He dropped the pot and ran back into the kitchen. He hoisted himself up onto the counter so that he could reach one of the tin cups that hung on hooks below the cupboard. Coming back to the door he paused, trying to think of anything else he might have forgotten.

Well tain't like yer goin ta the moon.

The assault on the corn had continued unabated, though now it seemed that some light sparred through its gloom. And there were more crows on the ground, picking over the remains of the cacklers, scores of which now pocked the field. New shadows ranged high against the blue, too large to be anything but hawks or maybe eagles. As he broke from the berth of pines the boy watched one of them dive, following its descent into the seething mass.

His mother lay on her side within the shade of the cedar hedge. Her eyes were open and their whites shone against the grey hollows engulfing them.

Gawd, he thought as he walked towards her, don't she look like that chicken ya found last winter, caught out in the rains. It had stared at ya too. Remember. So ya'd thought it was just sick but it weren't. It was dead. And it'd been yer fault. When the rains had started Pa'd sent ya to put em away but ya'd missed one. It must have been cowerin under the eaves. He hadn't blamed ya but there it was. Its feathers limp and dirt spackled. You'd cried so hard it'd made Pa laugh and pluck ya into his arms.

He'd said, It's jus a chicken, son.

But here was his mother looking at him the same way.

The boy watched her and prayed for her to blink. He counted down from five, telling himself she'd blink before he'd reached one. When he got to two, he stopped and took a deep breath. Her eyelids quivered.

I brought ya some water, he said, setting the pot down beside her.

She licked her lips.

Taking off the pot's lid, he fetched the cup and dunked it in. When he turned back to his mother, her eyes were closed.

Ma? he said. I got the water.

She opened her eyes again. The boy tilted the cup to her lips. Most of it dribbled over her chin but enough got in her mouth to make her start coughing.

More, she said when she'd subsided.

Y'ought'n sit up, the boy said. You'll choke again.

I cain't.

Y'ain't even tried.

I cain't.

I don't believe ya.

He glared at her and she swallowed hard.

A'right.

She laid her hand flat on the ground and cocked her elbow. The muscles on her forearm tightened a moment then relaxed. A tear glistened at the corner of her eye.

I cain't.

Ya jus need some help, the boy said.

He straddled his feet, one on either side of her head, burrowing his hands under her shoulder and bending his legs and lifting, straining against her weight. After a moment, she cried out and her shoulder broke free from the ground. He felt her rise. Then the pressure was gone. She was resting propped on her arm.

I tol ya ya could.

The faintest smile parted her lips and then she was coughing again. She leant over and choked up a thick globule, its green, the boy could see, speckled with red. Wind plucked at the sinews of spit straddling the distance between her lips and the ground. Thunder rumbled. Belle raised her head, whimpering, and the boy looked skyward. Storm clouds broke against the treeline above the granite ridge on the far side of the field.

The rains is come early, he said.

His mother peered past him, her eyes growing wide under the threat.

I guess y' ought'n be gittin home then.

I ain goin leave ya.

She reached out and brushed the back of her hand against his cheek. Her touch was as light as a feather.

Yer goin have to walk, the boy said.

I cain't.

But Ma—

I cain't.

I'ma build ya a tent. Pa showed me how.

She groped for his hand and took it and squeezed it no harder than a baby would have.

If the rains come I'm done fer. I ain goin—

I'ma build ya a tent. I'll—

She squeezed his hand again and this time drove a sharp nail into his palm so he'd listen.

I'm done fer, y'understand. Ain't no two ways about it. If the rains come I won't make it and you'll be on yer own til yer pa gits back. Ya need to set yer mind to that. Look at me.

But the boy wouldn't. He stared up at the clouds boiling angry overtop of them. Raindrops fell on his cheeks as fine and as sharp as needlepoints.

Look at me, she said again. Her voice had gentled and the boy was powerless against it. When he turned back to her, sweat beaded her forehead and her cheeks heaved. She coughed again.

You can do it, she said. I know ya can.

Lightning flared from within a great black mass just now usurping the lesser clouds and the both of them waited for the thunder. The lightning flashed again. It lit a fringe around the cloud and there wasn't a sound in the world except his mother's wheezing breath. He reached into his pocket, searching out the tooth. His fingers dug past his knife and his magnifying glass and probed the crevices but found nothing there but a small hole.

Pa ain never comin back, he cried. He ain't!

N earing dusk, retinas of smoky-blue blinked at them through the clouds and patches of sunlight scoured the field. The birds had departed and in the fading light, the cornstalks looked like the shafts of arrows forgotten in some battle-ravaged land. The rains had amounted to no more than a sprinkle and the sky celebrated their fortune with a dazzle of deep reds streaked with orange.

Ain never seen a prettier sunset, his mother said, lying on her back and gazing up at it.

Flies buzzed about her and she made feeble swats at them. One probed about the boy's cheek but his thoughts were elsewhere and he minded it as little as the breeze plucking at the hairs curtained over his brow. Sitting there, cushioned against his mother, he was thinking of how, on any other evening such as this, his father'd be ambling back from the barn, whistling, his hands in his pockets, his shoulders shrugging to the laze of his stride. The boy, shooing the chickens towards the coop, would look after him as he mounted the porch steps, stopping momentarily to gaze down at his wife. Her head would be leant back upon the cedar rail chair, her hands cradled over its arms, her eyes closed, wearing the faintest of smiles — glorin in the day, she'd have called it. Pa'd kiss her forehead and ask her if she'd like a cup of tea. She'd open her eyes, blinking as if she were seeing him for the first time. Hmmm, she'd say and squeeze his hand. I shore would. When he'd turned to the kitchen she'd call lightly after him, And don't skimp on the honey.

By the time the boy had locked the coop and was making his way back to the house, his mother would be warming her hands round the cup in her lap, his father leaning against the post striking a flint-spark into the tobacco trailing over the bowl of his corncob pipe. The boy would step up beside him and man, woman and child would watch the last traces of sun leaking out of the sky.

Belle let out a sudden snarl and the boy sat up from his dreaming. The hair bristled along her back and her jowls quivered over the razored points of her teeth.

What is it, girl? the boy asked, reaching out for her.

Shirking his touch, she hunched low and then bolted for the forest path, yapping against the sin of whatever it was that was out there. The boy leapt to his feet and took a step but was unwilling to leave his mother.

There came a volley of barks, blistering the quiet and then fading without so much as an echo as if whatever it was that was out there had devoured them along with their mistress. The boy snatched up his three-pronged stick, never once taking his eyes off the black-walled corridor leading through the pines. He listened past it for a sign of what was to come but the encroaching dark locked away the secret of it in silence and shadow.

He listened and waited, holding the stick as a ward against the fear pitted in his belly. There came then the rush of paws thumping up the path and the boy thought of his father facing off against the dogs. He switched the stick to his left hand and fumbled the knife out of his pocket with his right. He pried the blade loose with his teeth. Its silver caught not a glint of the moon, buried now beneath a solitary cloud.

He clenched it tight and gritted his teeth.

Come and git me you sons of bitches. His voice cracked, his throat parched and his lips as sand.

The paws met with the crackle of leaves and their canter took form against the nightshade. The boy could see the flap of the dog's ears and saw in its stride a familiar gait.

Gawd, Belle, he said, y'ever gave me a fright.

He folded his knife and pocketed it and still she came at him, her pace unrelenting.

Whoa now, had barely parted his lips when she was on him, tackling him to the ground and pinning him beneath her, licking at his face.

Wha's got into ya? he said.

He pushed her off and sat up.

She barked at him, her head bent over her two front paws, and it struck the boy as odd, seeing her that way, for she'd never been one for such play. Then he caught sight of her eyes, their colour straining against the dusk. They were blue. Blue like his father's.

Sky! he cried.

Hearing his name, the dog slunk towards him, humbled and shy, his head lowered, repentant of the trick he'd just played. The boy wrapped his arms around his neck and buried his nose in his fur. He smelled of river mud and for a moment the boy didn't see the meaning behind his return, so glad was he to feel the pulse of his dog's breath against his chest. Sky, here again when he'd never thought—

And then its import wedged itself inside of him. He looked again to the wall of darkness, barricading the forest against the field. An orange ember burned a hole in the pitch at the height of a man. Belle jittered below it and his father's pipe smoke flavoured the breeze.

Pa! he yelled and rushed to his feet.

The moon's swollen crescent pried itself from under the cloudscape, birthing his father into light.

Land's end boy, what the hell are ya . . . His voice trailing off as he caught sight of the ravaged field.

It's Ma!

In the next instant, his father was kneeling beside his mother, forcing his hands under her back and lifting, all of it happening at once so that time seemed to have loosed its hold over them. Her body convulsed against his. She let out a pained sob and never had the boy heard a more joyful sound.

Her arms latched around her husband's neck and the man turned, hurtling past his son, the dogs nipping at his heels, chasing him down the path towards home.

II

The rains had been threatening all day, the clouds turning from grey to black, the wind rising into a furious gale, then just as she was ladling out stew from the cast-iron pot hung over the fire, the distant rumble of thunder.

Her father was sitting at the kitchen table, carving a new handle for his axe from a length of rock maple. The old one had cracked that morning and lay on the table's top in front of him, still attached to the steel head that had been passed down from his father and his father before him and on and on, perhaps, to the beginning of his line. The endless succession of owners had worn it down to a nub not much bigger than the size of his daughter's hand, though it was four times as thick. Still, he'd as soon have parted with it as he would have his right arm. He'd finished the shaft's general outline and was scraping his spokeshave over its butt end to fashion the fawn's foot. Wood shavings were scattered around it. When his daughter brought his plate to the table she bent low and blew at them, chasing the curls into her father's lap to tell him what she thought of him bringing work into her kitchen. He made no sign to say he'd noticed and she set his plate down heavily in front of him, sloshing stew up over its sides. Only then did he look up, but all he saw of her was her back as she went to fetch the broom from beside the door.

Don't ya worry bout that, he said, propping the handle against his chair, I'll clean up afta.

If'n I believed that, she answered, I wun't fetcht the broom.

Jus leave it.

I'm almost done aryhow.

He picked up his spoon, then thought better of it. Setting it aside, he scraped the tailings from the table into his palm then stood and carried them to the stone oven set in the wall. He tossed them onto the coals under the pot and when he turned back, she was standing behind him, leaning on the broom and scowling. Strawberry-tinged coils of hair hung loose over her pale and freckled face, the crooked nub of her nose parting its drape.

Gawd, he thought, don she looked like her mother on the day we were married. And thinking of the night that had followed, he felt his cheeks flush red. She hadn't been much older than his daughter was now.

Scuse me, he said, lowering his eyes and burying his sudden discomfort by sidestepping her with a playful jig as she swept the scraps of wood into the oven.

He was just about to sit back down when she said, You jus goin leave that ol axe on the table while we et?

She was glaring at him and he knew that if he said anything but, No ma'am, while she was looking at him like that she'd be apt to mix a pebble or two into his stew when she reheated it for supper, a trick she'd learned from her mother, God rest her soul.

So he said, No ma'am, I ain't, and took up the old axe and

the new handle too. He walked over and stowed them beside the door.

She was sitting at the table when he returned, a spoonful of stew at her lips, blowing at its heat. Thunder rumbled again and he shook his head, taking up his own spoon.

Helluva a time for that handle ta break, he said. That new field ain but half cleart and it'll be three weeks afore I can use the new one.

You can always ast Mr. Edgars to borrow his.

I wun't ast Edgars for a rope if'n I was drownin.

Even the thought of Edgars was enough to sour his mood. Thinking maybe that's why she'd brought him up in the first place, he looked to his daughter. She was grinning and he took that to mean he was right.

I guess'n it'll have to wait then, she said.

Well I guess'n it will.

Another clap, this one rattling the window's glass. The girl's hand stalled on her spoon.

Will'll be some afeared, she said. He jus hates the thunder.

I'll go and see him when I'ma done. I got to git some pine tar to seal off the ends of that handle while it dries aryway.

I'ma the only one who can soothe him when a storm's a-brewin.

I'll manage.

He went back to eating. The thunder was fading now, and when it had gone his daughter started eating again too.

You'll sing him the song? she said between bites.

The one bout the ol lady swallered a fly?

No, the other.

I thought tha was his fav'rit.

It is. But it'll just keep him up. He always laughs somethin fierce when ya get to the part about her swallerin that horse. Ya got to sing the other, if'n ya wan him to fall asleep.

How'n that go again?

Setting her spoon aside, she cleared her throat and began to sing.

Hush little baby, don't say a word, mama's goin fetch ya a mockin bird.

Her voice was sweet and pure. It did not rise above a whisper.

I member it now, her father said and she picked up her spoon.

I din't mean fer ya to stop.

Cain't eat and sing at the same time, now can I?

You hardly ever sing arymore.

Tha's because ya never ast me to.

I miss it.

All ya have to do is ast.

He watched his daughter eat. After a few bites she looked up at him smiling, and he went back to his meal.

I don't know what all the fuss is bout aryhow, she said chasing a chunk of potato around her plate. Mr. Levin comes ever year, I ain never had to hide out in the house afore.

Is different this year.

How?

It jus is.

But—

Tha's the end of it.

He levelled a hard stare at her so that she would know that it was, pebbles in his stew be damned.

They ate the rest of their dinner in silence. Then, just as he was mopping up the gravy from his plate with his finger, three sharp raps sounded.

They both froze, he licking the grease off his finger, she staring over his shoulder at the door.

Go on upstairs, he whispered to her.

Is just Barlow, she whispered back, I'da know his knock ary-where.

He shushed her but heedless she called out, That you, Barlow?

A muffled What? sounded in response.

I done tol ya it was.

Cursing under his breath and shakin his head, her father rose and walked to the door.

Scared of a skinny little runt like Barlow, she called after him. Ain that a thang?

When he opened the door, Barlow was standing on the porch holding his hat against the wind's bluster and looking like someone maybe ought to be holding on to him too.

Well there's a surprise, the man said, Mr. Barlow knocking at ma door come feedin time.

I ain here about feedin, Mr. Henry.

I guess'n they's right then.

Sorry?

They's a first time for everythin.

Barlow looked at him as if he couldn't tell whether he should take offence.

What can I do ya fer, Mr. Barlow?

The oats is gone.

The oats?

From the allotment.

Alla it?

The whole sack.

How— then gritting his teeth — Edgars.

Mr. Thomas said he saw him spookin around the barn lass night.

Speak of the devil and he shall appear.

Scuse me?

59

Nothin. You talk to him?

Mr. Edgars?

Yeah.

I did.

And wha'd he say?

He called Mr. Thomas a lyin— then glancing to the girl sitting at the table — somethin or other I can't repeat in the presence of a lady.

My daughter thanks ya for that.

Barlow grinned like a dog that had done his master right and it was all Henry could do to keep from patting him on the head.

Where's Edgars now?

Last I saw of him he was slammin his door in ma face. Whadya goin do?

I guess'n I'm goin ave a talk wit him. He reached for his jacket on the hook beside the door.

He'da buried them oats by now. He ain never goin give em back.

Then ya best see how much ya can scrounge from the others.

They ain goin be happy, the must took most of the crop already.

I know it.

They's goin shivaree him fer shore when they find out.

I've haffa mind to let em this time. Then cursing, Gawd, if it ain but one thing is another, he cinched his hat on his head and was just stepping onto the porch, bracing himself against the wind, when he caught himself and turned back.

I won be long, he said to his daughter. You stay in the house till I git back.

I's jus goin to mend them ol boots a yers aryhow, she said, collecting the plates.

He frowned like he wasn't sure he should believe her.

Ya can lock me in ma room if ya want.

60

She was glaring at him fierce and defiant, and he paused, thinking maybe he should, but shut the door behind him nevertheless. As the girl set the plates to soak in the bucket of water on the counter, she watched him chasing after Barlow through the window, the both of them tilted forward, fighting against the wind as they hurried down the yard's slope towards the dirt road leading into town.

Lightning quartered the sky's black and she held her breath, thinking of her brother out there all alone and how he'd tremble when the thunder came.

The wagon trail cut a straight path through the forest that ringed the settlement. It dead-ended at the river, a few hundred paces from where it started, though she was only going halfway there. Cedars crowded the path, blocking out the wind, but she could hear its roar lashing against the treetops. The air was cool and tasted of rain.

She hadn't taken the time to buttonhook her jacket, and as she hurried on she held its flaps tight against her body with one hand, the other clasping the cornhusk doll she'd made for her brother from this year's harvest. A spot of light appeared through the bracken ahead and she chanced a look behind. One of the settlement's stray dogs was following her — dirty and mange-ridden, trotting along with the peculiar sideways gait that seemed particular to its breed, its paws cross-stepping over themselves and its head craned towards the forest as if it was expecting something to jump out at any moment.

Slowing her pace, she let it catch up. It circled her warily, casting her a skittish glance, and she made as if to grab the tattered fray of its tail as it passed. It tucked it under its hinds, scampering away, and she chased after it until she'd come to the clearing hewn into the forest around the settlement's Memory Stone.

It was a square block of charcoal-grey granite carved from a boulder of a kind that was common to these woods, deposited, she had been told, by the hand of God when humankind was but a notion. The founders had chiselled its sides flat so that each of the original four families would have a place to mark their dead. Whenever a child was born it would be brought here and the names would be read, starting with the kin on its father's side, and in this way it'd come to know its place in the world.

She found her brother's name at the bottom of the tally on the near side and kissed the tips of her fingers, dabbing them against her father's scrawl. There were nine other Williams listed above and she recalled how she had fought with her father to have her brother entered, instead, as Will, like it would have meant the end of the world if he didn't. But tha's his name, she'd screamed when he'd refused. When he still wouldn't give in she'd pounded on his chest and kicked at his shins, her father taking the punishment as if it was his due, and finally, her anger succumbing to grief, holding her as she cried like there could be no end to her sorrow.

Thinking of it now, sorrow again threatened to swallow her into its pit. Thunder rolled over the roar of the wind and she circled the stone, towards her brother's plot.

It was the only one that had been laid that summer and the dog was already nosing at the fresh-dug earth. She shooed him away and knelt beside it.

I'ma here, Will, she said. Then holding out the cornhusk doll: I brought ya somethin to keep ya comp'ny.

Placing it at the head of the grave, she pressed the toy into the earth, patting down the dirt at its feet to bolster it, then lay down with her back against the mound.

The thunder was subsiding but another crack eclipsed it, startling her and causing the stray to whine and draw closer, though it would still not come within arm's reach.

Don't fret, is okay, she said, leaning on her side like she was peering over the bunk bed that she had shared with Will. It ain goin hurt ya.

The dog's whimper could just as well have been her brother, who would also cry when a storm awoke him in the night so that, closing her eyes and laying back down, it was easy to imagine that she was back in her bed and Will was still alive, though he'd been in the ground for almost two moons.

The only thing that would calm him would be to sing the lullaby that her mother had sung to her and then to Will for the first time when he was but a bump in her belly and she'd said it was the only way to get him to stop from kicking.

As she sang it now, her voice rose from its whisper to fight against the thunder's peal. She'd almost got to the end when the dog let out a sharp growl. The last line choked in her throat and she sat up, opening her eyes. There were four men walking towards her, none of them seeming to mind that they were treading over the graves of her ancestors. She recognized two of them right away — Mr. Levin, grey bearded and cradling an ancient and weathered rifle in his arms, and the giant whom she knew to be called Yoke. He was as tall as the Memory Stone was high, though her father could hardly reach its top, and true to his name, his shoulders were as broad as a team of oxen, his legs and arms as thick as tree trunks, his bald head residing like a fire-scarred mountaintop above them.

The other two she had never seen before, the both of them dirty-faced and neither with more than a few sprouts of hair on their chins. The younger one wasn't much older than she was. He was tall and as thin as a sapling and had the heavy sloping brow of a simpleton. The older was shorter by a head but had two stone on the other and wore a pained expression like he was trying to dig a sore tooth loose with his tongue.

The dog was snarling as they advanced but none of them had eyes for anything but the girl, now thrusting herself to her feet and backing away.

Tha's a real purdy song you'ns singin, Mr. Levin said, smiling as if he was sorely out of practice so that it had the opposite effect he'd intended.

She turned to bolt and ran headlong into the one named Briar, standing not a half a pace behind her. His cheeks were windburnt and pocked so that they appeared from beneath his whiskers as slabs of raw meat, rotted and ravaged by worms. But his eyes were keen and clear and brimming with malicious intent.

She dodged away from him but his hand was too fast. He grabbed her arm just below the shoulder, jerking her to his chest and holding fast to her wrists, crossing her arms over the small mounds at her breast.

Now where ya runnin to, little miss? he said.

She struggled against his grip, kicking at his legs with her heels and squirming, trying to wrestle free.

She shore is a feisty one, ain she? Briar said, burying his face into her hair. And, Gawd, but don't she smell good.

Tha's Henry's daughter, Levin said.

Well he ought'n know better'n to let her wander in the woods all by her lonesome. Is dangerous.

A'right now, let her go. You've had yer fun.

Briar grimaced as if he was thinking of arguing the point, then released her anyway, raising his arms above his head to sign his surrender.

The moment the girl was free, she hurried from his reach.

I din't mean no harm, Briar said. I's jus having some fun, like he said.

She turned towards them and backed away, her chest heaving.

Be a good girl now, the old man told her. Run along and tell yer pa we's comin.

She didn't need to be told twice and wheeled around, bolting for the path. The stray dog scurried after her until he'd made the forest then turned back, growling at the men one last time, all of them watching after the girl as she disappeared into the cedars.

Gawd, Levin said when she'd gone, seems she was but a little girl lass time I saw her.

Briar sucked on his teeth.

Well she shore ain now.

W hen they came out of the forest, she was hurrying up the slope leading to her house, perched atop the hill overlooking the village. Her father was coming up the road alongside Barlow. He'd spotted her too. He was yelling something that was lost to the wind and making as if to set off after her before he caught sight of the five men walking towards him. Stopping short, he looked to Barlow and a moment later Barlow turned back at a stiff jog towards the barn set a ways back from the half-dozen houses bunched around the gristmill where the river flowed at a steep pitch into the lake. Each house was made of logs patched with limestone and clay, except Henry's, which was made of hewed lumber and was also the only one that had glass in its windows.

As Levin passed it by, the curtain over a window on the second floor opened and the girl's face appeared through the crack.

Henry had seen it too. He was shaking his head and cursing under his breath as the others approached.

Children, huh? Levin called out to him. Ever under foot unless'n you'ns lookin fer em.

Henry smiled.

Tha's a good one.

Is what ma ma used to say.

I'll have to member that. Now holding out his hand. Howdo, Mr. Levin?

Cain't complain, the old man said shaking, and even if'n I did wun't make a damn bit of difference aryhow.

Ain tha the truth?

Taking his hand back, Henry passed a clipped glance over the other men, pausing ever so slightly at Briar, staring up at his daughter's window. His eyes were narrowed to slits and his tongue was just touching at the cleft in his top lip. He caught him looking and Henry covered by wiping something from his eye as he turned back to the old man.

We found yer daughter up at the graves, he was saying.

Yeah. She spends half her days there ever since her brother died.

Will's dead?

Fever took him two moons back.

I'ma real sorry to hear that.

Tha's kind of ya to say.

Ain nothin worse than losin a child.

Is been a trial, a'right.

He was getting choked up just thinking about it. Clearing his throat, he glanced back towards the barn.

I, uh, sent Mr. Barlow to fetch yer allotment. He won be but a moment.

I'll git the yearlins to give him a hand.

Craning his neck, he called to the two boys behind him, Lemon, Jude, go on up to the barn yonder, help Mr. Barlow with the allotment. Go on now, shake a leg.

The two boys hustled past. Levin started walking after them and Mr. Henry hurried to catch up.

They's two of them Kittredge boys, Henry said.

You know em?

Wun't be spring unless'n Clayton Kittredge's bangin at every door in town, begging for scraps. He lives wit his brood a half a day south of here. Then lowering his voice: Inbreds, ya know.

I wun't. I don't get down south much maself.

How's they come to be wit you?

We ran into em north of the forks when we's comin back from patrol. They'd been livin in the woods some time, I gather. Been wit us ever since. Never said nothin bout their pa.

I guess'n if Clayton was my pa, I'da have tried to forgit him too.

They'd reached the edge of the village. Aside from a couple of stray dogs sheltering from the wind against the houses there was no one about. They turned onto the path leading up to the barn and walked on until they came to its yard. It was ringed by a cedar rail fence that funnelled into a narrow passage at the river so the cattle could escape the summer's heat by grazing in the forest on the other side. Jude was leading a steer out through the barn doors and Lemon was walking behind it, crimping its tail whenever it slowed. Hitched to its back was a wooden box, covered over with cowhide to keep the rains off the sacks of grain and potatoes, apples and corn. The barn doors clattered violently at mercy to the wind and Barlow was fighting to close them.

How was the harvest this year? Levin asked, stopping at the open gate.

Oh, it was a might lean, Henry answered. On account the must got into the oats and some of the greens.

The must gits in the soil, you'll never git ridda it.

Ya don't ave to tell me. We's clearin another field but I cain't see how is goin be ready come seedin time.

What bout the t'backy?

Must don't care much fer t'backy.

Well thank Gawd fer that.

Which reminds me. Henry reached into his pocket and pulled out a small leather pouch. The t'backy had a hell of a time drying this year, on account of the humidity.

It was some humid a'right.

I cured that myself, he said, handing the old man the pouch, so'n you'da have somethin to tide y'over.

I preciate it.

Levin packed his pipe with a plug of the weed and turned his back on the wind, crouching low and striking his flint against a piece of white rock to light the pipe. When he'd finally managed to get it to catch, Jude and Lemon had reached the gate and Briar was rooting through the allotment.

Seems a might light, he said.

Henry shook his head.

Is the same as it always is, ceptin the oats.

Ain but a quarter sack.

Tha's all there is. We lost the rest to the must.

So ya said. Not much to see us through the winter. Specially now that we got two more mouths to feed.

We'da give ya more if'n we'da had it.

Briar was peering at him through squinted eyes, trying to find evidence that he was lying. If he was, his face betrayed none of it.

It'll have to do, Levin said, expelling smoke through his nose. A spattering of raindrops drummed against the brim of his hat and he looked skyward.

We best get a move on, we goin beat them rains.

Ah hell, a little rain never kilt no one. Briar was still staring at Henry when he said it so it came out sounding like a threat.

Henry lowered his eyes.

I guess'n you'ns right there.

L yin sumbitch, Briar cursed as they passed the Memory Stone. The spattering had become a downpour. The cedar canopy spared them the worst of it but he could already feel the cold and damp trickling down his back.

A handful of goddamn oats and I'll bet ya stones fer apples them potatoes is half-moulded like they was lass year.

The must took the rest, Levin said, you heard him.

Must my ass. He's holdin out on us.

Henry ain the holdin out kind.

Maybe he ain and maybe he needs a reminder of what it is we's doin fer them out here.

We's protectin them, an tha's all we's doin.

Protectin them? From who? The Reds? The war ended years ago and they ain been hide nor hair of em in these parts ever since.

But they don know that.

If'n tha's whadya believe, then you'ns more of a fool than I took ya fer, an tha's plenty fool enough already.

Ahead of them, the others had reached the end of the cedars. Beyond, the rain sounded its patter on the bridge spanned over the river. Jude and Lemon were running across it, slipping and sliding over the slicked wood, and Yoke was dragging the steer bawling and stamping his feet behind.

The old man pulled his collar up and snugged his hat down over his ears, moving to pursue when Briar grabbed him by the arm.

He's playin ya. And you's the only one who don know it.

Levin snorted.

You's the only one tryin to play me, he said.

Briar's eyes widened, affronted, and he took a step back.

I don't know whadya mean.

But the old man was already pushing past him, charging into the rain's drench.

You leave that girl alone!

It was well dark when they reached the cave. They came out of the rain and stood sheltering under the awning of rock that leaned over its entrance. Water poured from their hair and over their cheeks and beaded in their beards. The steer was huffing from the climb and its breath rose white in the chill air.

This'n where y'alls live? Jude said, peering at the dark recess in the cliff.

It's where we winter, Levin answered, rubbing his hands together to relieve their numb.

But is jus a cave.

Don't ya never no mind bout that. Now go on, help em with that steer.

While the others unloaded the supplies, Levin tendered a pipe then crouched in furtive contemplation at the foot of the tunnel leading into the cave, propping his weight against his rifle. The hand on its stock trembled with the cold and with age and his knees ached from the same.

After a time, Briar knelt down beside him.

What is it? he asked.

Smells like bear, Levin said.

Briar leant forward, inhaling deeply and running his tongue along the pitted remains of his teeth.

Could be, he said.

Could be, hell. It smells like bear.

Both men rested stoop-legged peering into the dark, but no amount of trying could pry loose its mantle.

You member that time Yoke wrassled a bear, Briar said after a moment.

Hard to forgit.

Hey, Yoke, ya feel like wrasslin another bear?

In the rain-drenched dusk all he could make out was the giant's silhouette as Yoke raised his machete over the steer's neck. Briar had known the man for going on eight years and he'd never heard him speak a word. He did nothing to make him think he was going to change his ways now, and as Yoke brought the blade down, Briar turned to Lemon and Jude. The both of them looked like they'd crawled out of a swamp. Dirty and wilted and shivering against the cold. They flinched against the steer's startled bleat and Lemon turned away as it was driven to its knees.

We ought'n send the yearlins, Briar said after appraising them.

Tha's a fine idea, Levin agreed. Hey, boys, either of you'ns ever kilt a bear?

I— Lemon started then stopped.

Well spit it out. You'ns kilt a bear or not?

No, Jude said. We ain't.

Well then you'ns in fer a treat tonight.

I— Lemon said again.

His eyes widened and he shook his head and took a step backwards. Jude steadied him with a hand on his shoulder as Levin pulled his knife from within the sheath under his coat. Even in the grey light it was a cruel piece of hardware. Fourteen inches from haft to tip and notched along one side with barbed grooves. It had a point as sharp as a thorn.

I'ma goin want that back. I took it offa the first Red I ever kilt.

Jude accepted the knife with utmost sobriety and held it up before him as if trying to find some sort of truth in its heft.

Well, go on now, Briar said.

The entrance was four foot round — a black, gaping mouth or an eye, dark and malevolent. Jude bent to it and peered inside. The tunnel pitched upwards at a slight angle and there was nothing but the hiss of water running at a distance to tell him there was any end to its reach.

How'n we a'pposed to see? Jude asked.

God gave ya more sense than sight boy.

Whadya mean?

Levin frowned.

Once ya git through the tunnel, the cave opens into a dome, twenty paces deep. Jus keep to the right. Feel yer way along the wall. In the back, there's a nook. I'ma bettin that's where ya'll find it.

And if we do? Jude asked.

Well you got that knife, ain ya?

Not much of a plan.

You got a betta?

You could give us that rifle.

Yeah, Lemon agreed.

This old thing'd jus as like to misfire as fall apart in yer hands.

I'da take that chance.

And if'n there's more'n one? The shot'd wake the others and then wheredya be? Yer betta off with the knife.

You say so.

I do. Now if you'ns done yabberin.

Jude squared his jaw, then knelt with the blade pinioned to

his chest and walked bandy-legged into the hole. His feet slipped on the wet stone. Steadying himself on the walls, he pulled himself up and into the fold. Lemon followed after, casting spurious glances over his shoulder as if he was hoping the bear might come lumbering out of the rain to spare them.

Levin and Briar watched him scuffle into the dark. After a few moments they heard a muffled thud and Jude cursing.

What? What? Lemon's voice came back a frantic whisper.

Jude groaned and cursed some more.

Yer goin wanna duck, he said.

What?

Feet scuffled and then another muffled thud. This time it was Lemon swearing.

Shitjeesus. Goddamn!

Hurts don it, Jude said.

I hit my goddamn head.

Tha's why I done tol ya to duck.

Them two shore a pair, Briar said, laughing.

A pair a what though? Levin asked.

Tha's a fair question.

They listened awhile longer but the hole had gone as quiet as a tomb. Briar stood and slicked back the sopping cord of hair that coiled over his cheek. He looked back at Yoke slinging the dead steer up onto his shoulder as if it was nothing more than skin, then turned back to the old man.

How long we goin stand round out here? he said. I'ma bout done with this rain.

Give it another—

There was a startled yelp followed by a splash. Then one of them was yelling — Son of a bitch. Goddamn — they couldn't tell which.

A'right then.

B eyond the tunnel, the cave floor tilted up sharply on the left and then levelled off into a plateau some fifteen paces wide and as many deep. A raised ledge ran along its wall. Several cords of quartered birch logs had been piled there and left to dry.

Levin felt his way up the rise until he came to the flat. He reached in the dark for the torch he'd left propped against the wood before they'd departed in the spring. He could hear the rush of rain funnelling through a hole in the ceiling. Overtop it, the splash of water as Jude tried to extricate himself from the reservoir at the foot of the cave and the high wail of his voice, Give me yer hand. Hurry. Goddamnit, Lemon!

How'n I apposed to give ya ma hand, Lemon called back. I cain't even see ya.

I'ma drownin here, you sumbitch. Give me yer—

There came another splash and then Lemon was sputtering and coughing and Jude was laughing and splashing handfuls of water at him.

The sound of their frolic pursued Levin through the dark as he took out his tinder horn, struck a light and set it to the torch. The end of it was wound with frayed strips of birch bark smeared with pine resin and the flame lapped at it hungrily. Stepping to the ring of stone, he pushed the torch inside a stack of kindling made into a tent. It came to life at once and he stripped off his leathers. He sat down naked on a fox hide folded over the granite ledge, rubbing his hands over the fire, and then took out his pipe.

Briar was bringing in the last of the supplies, stacking the sacks against the wall, and Yoke was quartering the steer at the edge of the plateau, the steady slash of his knife sounding in tandem with the sop of wet feet struggling against the granite slope.

After a moment, Lemon and Jude came into the light and stood gaping at the fire as if such a marvel had only been known to them from legend.

Where's ma knife? Levin asked.

Jude took it out from where he'd wedged it in the cord wrapped around his pants and passed it over. Levin ran his thumb up its sharp. Satisfied that it hadn't been nicked, he slipped it back into its sheath.

Well, come on then, he said, git outta them wet clothes. You'll catch yer death.

They stripped under the old man's watchful recline. Setting their leathers to dry by the fire they sat side by side on a bench fashioned from a piece of slate, the both of them covering their shame with cupped hands, the old man smiling at their modesty, his own organ a mere curiosity to him, shrivelled and grey so that it amounted to little more than a drowned worm between his legs.

Briar had joined Yoke at the steer and as the cold and damp steamed from their skin the two young men listened to the cleave of their knives rending the meat and watched the smoke rising at a sharp pitch from the fire.

Hey, Lemon said, pointing to a crude drawing etched in the rock directly above them. Tha looks like us up there.

It was of five stick figures sitting around a hearth such as theirs. Jude squinted at it and shook his head.

Cain't be.

I'ma not sayin tis. Jus, it looks like us. Hey, Levin, ya see that picture on the wall up yonder?

Levin looked up from prodding the fire and sought out the engraving above him.

Who ya reckin that is? Lemon asked.

Hard to say. S'been there ever since I can recollect.

And how long's that?

We's found this'n here cave in the tenth year of the war.

What we in now?

The thirty-fifth.

Tha's— Jude tried to do the sum but the numbers got all muddled up in his head.

Twenty ought years, give or take, Levin told him.

So it cain't be us.

Tis doubtful.

Tol ya.

Lemon shook his head and went back to staring at the picture. Then: Whydya think he done it?

Who?

Whoever drawed it.

Ta pass the time I guess, Levin said. Ya got to have somethin or other to do, or ya like to get the stir-craze livin in a cave all winter.

Whyn't he jus go build himself a house, live there?

Levin leant back against the wood and fixed him with a careful gaze.

Whadya know about history, son?

Who's story?

Man's. You know, what come afore ya.

I spect it was my mas and my pa.

Levin barked a short, sharp laugh and slapped his naked thigh.

Ya hear that Briar? he called out. His mas and his pa. I done tol ya he was a keeper.

The rhythmic slash of the blades through bone and the chip of steel hitting rock stuttered a beat, and Levin waited to hear if anything would come of it. When it started up as before, he leaned forward and poked the fire with his stick, sending a fresh volley of sparks towards the cave's ceiling.

History goes a might deeper than yer mas and pa, son.

Whadya mean?

It goes all the way back to the begin.

The begin?

Creatin, boy.

When's that?

Well tha's been a matter of some debate.

So ya don't know?

I din't say that.

Well then, what do ya say?

Five, maybe six thousand years.

That a long time?

Helluva a long time. And in all that span, man'd be livin in caves. Sometimes he gits in his mind that a cave's not good enough for him. He builds hisself a house and maybe a barn, domesticates hisself. But it is to the cave he will always return.

When Briar and Yoke were done with the steer they shed their leathers. They sat beside Levin on the ledge and there was no shame at all between them as they smoked their pipes, watching the old man roll the strips of the meat they'd cut around thin slices of wild garlic and fresh basil. He skewered them on sharpened sticks and they cooked them over the fire until the meat was blackened on the outside but tender and juicy on the in. Neither Lemon nor Jude could remember ever having tasted such a thing and they ate until they were sick with the weight of meat. Levin then gave each of the boys a tattered wolf hide and a coarse wool blanket. They lay them down on the floor, stretching their backs out on the mattress and rubbing their filled bellies as they listened to the old man tell stories of the war.

They were all of a similar strain, and it was not long before they could detect within them a clear design. A few men stood against a horde of the heathen savages. Most were killed and yet always Levin survived, through stunning feats of cunning and bravado, or sometimes just plain old dumb luck. Yet they did not tire of hearing them, for he told of these battles and of his escapes from certain death with such suspense that he cast doubt within the boys as to his own fate, though he sat there right before them.

I cain't magine, Jude said after a particularly harrowing tale.

What?

Livin through all that.

Prudence, Levin said. Tha's the key. Whoever strays from the path of prudence shall come to rest in the company of the dead. Tha's the first lesson ya must learn. It's why'n I've lasted so long and the others have not.

There's another name fer prudence, Briar said, and Levin cast him a reproachful glare.

Do not mind our narrow-sighted friend, he said. His war is not mine. It is a cruel and lowly path he treads and I cain't act as a broker for the reasons why'n he engages in it thusly.

Old man, Briar hissed at him, ya shore have a dainty tongue. Ya could talk the devil outta his horns I'da bet, but when ya git to sermonizin I'da soon be swallerin a porcupine tail-end first. So go on now, fore I take offence. How's bout ya tell em how Yoke come to wrasslin that bear.

Levin tapped his one remaining tooth with his index finger then leant over and took a stick from the fire. He stood and held the torch against the darkness as if he was hoping it might illuminate the story's begin.

A most remarkable tale, he finally said. It started on a night afore the rains had come, some eleven, twelve, years ago. It was me, Galvin, Val and Duke—

And me, Briar said.

The old man shook his head.

This'n afore yer time.

The hell it were.

You shore?

How else'n I remember it?

I could have sworn—

I was there.

You say so.

I do.

A'right then. So it was me and Galvin and Val and Duke and some say Briar was there too even if nobody seems to member it that way but hisself.

I was goddamn there, he shrieked, turning to Lemon and Jude and stabbing at his chest with a pointed finger. I's the one who found him tied to that tree—

I know how it goes, but you'ns gittin ahead of the tale.

Well then git on with it.

We was followin The Blood south—

What's that? Jude asked.

A river. Named on account it flowed red one year from spring to the winter rains, such was it impregnated by the blood of the savages we'd kilt. The harvest moon was yet but a sickle and we were tired beyond the limits of man. We'd lost most of our party at Settlers' Ridge, which I mentioned afore, it being the focal point of the war to that date. We'd taken the fort back in the spring and held it all summer, but them Reds had amassed an army of some ten thousand. There weren't but a hun'ed of us. They burnt us out and the only one's made it out alive were me, Galvin, Val and Duke, and maybe Briar, if'n ya can believe what he says.

Ya know I did. How else am I settin here?

Of the four or, possibly, five of us there weren't a man not injured in some fashion or nother. None of us had eaten in nigh on a week. We were a most pitiable lot and there weren't a single thought between us but puttin one foot in front of the other. We was headed south along The Blood, back to this here cave as a point of fact, when we picked up the scent of meat cooking o'er a fire. I tell ya, ain nothin so mean on a man with an empty belly than the smell of meat cookin o'er an open fire.

He paused a moment here and looked to Jude, who was nodding his head with eyes alight like he was imagining himself inside the story just like Briar.

Ya know of what I spek? Levin said.

Boy, do I ever, Jude answered.

Then y'also know how it's damn near impossible to put it out of yer mind.

Tha's the truth and then some. It gets to feelin like the very air's conspired against ya.

I couldna put it better maself.

Hearing that, Jude grinned and turned to his brother but Lemon was once against staring up at the drawing on the wall and seemed not to have heard what he'd said.

The wind was folldown us, Levin started again, and, like ya said, it did damn near feel like it was conspirin ta drive us out of our wits with hunger. Finally, Duke, he cain't take it no more. He turns to the west and sets off on a stiff course into the breeze.

Well that's a load a bull, Briar said. It was me who'd set off first and ya know it, jus like'n I's the first one to see Yoke. Tell the story right, or don't tell it atall.

As I said, Duke—

Lying sumbitch.

—turned west. Whadya doin? I called after him but he didn't hear me, lost as he was in the grips of that mania set upon a man when his belly's taken to chewin on itself fer sustenance. And it's contagious too, so it weren't a heartbeat afore the rest of the party set after him, with me trailin behind, urging prudence.

Now I done tol ya prior that they's about as many kin'a Reds
as they is animals, but what I din't relate was how they each have
their ways of making a man feel welcome when he's wandered
onto their land. The Cougar clan prefer to skin a man from
his toenails to his teeth and then smear burnin pine pitch over
him to keep him alive so as he don't miss nary the fun. And the
Kiyotes'll bury ya to yer neck in the dirt and smear yer head with
rancid meat and then set a pack of their namesakes upon ya.
Then there's the Jackals. They's downright hospitable. They's'll
dig out yer eyes with a sharpened stick and replace em with hot
coals and set ya to a slow roast o'er the fire. But there ain't nothin
worse than the Crows. They's not a more bloodthirsty race on
God's green earth. They's a people without a home, wanderin
the world, hunting the livin when they could and livin off the
dead when they could not.

They'da et ya? Jude asked, sitting bolt upright.

And boiled yer bones fer soup after.

I hope I ain't never meet a Crow.

And that was exactly what I was thinkin as I followed Duke—

Pfft.

—and the rest through that forest all them years ago.

Levin settled then against the pile of wood at his back. The
light from the fire struggled to ordain his features, ever changing
in the vigorous folds of shadow from which his voice seemed
to sprout like the lost spirits of the dead forcing their memories
back upon the living.

We could hear em long before we came into sight of their
camp. Whoopin and hollerin and beatin their drums. We knew,
somehow, that they was celebratin their victory at Settlers' Ridge
and how many of our kith and kin they'd kilt. Anger quickened
our pace t'wards what I was certain to be a most grisly fate.
Shortly, we could see their fire tarryin through the gloom. It

sprung upon us like the vision of a waterfall before a man dying of thirst, but Duke had enough sense to hold up, which Briar never would have, mind you, so I knows it musta been Duke.

Keep it up, old man.

We's all stood there starin through the dark and thinkin as to how we's might'n fill our bellies with somethin other than the sharp end of a knife or, if we's lucky, a half-dozen arrows. And then—

And then that's when I said, Briar interjected, I'sa betta check things out.

Maybe that's how it happened or maybe it was Duke who'd said the same.

The hell it was.

Don't matter a speck now, since Duke ain't here to prove the truth of it. One of you'ns took a wander round their camp and came back and told us that they was maybe a dozen of em and—

And they had a man tied to one tree and a short ways off a bear tied to another, Briar said. And they was so busy watchin em fight that we could have walked right into their camp and lit off with the deer they'd spitted o'er their fire fore they'da even know'd we was there. Tha's what I done told y'all and lightnin strike me dim if I'ma lyin.

It was exactly as Briar said, though I'sa told the story so many times tain't no mystery as to how he recollects it so. Now there ain't a one of us'd take such words fer the gospel. Reds is betta at trackin than a wolf and tha's a lesson I hope y'all never have to learn in the flesh. Theyda followed us through hell's half acre, we lit out with their feed. Weren't nothin fer us to do but kill the lot of em if'n we had ary a hope of gittin our teeth into that deer. They was round bout a dozen of em, as I said—

Was they Crows? Jude asked.

No, they was Minx but that weren't much consolation. Theyda flayed us alive and wore our skins fer britches they had haffa chance. If'n I was with ary other men ceptin Galvin and Duke, I'da lit right outta there but I'da seen each man take on as many in open battle. I'da figured I was good fer two myself, not yet being reduced to the todderin old man that sits here afore ya. Val could be counted on fer two or three on top, and well if Briar was there like he says, he might be able to manage one, if'n maybe he was lame and blind in one eye.

Yoke let out a snort that could have been a laugh. Briar spat and fixed him with a cruel look.

At least I weren't the one who got hisself tied to a tree by no Red, he said and his eyes meandered back to the old man. I kilt four on that night and a hun'ed since so I's know yer jus havin fun. And ya best be departin it soon afore I git in mind to prove the truth of what I spek.

You'ns about done?

I'ma gittin there.

A'right then. Now where was I?

Y'alls about to have at them Reds, Jude prompted.

Right, right, Levin said. We had spread out in a circle round the camp.

Closing his eyes, Jude imagined how it must have been, and in the dark, the old man's words formed into pictures as clear as any dream so that it came to seem like he was actually there along with him in the woods, those years ago.

All at once we came into that glade as if God hisself had transformed us into a tempest to lay waste to them ungodly heathens, nary a one layin a finger on ary of us. When they was all dead, we turned our eyes upon the man and the bear. Y'all know it was Yoke and that he's settin among us still with nothin to show fer his part in the story ceptin four ribbed lines over his shoulder where the bear tagged him, so I won't bother providin a proper descript of what he looked like then. Much the same as he does now, ceptin they'd only just scalped him. He had in his hand a sharpened stick maybe four finger-widths long, which they'd given him, good sports like they is. We could see that he'd already used it to blank one of the bear's eyes and had peppered its chest with such thrusts that the ground between them was sodden with its blood. I cut Yoke loose, unless'n Briar wants to lay claim to that feat as well.

I'll give ya that, old man, I was already four hands deep into that deer by then.

When Yoke was free, he turned to me. Instead of some gesture of gratitude, like'n I was spectin, he grabbed fer ma knife. I thought he meant to use it on me and was just cursin the fates fer their whimsy when he turns back to the bear.

I reckin he ain't done with it, Briar said. Ya recollect I said that?

I recollect someone did.

I reckin he ain't done with it, Briar said again, slapping Jude on the leg and laughing at his own wit.

Whadya make of that?

The rain carried on through the night and did not relent even as a dull light skewed through the crack in the back of the cave. Levin's stories had been knocking around Jude's head all night, keeping him awake thinking of the adventures that might be in store for him, and he greeted the coming of the dawn as he might have a snake that had crawled under his blanket. He was cold and he urged himself to get up and light a fire but he lay there still, watching the light parse the ceiling. He looked for the picture on the wall but the limestone was as black as slate. He closed his eyes and when he opened them there was a fire in the hearth and Lemon was standing beyond it scratching something into the wall with a sharply knapped stone.

Jude sat up, rubbing his eyes. Yoke and Briar were sitting on the ledge sipping past the steam rising out of the tin cups pressed to their lips.

That there chicory? he asked.

What? Briar answered.

What you'ns drinkin.

No.

Pa used to drink chicory. Never had much of a taste fer it maself.

Tain't chicory.

Jude stretched his arms and stood and walked naked to the fire. There was a cast-iron pot set on a rusted metal grill. Inside it, the water boiled red.

Sumac?

What? Briar grunted.

I said, is it sumac?

Yeah.

Pa drank that too. Said it keeps away the winter shake. Hardly worth drinkin without a drop a honey.

Ain got no honey.

How bout a cup?

Shaking his head, Briar upended his cup into his mouth and tossed it to Jude. He shook it out against the ground and dipped it into the pot. He blew at the steam until the tin grew too hot in his hand, then set it on the bench to cool and bent to his clothes. They were dry and stiff. He kneaded the leather between his fingers until it was supple again, dressed and sat on the bench. While he drank his tea, he watched Lemon scratching at the wall.

It's the same as the other one, he said after a time.

What?

The picture ya drawed.

Lemon took a step back to appraise it.

Tain't.

Five stick men settin around a fire. It's the same damn picture.

No, it's us. He pointed at the largest of the figures. Tha's Yoke. And thisn's Levin and here's Briar and that's me and you.

Its looks the same to me.

Drinking the last of his sumac in one gulp, he stood and let the slope pull him down towards the tunnel. He crawled through it and stood under the rock awning looking down at the earth washing in great sodden streams into the river some fifty feet beneath a rubble-strewn slope. The downpour was such that he could not see the far bank. He looked to the sky but could find no seam within its shroud.

He relieved himself at the edge of the awning and shimmied back up through the tunnel. Lemon was at the reservoir filling a cup with water. He smiled at Jude as he passed by like they held a secret between them, though for the life of him Jude couldn't figure on what it might have been. When he came back up the slope, Yoke was sharpening his machete with a flat stone and Briar was puffing on his pipe.

Levin's lookin fer ya, Briar said as Jude came back to the fire.

Where's he at?

In the nook.

The nook?

Back yonder.

Briar pointed to the rear of the cave with his pipe.

What the Sam Hill he doin there?

Killin a bear, I guess. Briar smiled wide through rust-coloured teeth and Jude shook his head but couldn't stop himself from grinning back.

Hey, Levin, he called out.

His voice echoed off the walls and he listened for a response but there was nothing beyond the lap of water. He took up a stick from the fire and walked along the plateau towards the rear of the cave. The shadows shrunk from his torch, hiding amongst the cracks. He came to the waterfall flowing through a hole in the cave's ceiling. Beyond this thin artery, he could see a red light as bright as the sun. A shadow passed in front of it and he called out, Levin, you in there?

Who's that? the old man called back.

Jude.

Well don't jus stand there, boy.

He followed the torch past the waterfall. Beyond, there was a cavern manufactured into a perfect steeple by some upheaval pre-dating the advent of man. On the far side of it, Levin stood in front of a small oven cut into the stone from which the sun-glow emanated. He was naked, save for a leather apron tied at his waist, and smudged with soot from head to tail. He pumped his foot on a bellows on the floor. With each blast the coal piled within the forge glared red and the glow licked at the bottom of a small cast-iron pot set just above it upon iron girders. It was hotter than summer back there and an acrid smoke choked the breath out of the air.

Gawd, Jude said coughing into his arm, don't it reek. I ain't never— What the hell's ya cookin back here?

The old man smiled.

Lead.

Lead?

Fer ma rifle. Come on then. Ya can work the bellows while I tend to the powder.

The old man stepped aside. Jude took his place and peered into the cauldron. Inside it there was a thin grey tube, hollow and

87

as long as his forearm but no wider than his thumb. Its low end was submerged in a bubbling pool the colour of granite.

Go on, now, Levin urged.

Jude pumped at the bellows with his foot as he'd seen the old man do.

Y'ain't suckin a tit, boy. It's got to be slow and even. Slow and even. Slow and— There ya go.

Nodding, the old man took up a wooden bowl from the ledge beside the oven. He urinated three quick squirts into it, tapped out a few extra drops and lowered his apron. He then sat on the ledge and poured from his powder horn a mixture of black and yellow sand into the bowl. When it was half full he stirred it with a stick whittled into a crude spoon. After a while, he stood, set the bowl on a flat shelf of rock beside him and walked to the cauldron. The whole tube had succumbed to liquid bubbling under the heat.

Levin then took from the pocket of his apron a small tin with a hinged lid. He opened it and scooped from within a fingerful of thick yellow paste.

Now fer the secret gredient, he said.

He dropped the paste into the molten lead and stirred the pot with a black metal rod.

Wha's that? Jude asked him.

What?

The secret gredient.

Wax.

Like'n from bees?

Like'n from what come out of yer ear when ya pick it.

Ear wax?

I been savin it up all year.

Why'n ya'd wanna do that?

It drives out the impur'tie so the shot'll fly straight.

And how'n the hell it do that?

It's science, boy.

What?

Science. Tha's the rules that govern all things. Even these here rocks are slaves to them.

Rocks got to obey rules?

Yeah.

Like'n what?

Like'n about stayin hard. And like some bein able to burn like this here coal and, hell, I don't pretend to have knowledge of every last one of em. But I do know that without wax that lead'd be bout as good fer shot as if'n I'd boiled up a pot of pig shit.

Jude shook his head.

Is a strange world, ain't it, son?

And then some.

It rained hard for nearly a week. Then one morning when Jude awoke, the waterfall's rush had dwindled to a trickle. Levin, Yoke and Briar were nowhere to be seen and the fire had burnt down to embers. The only light save the greyed dawn probing through the hole came from the torch that Lemon held in his hand to illuminate the picture he was scratching into the wall.

Jude sat up, shivering, and yelled over to him, Ya let the fire go out.

His brother didn't so much as twitch to say he'd heard him.

Unfurling from his blanket, Jude stood and walked to the stack of corded wood. He took two quartered logs from it, set them onto the coals and blew beneath them. The coals fired red and flames lapped at the curls of birch bark. He then took up the pot and lifted the lid. There were only a few dregs left in the bottom of it. Setting it back down, he called out to Lemon, Where's everyone at?

Yoke and Briar left in the middle of the night, his brother answered, not taking his eyes off his creation.

Why'n they do dat?

I don know. But Levin was in a right mood when he woke up and found em gone.

And where's he at now?

I guess'n he musta gone after em.

But when Jude came out of the cave the old man was standing at the edge of the awning, smoking his pipe and staring out at the drizzle as if it had done him some great wrong.

We got arymore of that sumac? Jude asked as he stepped up beside him.

Levin didn't reply and Jude opened his mouth to ask again, but the look on the old man's face told him he'd better not. After he'd relieved himself he crawled back inside and sat by the fire, chewing on a strip of dried meat and watching Lemon scratch at the wall.

He'd drawn a picture of Yoke fighting the bear and beside it he'd etched a house and a barn in boxed lines with the frilled bloom of a tree between them. The scene was peopled with six hands worth of half-sized stick figures, which Jude took to be children, and a few taller ones he took to be mothers.

Tha's the farm, Jude said, stepping up beside him.

It's the day we left. See, there's Pa.

He pointed to the figure strung from the tree's lowest branch with a line looped around his neck.

They's a crow peckin at his eye, last I recall.

I'ma gittin ta it.

On the far side of the barn, the smooth limestone broke into a vein of quartz bespeckled by the torch's flicker and Jude saw that Lemon had envisioned in this a river. There were two figures on the near side moving, from the stretch of their legs, at a desperate run towards three other figures north of where the vein forked in two. It recalled to him the day they'd met up with Levin, Briar and Yoke.

Whadya reckin happened to em? Lemon asked as he stencilled a bird's head suspended over his pa's shoulder.

Ya knows what happened. They's us.

Not us, them.

Lemon waved the torch at the crowd of stick figures beneath the tree.

Afta we left, I mean.

Theyda made out.

They's not a one of em had the sense God gave even the lowest creature. Tha's what Pa said.

He'da know a'right.

I'ma bettin they's dead.

Then they's betta off.

Ya reckin?

Y'ought'n just forgit about em.

They's our kin.

No they's ain't.

We's from the same mothers.

We ain't like them, Jude said. They was animals. Worse than animals. Our mothers too. Livin in their own shit. Eatin it. And— now whispering — fornicatin. Like mangy half-breeds never outta heat. Pa whippin em to beat the devil. Ya member that? He shook his head to release himself from the memory. Pa ought'n to ave burned the whole damn lot of em afore he hung himself from that tree. Forgit about em.

I cain't.

Try.

I did.

Well, scratchin it in the wall shore as hell ain goin help. Ya shun't never have drawed that. What was ya thinkin?

I don't know. It's like— what Levin said.

Howdya mean?

Is history.

History's somethin happened to other people. Ones who's dead. That's what Levin said.

Ya shore?

Ast him yerself. ·

Lemon blew dust from the crow's head and stood back to appraise it.

It's ourstory then, he said.

What?

It'd be ourstory then.

There ain't no such a thing. They's just—

What?

I don't know. Us. Here. Livin in a cave. Ain't nothin worth scratchin on a wall, tha's fer shore.

But—

Y'ought'n jus scratch the whole mess out!

Towards dusk, the rain picked up again, turning the trickle back into a geyser. Levin had not left his vigil and Jude bided his time swinging an axe at the birch tree Yoke had dragged up onto the plateau the day before. He'd cut it into logs and was just setting up the first of these on the chopping block when he heard a sharp crack like thunder, though if it was its lightning must have struck at the old man himself, the way the sound pierced the cave, echoing about the walls, loud enough to make Jude's ears begin to ring.

A moment later he heard Briar's voice raised in alarm, Ya gone crazy, old man, y'almost kilt me, and Jude scuttled down the rise and into the tunnel. When he came to the edge of its dark he saw Levin packing fresh shot into his rifle with a thin dowel and Briar striding towards him. In the fading light he could just make out three black lines over each of his cheeks, charcoal maybe or blood.

He didn't have long to ponder what they could have meant before Levin was raising the rifle, pointing it straight at the other's chest, Briar stuttering to a stop not two paces from the tip of its barrel.

I done tol ya to leave that girl alone, Levin growled.

It weren't like that. We's-a huntin. Ain that right, Yoke?

He looked over his shoulder at Yoke standing behind him, a deer slumped over his shoulders. The giant nodded and it seemed to reassure Levin, for he let the rifle's barrel sag from its sentry.

You'ns jus huntin?

That's right.

Then maybe you'ns wanna splain why'n you's wearin war paint.

Briar blanched and his hand moved to touch at his face, his fingers dabbing at the marks on his cheek.

I— he started but was cut off by Levin jamming the rifle's barrel up under his chin hard enough to make him bite his tongue.

Go ahead, the old man said, cocking back the hammer with his thumb. Tell me another lie.

Blood foamed at Briar's lips and he licked at them, swallowing hard.

Okay, okay, he said. Don't get yer britches in a bind. We did go back to the settlement. But it weren't fer the girl. It was fer the oats. I's goin prove to ya they was holdin out.

I'ma s'posed to believe that.

Believe what ya will, don't make a damn bit of diff'rence aryhow.

Levin pushed the barrel deeper into Briar's throat.

You touch that girl?

Tha's what I's tryin to tell ya, Briar choked out. We din't see the girl. We din't see aryone. None's that livin aryway.

Whadya talkin bout?

Henry and Barlow. We found their bodies on the road. They's missin their heads.

Missin they's heads?

Yeah. And they's houses all burnt down too. They ain't nothin left. Go on and see fer yerself, ya don believe me.

Levin chewed on his lip a moment, then unhitched his rifle from under Briar's chin. Briar commenced to rubbing at his throat and stretching his neck to get the cramp out of it as the old man ran his fingers through his beard, trying to find some sort of sense in what he'd said.

Was it Reds? Jude asked.

Levin looked back towards the tunnel. All he could see of the young man was two white globes peering anxiously from within its dark.

Musta been, I guess.

Now scratching at the top of his head.

Shoot, he said. Well don't that beat all.

It rained steady for three moons.

Then one morning, Jude awoke to the tack-tack-tack of water

dripping onto stone. He sat up and saw a shaft of sunlight like an arrow splintering the head of the bear Lemon had drawn fighting Yoke. At the rear of the cave, the orange flame from a torch dipped and bowed towards the rock where Lemon was enslaved to his latest creation, a mural depicting The Battle of Settler's Ridge. He'd been working on it for two moons and hadn't yet finished half of it.

The rain's stopped! Jude called out.

He listened for a response but there was nothing but the sharp tack-tack-tack. He hastened to the tunnel and drew himself through it and into the bright. Sunlight winked through the fleeting turbulence of white-frocked clouds rolling out from behind the ridge. Levin crouched at the edge of the perch with his hand stretched out before him. A sunbeam bandied over his fingers and he stared at it with the wonder of a child seeing his first dawn.

Yoke and Briar stood a short ways off, the former with a pack laden and heavy on his back, pitching stones into the tyrannical seethe of the water below, the latter unburdened and using the lash of his rawhide whip to mark a knot in a tree some fifteen paces away.

. . . scratchin at the goddamn wall, Briar was saying. And the other's just about as useful. Ain't done a damn thing all winter but eat, sleep and shit. We ought'n jus leave em behind.

Yoke grunted, in assent or its opposite it was impossible to tell. The scuffling of feet turned them to the cave's entrance where Jude stood shielding his eyes against the glare.

Ya shit yer bed? Briar asked.

What?

I say, ya shit yer bed?

No.

Figured ya musta, bein up so early.

I din't.

Briar glared at him as if he was thinking of contesting the point. Then: Where's the other?

Lemon?

I ain goin dignify that, boy.

Huh?

Sweetjeesus!

He snapped the whip in Jude's direction. Jude ducked and it cracked a hand's width above his head.

He still scratchin at that wall?

Jude nodded.

Well, whadya waitin on? Go on, then, fetch him. Hurry now.

He cracked the whip again to speed his flight.

There's Reds in them thar hills!

III

H e awoke into a hazy dawn.

He'd slept in the hollow under the lip of a sandwashed bank. The only vestige of the river that had corroded its shores was a thin stream pissing into a shallow pool a few feet from where he sat trying to figure whether it was early or late, the grey light prying through the dense mist providing no clue beyond telling him that the night had passed. He rubbed his arms against the chill, crumbling the hardened mud that he'd plastered on the night before to keep the bugs at bay. Still, he could feel the itch of bites on the back of his neck and he scratched at them with the leisure of drawing smoke through a pipe.

The air smelled of ash and tasted of grit, and it recalled to him the dream he'd just awoken from. He was a boy again, wandering through his village. The houses he could see as only vague impressions through a heavy fog. All was quiet save for an intermittent lark's twitter, which he knew to be coming from his brother. It was a game they'd always played when *kaskawahkamic* rolled in off the lake, entombing their village and remaking it into a spirit world full of mischievous ghosts. He was following Ostes's whistle like he'd been made one of them: a revenant called from the underworld by thoughts of home and now trapped in a halfway land by some creeping malevolence that he couldn't see but which he felt in the way the chilled morning air suddenly turned hot. Ash clung to his skin, greying it to stone, and the air was so thick he could hardly breathe. There were monstrous black masses pressing against the gloom and he could hear the thud of footsteps like thunder rolling over a barren land. A red glow crackled all around and out of the murk a firewhip tongue lashed out, startling him awake.

L ater, as he bent to the edge of the pool, he heard his brother's voice whispering out of the fog.

Nisi, it said. Are you awake?

He looked up but couldn't see beyond the borders of the river's raised banks, the haze was so thick. He cupped his hand in the water. It was cool and the current flowed through his fingers, pulling downstream. He drew a palmful to his lips. It tasted pungent of minerals and algae and, like everything else, of smoke.

Nisi, Ostes said again, this time more urgent.

Nisi rose and followed his brother's tracks to a fallen pine tree spanning the distance between the riverbed and the bank, some ten feet above him. He tightrope-walked up it. When he'd reached its upended crown he could see his older brother crouched on the lowest branch of an elm tree. He had a fevered look about his eyes, impatient and harried, as he often did when currying for his brother's attention.

Why did you not answer me? he asked.

Ignoring him still, Nisi stepped lightly off the log. He turned his back on his brother and walked to the edge of the riverbank.

It worries me, brother, that you sleep so much, Ostes chided. Too much sleep dulls the senses. On a day such as this, you should have been up well before dawn.

And I would have, brother, Nisi said as he relieved himself, but I was awake most of the night.

A true warrior knows how to still his troubled mind.

It was not that. You were crying out in your sleep.

I was not.

Naakaa. Naakaa, you called.

You lie.

Then you made suckling sounds. I believe Naakaa had proffered to you her breast and you were drinking from it her milk. And never before have I seen such a serene smile amongst the gentle cooing of a baby well satisfied at his mother's tit.

This is no time for jokes, Ostes said, standing and reaching for the branch above him. Come, I have something to show you.

Nisi folded himself back into his pants and turned back to his brother.

What?

It is important.

It is always important.

And never more so.

I am hungry.

You will not be when you have seen what I have. Come. Hurry!

The elm's lowest branch was half again Nisi's height above him. He took three running strides and leapt at it, grabbing hold of the branch and pulling himself up and into the tree. He was already breathing heavy as he stood, watching his brother clambering above him, envious of how he shimmied towards the elm's summit with the ease of a bird in flight and of the taut prowess of his physique, his own shading towards the fat that his father wore with a pride befitting his birthright as chief of the Omushkego.

As he laboured after Ostes, Nisi's arms grew damp with the mist, and brown streams drained the mud from them. The fog thinned and he saw it for what it was — a grey tide drowning the land on all sides. Towards the south, *pikihtew* — the smoke on the horizon — leaked into the sky. He watched the great black stain roiling out of the mist, thinking the same thought that he had the first time he'd seen it from the watchtower presiding over their village: that the earth was waging war upon the sky and woe to any man who stood between them.

The sun was but a pale yellow dot low within the billowing plume and the air burned his throat.

It is as if the world has been set on fire, Nisi said, pulling himself up onto a high branch beside his brother.

Towards the southwest, there was a funnelled cloud of feathered black — several dozen vultures circling among twice as many crows. Ostes was sighting on them through his binoculars.

It worries you, he said.

It should worry you as well.

Perhaps, but you are worried enough for the both of us so I let my thoughts seek more pleasant company.

And what is that?

The stories they will tell of Nisi and Ostes, two great Omushkego warriors who followed pikihtew into the southern wilds and found glory.

It is just as likely that they will tell the story of two brothers who defied their father and were cast out of their village.

That is only your own fear given voice, for you know that father would never do such a thing. Was it not he himself who led the charge during The Battle of White Rock, who pushed back the *waapishtim*, who—

I know the stories well. But that was in a different age, brother.

Yes, an age when fathers did not begrudge their sons for seeking their own paths to glory.

Kimi will give me all the glory I need.

And fear not brother, you will be lying with her before the moon is yet full.

It does not seem likely.

But it is, for I have seen our future.

Ostes passed him his looking glasses, and his brother sighted on the crows.

Something's died.

That is obvious, Nisi said foraging his pipe from his pouch and packing it with *kaapii* leaf, But not what.

Nisi followed the birds' swirling descent to a tree standing alone upon a hilltop, suspended just above the fog. It was a cherry tree, that much he could tell. Its limbs were weighted with globes strung beneath its branches like giant sun-wrinkled apples. He lowered the binoculars and looked to his brother, expelling smoke in twin streams through his nose.

They're heads.

Yes, his brother replied. Have you ever heard of such a thing?

No.

It is something new then.

And terrible.

All the better for our intent.

They ran southwest under a roof of evergreens reared in darkness, the ground oppressed by pine needles and their footfalls light and leaving little trace of their passing. They ran until they came to a gully eroded between two gentle slopes by a long-dead tributary of the dying river. Here they stopped to breathe and to drink from their bladders. Both inhaled deeply the smell of rotting meat, which came to them along the cross-current.

Why so grim? his brother asked after Nisi had drank his fill. When the day is finally upon us?

Nisi wiped his mouth.

You are thinking again of Kimi perhaps, Ostes said.

No.

Still warm in her bed.

I was not thinking of her.

Fresh seed between her legs. Who do you suppose is trying to slip from her embrace without waking her?

Nisi lowered his eyes but could not contain a smile.

Whoever it is, he said, he is not long for this world.

His brother laughed and slapped him hard on the back.

That's the spirit.

J ogging up the gully, they came into a deep gorge between two granite walls softened by moss and draped with roots from the cedar trees leaning at drastic angles over their bluffs. The ground between them was cluttered with a deluge of skull-sized rocks. They picked their way through the scree to where the gorge dead-ended in stone steps leaking drizzle over silt-filled pocks. They stopped there to fill their bladders and afterwards climbed side by side up the rockfall.

At its summit were the remains of a fence — a few corroded posts and cedar rails softened on the ground by moss. On one side of it, the forest continued its unrepentant tangle, but on the other the old growth gave way to the new — a field overgrown with poplars and aspen, none thicker than their legs and most with no more girth than their arms. Timothy grass grew to the height of their waists amongst them.

Ducking under the wire, they wended their way through the thicket. Beyond, they could espy the hillside rising like the back of some great, black, hairy beast. The odour here was beyond the tolerance of man. Ostes carved a deep line into the closest poplar tree and dug under the bark with the blade of his knife. When he drew it out, its sheen was dulled by a clear pitch. He smeared it over his top lip and held the knife out to Nisi.

It will help with the smell, he said.

Nisi took some on his finger. He plastered the smooth cleft beneath his nose with the bitter sap, then followed Ostes to the foot of the hill. Its slopes were burnt to a cinder and littered with stumps, shorn coarsely with crude axes at a height of two or three finger-widths. Nisi looked to its summit. The crows and the vultures had beset the cherry tree with boisterous delight. No sound could penetrate their squabble.

When they came halfway around the base of the hill they found a narrow path tramped in a straight line all the way to its crest and another path leading away through the forest, no less straight but three times wider. Ostes walked a short way into the sun-dappled tunnel and bent to a patch of mud.

They were careful about walking single file, he said when he'd returned to Nisi. But their dogs weren't.

Dogs?

At least three, maybe more.

They don't mean to make it easy, then.

Let us hope.

At the top of the rise, crows squawked their defiance and red drips rained from the tree, forming brackish pools on the ground. Nisi's stomach turned against the smell, the sap powerless against its fervour. He cupped his hand to his mouth and looked up at the heads, each one hanging from a limb by a rope, tilting in the wind and dancing against the onslaught of their winged oppressors. The heads were varied — pink and black, some jaundiced and others mottled grey, some old and the rest young or of indeterminate age — but all were removed from the necks of men. None had any teeth in their yawning mouths and each bore the same expression: horror and torment in a slow decline towards an endless boredom.

The ones at the top are still fresh, Ostes said. Not more than a day old. The ones near the bottom, perhaps a week.

Nisi turned from the tree and cast trolling eyes over the wilds to the south. A short distance through the forest, a thin spire of smoke curled out of the green. He took out his compass and sighted a bearing on it.

What do you make of this? Ostes said, motioning to a slat of wood nailed to the trunk of the tree. Crude etchings riddled its surface.

It is the old tongue.

Can you read it?

Chiishaayiyu taught you to read it as well.

I was not a good student.

You were not good at many things.

Get on with it then. What does it say?

Nisi studied the words.

So?

It has been a while.

Perhaps we should go fetch Chiishaayiyu.

Nisi held up his hand and his brother froze into a mocking portrait of stillness.

A moment passed and then Nisi read in a halting stutter: And . . . God . . . said . . . the . . . end . . . of . . . all . . . flesh . . . has . . . come . . . before . . . Me . . . for . . . the . . . earth . . . is . . . filled . . . with . . . violence . . . through . . . them.

A prophecy?

Perhaps.

Ours to fulfill then, brother.

They travelled southeast away from the hill, following the needlepoint of Nisi's compass through the bracken that had nettled the woods into a vast briar. They moved slowly, soundlessly, until they came to a wide swath that had been plundered by some ancient storm. Uprooted trees lay among others that had been snapped off halfway up their trunk. Moss grew in a thick carpet over everything so that at first glance it looked to Nisi as if an invisible river were flowing through the forest, its current impregnated with the smell of smoke flavoured by the simmer of meat cooking over an open fire.

They crouched low and threaded through the forest's undergrowth to a toppled pine tree not fifty paces from the camp. There they lay bellystretched beneath its branches and took turns sighting through the binoculars.

In the centre of the camp sat a large tent canvassed by a ragged patchwork of deer hides stretched over a wooden frame. In front of it, heat shimmered from a stone-ringed firepit over which a tanned and gutted pig was skewered. A woman, bedraggled, dirty and clothed in a crudely stitched leather dress, turned the spit's handle. One of her breasts hung loose from her wrap and drool leaked from her downturned mouth, borne in the expression of an idiot. A naked infant sat at her feet stuffing handfuls of dirt into its mouth and she stared down at it in static wonderment or perhaps futility.

Elsewhere they looked, the camp was quiet and empty.

There are women and children, Nisi whispered, handing the binoculars back to his brother.

You are not afraid of women and children, are you?

No. Only of what I cannot see.

Do not fret, that future will be upon us soon enough.

One of us should take a wander.

Nisi made as to rise.

Wait. Look there. Perhaps he is more to your liking.

Ostes passed him the binoculars and Nisi sighted on the skinny stick figure of a manchild standing in front of the tent flap. He was as pale as ash and naked save for a loincloth and the bones pierced through his flesh — sharpened ribs running in rungs down his chest like plated armour and metacarpals whittled into slivers and impaled through his cheeks and nose. His head was shorn clean and his bald plate dipped in red so that it looked like he had shed his skin along with his hair. On his face there was tattooed the faint imprint of a skull and each of his ears was punctured with the bite of a half-dozen teeth. He couldn't have been older than fifteen.

He is but a skeleton, Nisi said, passing the binoculars back to his brother.

Yet fierce. See how he wears the bones of his victims.

They watched the manchild walk to the fire and tear a strip of meat from the carcass. Chewing on it, he stepped behind the woman and lifted her dress. She spread her legs for him, offering up her sex like an animal. As he thrust into her, red juice from the meat slathered from his mouth so that he looked to be in the throes of some horrible sickness. The infant watched with curious amusement, clapping its hands and laughing, and the woman's hand stalled on the spit until the manchild was done then started up again the moment he pulled himself out.

It he fights like he fucks, Nisi said, nudging his brother and grinning, we must be careful.

Yes, he was very quick.

The manchild wiped his member on the back of the woman's dress and wandered from their sight. Ostes shimmied out from under their blind.

Where are you going? Nisi asked.

I felt the ground quiver beneath us. I think you are in need of a moment alone.

Had I been aroused the ground would not have quivered, it would have cracked open. It must be you then who needs a moment.

You are right, Nisi. I heard Kimi calling to me and must now give her my reply.

Tell her then, that I will be along shortly to finish what you could not.

I would but I fear that such a frail creature as she would not survive the encounter.

She is not so frail as she is easily bored. If she were to die of anything in your arms, it would be only of that.

Ostes rose to a squat and studied his brother with a rueful leer.

I should know not to spar with you, Nisi. You have Chiishaayiyu's gift for turning words.

You, at least, have father's gift for stating the obvious.

Nisi set the binoculars once more to his eyes and gathered the woman again in its scope. She was staring directly at him, her focus so intent that it seemed to Nisi that she must have heard them.

Ostes, he whispered, and when he did not reply he looked to where his brother had been only a moment ago, but he was gone.

While he awaited his brother's return, he maintained his vigil upon the woman who, for her part, continued turning the spit and staring back at him. Under her stalwart gaze he grew more and more uneasy, until there was no doubt in his mind that she knew of his presence. He watched for a sign that she meant to raise the alarm but she just went on rotating the meat and staring vacant-eyed back at him.

After a time, the infant at her feet wearied of eating dirt and let out a sharp cry. She bent to pick him up and Nisi slipped out from under the pine tree. He crept to an upended spruce and huddled behind its crown of splintered roots clung fast with dirt. He was breathing hard and felt as he had in his dream: that the world was coming undone around him. Cursing himself for letting the woman play such havoc with his calm, he closed his eyes and concentrated on the beat of his heart. When it had once again slowed to a languorous throb, he chanced a look at the woman.

The infant was suckling at her breast and her eyes were still trained on the pine tree.

A short while later, the skeletal manchild returned. Again he lifted the back of her dress and Nisi turned away. He leaned his back against the tree's crown of roots, listening to the manchild's feral grunting. Once it had quieted, he chanced another look. The manchild was parting the flap of the tent and slipping inside, and the woman was setting the infant on the ground. Rising, she took up the spit's lever and resumed turning it. Her eyes settled on their previous line, yet something about it appeared not to satisfy her. Her mouth crooked and her brow furrowed and her eyes took to roving over the morass of shattered trees and splintered stumps until they'd settled on the frayed blind of roots behind which Nisi was hiding. Her mouth then fell open again, resuming its idiot grin.

She is a witch, Nisi thought, ducking out of sight. He held his breath, certain that naming her thus would call her sorcery down upon him.

He had yet to exhale when there arose the halting cry of a whippoorwill. He recognized it as his brother and returned a call of his own.

Is that old hag still looking this way? Nisi asked after his brother had tracked him to his blind.

Ostes hazarded a glance at the encampment.

She is, he said. She must have seen you move.

She was looking thus at our old station. It is why I relocated.

She heard you then.

No, she is a witch.

A witch?

I am most certain. She has divined our presence and when the others return she will tell them and our night will be spent in flight.

She will say nothing.

How can you be so certain?

She is a prisoner.

She does not appear to be.

It is true all the same, Ostes said. Then, pointing towards a fringe of cedars at the western edge of the camp: You cannot see him, but there is an old man, adorned much as the other except he possesses a blade such as we would use to clear brush. He is watching over her and five others beside. Two of them also have babes in arms, and another has a belly as round as an overripe pumpkin. All of them are bound together with rope and sit in squalor under shelter of an oak tree. The old man holds the end of the rope in one hand and idles his time, as far as I could tell, clutching at his manhood with the other, trying to get it to rouse. It is a most fruitless endeavour for it is as lifeless as the cord. I came up behind him close enough to touch his shoulder—

That was foolish, brother.

It may have been, but if I have not the wits to sneak up behind an impotent old man then I fear our venture is doomed. The smell there, brother, is like Achaan's shitting ground. You would not believe it. These women are in the worst state and their children grovel about in the dirt swathed only in their own filth and suckle off breasts so deprived that they would likely get more sustenance suckling their captor's limp cock.

Such a sentiment, Ostes. It is not becoming.

I am sorry, Nisi, my mind is fouled by having witnessed such a sorrowful crop of humanity. But— he shook his head, unsure of how to continue.

What is it, Ostes?

There was one. How can I explain to you in words that would make you understand? It was as if there was a light, brother, radiating out from her so that she appeared removed from her surroundings, apart from the world of dirt and shit and even the desperate wantonness of the old man tugging at himself and laughing — Nisi, his laugh, such a sound I have never heard. It was like he'd been struck by lightning and it had cracked open the part of him that contained his malignant spirit and now it was leaking out, singed at once by the electrical current that had freed it, soaking up the sour acids of his belly and the malodious humours in his rotten lungs so that when it issued forth from his mouth it was disfavoured beyond the recognition of mirth or joy: it was the laugh of a man dying and taking comfort in the knowledge that the world was dying along with him.

Ostes, I have never heard you speak as thus.

I have never even thought as much, brother, but this woman — though I should call her yet a girl for she could not be much older than her first bleeding — has done something to me. I have yet to resolve what it is but, Nisi, I am changed.

And our venture?

The same. Only the stakes have risen. This girl is to become my wife.

She cannot, Nisi protested, clutching at his brother's arm. If you bring her home, Father will know that we had travelled south to wage war, not as emissaries of peace, as you promised. You swore an oath to me, on our mother's life, that he would never discover our true intent.

But that was before I saw *her*.

His eyes now became narrowed slits that would broker no dispute.

I must possess her, Nisi. I tell you, I must.

T he wind shifted just as the sun fell behind the treeline. Under cover of the dying light, they moved to a small grove of cedar trees very near the western edge of the encampment. Within it there was an open hearth, big enough for two men to lie down in or to stand, and there were ample openings in the layered green boughs to spy on the camp without threat of being seen.

From this new angle, Nisi was able to view the women that Ostes had spoken of. They were huddled, as he'd said, around an oak tree not thirty paces from the cedars. Their backs were to the grove, their faces hidden, and none shone with an inner, or outer, light so that he could not distinguish among them the young girl who had so fetched his brother. The old man's hideous visage he could see clearly though — a laughing skull-face that never seemed to tire of its solitary amusement.

While Ostes reclined against the trunk of the largest cedar, Nisi turned from the old man and renewed his preoccupation with the witchwoman. The infant in her charge now lay sprawled in a deep slumber on the ground behind her and she was once again staring at him with the docile infirmity of a retarded child.

The scene faded under telescoping shadows. When all that Nisi could see of the encampment was the weary fret of the fire licking at the blackened carcass and dancing in webbed lines over the witchwoman's face, the old hag stopped turning the spit's lever and cocked her ear to the darkened sky. On her face there flickered an expression akin to terror, though it wasn't so definite — the remembrance of past horrors or, perhaps, those yet to come. It appeared so reasoned that it made Nisi think for a moment that her enfeeblement had been but a ruse.

She turned to the tent as four black dogs stalked into the firelight. They stood almost as tall as she did and the thick mat of their coats was woven with bones that rattled as they moved, their eyes dark pits and their maws like open wounds festering with blooded drool.

Such wretched creatures Nisi had never set eyes upon, and he watched with muted awe as their leader advanced upon the witchwoman's child. It sniffed at the infant as if it meant to gobble it whole, then seeming to reconsider, licked the infant's face with its prodigious tongue. The child pushed out with clawed hands and the dog left him to his slumber. It traipsed in a slow arc around the child's mother, regarding the witchwoman with stilted caution while its subordinates took up sentry within the incandescent ring emanating from the fire. Their gazes roved over the women, now pouring forth from their refuge, carrying their children, some also with earthen jugs and others with sharpened sticks. The old man walked past them, coiling the manacled rope that had bound them. He hung it on the tent's corner post then walked to the flap and disappeared inside.

A moment later, the manchild cantered forth from within. He moved with the gait of a chieftain's son given leave from the hunt to assume his birthright overseeing the manor, now recalled from his indulgences by the clatter of hooves and the siren call of his father's horn. He stood and appraised the women as they set their children on the ground. The ones holding sticks lined up in front of the witch and those with jugs stood at intervals around the fire. The children, freed, crawled or tottered away from their mothers, coming to the dogs as moths drawn to a flame. When they reached these maleficent creatures, they clung to the hair sprouting from their chests, trying to raise themselves up, and pulled on their tongues as if they meant to make swings of them. If any of this abuse bothered the dogs, they made no sign of it.

Shortly, there appeared from within the forestshade glints of light such as a torch would make on the mineralled walls of a cave. Nisi bent to his sleeping brother and placed his hand firmly over his lips.

Ostes awoke at once and shrugged out from beneath his younger brother's censure.

They are back, Nisi signed in the secret hand-language of their clan.

Ostes gathered himself to his feet, and both brothers peered through a crack in the cedar boughs. Nisi now recognized the glints that he had seen as a brigade of torches. As the men holding them streamed into the encampment, they broke into two lines and encircled the women assembled around the red-pocketed char-pit. The torches were held by men adorned with bone-piercings the same as the old man and the manchild, though most were larger, some by thrice. Two of them seemed to have sprouted upon their shoulders second heads. Or so it seemed to Nisi before his eyes adjusted and he saw these were not appendages but children sitting in grim transport upon their shoulders. Walking among them was an older child, perhaps eleven or twelve. He was tall and thin and bore the same litany of piercings that marked his elders.

I have counted twelve men, Ostes signed. And four dogs.

I have counted the same, Nisi signed back.

They appear to have returned without any trophies.

The dogs will be hungry then.

Let us hope.

Coming to the fire, the men unslung crude weapons from unseen scabbards — machetes and sharpened pikes and axes and sledges, all seemingly made of the same grey steel and baring patches of ochre, rust or blood it was impossible to tell. They dropped them in a pile at the foot of the tent and stood their torches in stands fashioned from two pronged saplings, spaced at intervals. The two carrying children lowered their charges while the others slumped to the ground, weary from their travels.

In this moment, they were like any group of men returning from the hunt empty-handed. They stretched out their legs and the women proffered water poured straight into their mouths from the earthen jugs. The children reclined into their laps and the babies squeezed between their legs as sea mammals seeking shelter in some peaceable cove as haven against a storm. The men raised them in their arms and the children giggled their delight.

They are not so fierce, after all, Nisi signed.

Step into their light and we shall see if you are right.

That time will come, brother.

Have you noticed that none of them speak?

Yes. And look at the way they eat. It is almost as if they have no tongues.

There are many mysteries among these people.

There is the only mystery that beguiles me, Ostes signed. On the right, holding the stick out to your witch. Do you see her?

Yes.

Was I not right? Is she not a vision?

The girl was plain to Nisi's eyes, and even filthier than the others. He watched her standing at the firepit holding out the stake to the witchwoman. The hag tore a chunk of meat from the pig with her bare hands and impaled it on the sharpened stick. The girl then took a direct line for the largest of the men — a creature so immense that even sitting he nearly equalled her height. There was nothing about her that Nisi could see to elevate her above her peers.

It must have been some trick perpetrated on Ostes by the light, he thought, or perhaps by black magic.

Then, as the girl leant towards the giant, the torch's flame seemed to bend its will towards her. Its glow sparkled within the orange-tinged curls of her hair and haloed about her face, producing the most subtle effects upon her delicate features. At once, she seemed to stand apart from the scene — as a moon stands apart in its eclipse of the sun — and in that aperture Nisi had never witnessed such beauty.

I— he started but his fingers stalled.

Ostes patted him on the shoulder.

Do not begrudge me that I saw her first, he signed.

As she turned from the light, the aperture closed and once again she was only a dishevelled and wretched-looking little girl. She started away from the giant and he reached out and grabbed her by one of her calves. A look of stark terror descended upon her face as he ran his hand up her thigh, pressing it under the hem of her dress. She made to pull free from his grasp but the giant grabbed her around the waist, wrenching her towards him then bending her over and lifting her dress, burying his face within her sex.

Ostes grit his teeth and tightened his hand on the hilt of his knife. Nisi gripped his arm, staying him.

That future is not yet upon us, he whispered into his ear, holding his brother firm until his arm had relaxed.

The girl's body vexed to the man's savage appetite and all eyes in the camp set to watching her writhe and wallow. Finally she let out such a wail that Nisi and Ostes could see it written on the stunned looks of the children, as enraptured by the sight of this girl's pang as were their elders. The giant then pushed aside the loin cloth concealing his erect manhood and pulled her down into his lap. Pain flattened her features.

Do not lose heart, brother, Nisi signed. Kimi was broken also when I first lay with her.

But Ostes would not answer and stood with his back to his brother, listening to the girl's muffled cries and palming the hilt of his knife.

N isi watched her ordeal long into the night.

Above the camp, the moon peered through a hazy drift of smoke and the stars were but motes coruscate against the void, indifferent and laggard in their contemplation of the mortal world below.

Ostes sat against the cedar post in sullen recompose, following the girl's slavish progress among the men as a child might hunt the rustle of a snake in tall grass. Shortly, he heard her fury break into baleful lamentations. These too soon diminished with the languor of a fire succumbing to ash until finally there was no sound at all but the buzz of mosquitoes. He felt the touch of his brother's hand on his arm.

Your girl possesses an uncommon stamina, Nisi signed. I feared she would be at it until dawn.

What of the men?

They are not so remarkable. They have all retired to the tent.

And the dogs?

They sleep round the hearth.

It is just like in the story Nuuhkimus tells of the first settlers who came to White Rock.

Yes.

Do you recall how many dogs *they* possessed?

Five.

And they slew but two before the others awoke, all without the favour of bows.

Nuuhkimus has been known to exaggerate.

Still.

Nisi thought on it.

There are many paths to glory, he signed at last.

But none so fine as in bettering your elders.

We have only four dogs before us.

Then we must be as the wind.

L eaving their bows propped against the cedar's trunk with their quivers nettled beside them, they slipped from the hollow. The shadows of fractured trees drew away from the moonlight and they moved among these rails, skirting from fallen tree to fallen tree, their feet never once touching the ground. At last, they came to a ridge of moss — a great ancestral tree fallen and turning to sod. It ran in a straight line to the edge of the clearing and they crept along its cushioned bank.

Only a lone torch remained lit. A thin ribbon of black smoke trailed from its tip, lacing the air with the smell of burning pig fat and drafting over the dogs lounged in a loose formation around the firepit.

Ostes stepped onto the clearing's tramped earthen floor and Nisi padded after him, holding his breath against a sudden movement from under the oak tree where the women had resettled. The two brothers waited until its shadow was absorbed back into the greater dark and all was still again.

Drawing his blade from its scabbard, Ostes hid its moonglint behind his back. Nisi did the same and turned to his brother. Splitting his face was a smile so ominous in its delight that he saw nothing there but dread. He cursed his brother's devilry as Ostes stood to his full height and leant back his head, emitting a traitorous howl. The dogs by the fire snapped to their feet like mechanical creatures given current. They released short snarls and came at the two brothers as a single force. There was not a moment for thought or regret, nor for curses or hesitation — only the blades in their hands slashing out.

Nisi felt the cleave of flesh and saw the one splinter into two. The dog he'd struck careened past him, its snout bent at a drastic angle into the turf, but the other stayed its course. He swung at it and the second dog toppled over him, its neck slit, its teeth still grasping for his throat. Blood washed over his face and Nisi struck out again. His knife rattled against its teeth as it made swift entry into its mouth, taking a sharp angle upwards and severing the dog's palate.

Rolling out from under its body, he stood, looking to his brother slinging his knife from within the neck of another of the beasts. The fourth was dead beside it, a tangle of guts weeping through a gash in its stomach.

You are too slow brother, Ostes chided then bent into a quick lope towards the tent.

The flap opened and the giant strode from within, naked and fierce beyond the recollection of either man. He found Ostes within his menace and drew from his chest two of the sharpened ribs pinioned there, holding them as daggers. But their supple curves and razored edges were no match for Ostes's speed. The giant had barely raised his arms to strike when there was a blade puncturing his gut and driving upwards, slicing a trench to his chin. With his free hand, Ostes reached into this gored manifold and clutched at the giant's heart, playing him as a puppet and pushing him back into the tent.

Nisi was in full flight behind him when an infant let out a squawk. He turned towards the oak tree. The women had roused and their eyes were upon him. He fled their gaze, snatching up the torch and slipping into the tent, no more than five or six steps behind his brother. His light shone over a writhing sea awash in blood and entrails. The ground was a cluttered wreck of arms and legs and bodies hacked into pieces, the trail of woe enlivened only by the spasmodic tremors of life in retreat of its foe — hands clutching at spilled guts and stemming geysers and one severed from its master and twitching on its back like an overturned turtle.

The smell of shit and piss had Nisi choking on the stench, reeling, and then the manchild was rising from the ground beside the tent flap. Nisi swung his blade and caught him across his eyes, transforming him Cyclops. He fell away without a sound. Other bodies were now rising from the floor, their faces tortured by confusion and ink, the skeletal stain to their skin making them appear as the newly dead sprung to life. He lashed out at them, hewing a path beside his brother. The ground muddied beneath him and the sour taste in his mouth gave way to the salt-spray of blood upon his lips.

As he cleaved his way through the tent nothing touched him and the vanquished made no sounds beyond muffled groans and the wretch of blood vomiting from newly wrought mouths. He came at last to the far corner where the clan's three children huddled within a parapet of shadow. He chased away their darkness with the torch's light and stood before the eldest. He was still a cycle or two from becoming a man but his lean body was already mapped with rivulets of muscle.

What a fine warrior he would make, Nisi thought as he faced the boy.

The warriorchild stood brazen in front of the two others, each rousing into a nightmare stream of delirious macabre, rubbing their eyes as little ones are wont to relieve their drowse and peering up into the ghost-lit face of their assassin.

The blade stalled in Nisi's hand.

Behind him he could hear men coughing and the suction of air through punctured lungs and perforated throats. Overtop of them: his brother's riotous cavort calling out his name and entreating his victims to remember it upon the netherbridge where his ancestors would demand a full account of his deeds.

And if you do not give it to them, your last moments on earth will be like a memory of heaven, Ostes growled as he loosened a man's scalp with the tip of his knife.

Nisi cast the torchlight wide over the tent and saw that this man was the last among the living except for the children before him. He also saw, in his brother's deliberate stride through the labyrinth of dead, a witness to his reticence.

Brushing past him, Ostes raised his knife over the warrior-child's head.

No!

Such torment within the scream that for a moment Nisi thought it must have spawned from his own heart. The brothers turned as one to the witchwoman standing at the open tent flap. Her hair was as a snake's hive and her idiot's grin was supplanted by a look Nisi had seen once before, borne by his own mother on a night when his father had dragged him from his bed to be tanned for some misdeed. His mother had trailed after him, pleading with her husband for the boy's sake though his father had tanned him before and she had not paid more than a passing heed. Yet, there she was begging for the boy to be spared, weeping as she clutched at his father's arm.

Ostes touched Nisi's shoulder, drawing him back to the tent as the witchwoman came at them. She was muttering exaltations in her foreign tongue, indecipherable to Ostes but which Nisi could recognize as a single word: please, please, please. Stumbling over the field of carnage, drunk with worry and fear, pursued by the other women, streaming into the tent like a legion of crazed lemmings bent upon the precipice.

No mercy, Ostes whispered to his brother, is the only real mercy.

Nisi nodded, though he found no consolation in this, his warrior's creed. Still, he brandished his weapon, preparing his fury, shoulder to shoulder with his brother. When the moment to unleash it was upon him, he felt Ostes stiffen at his side. Nisi turned to him, trying to find some sense in the way the blood-mask upon his brother's face seemed to curdle under the flickering light and how his eyes seemed void of any reasoning. Ostes's hand drooped at his side and the knife slid from its grip.

Brother, Nisi said.

He reached out to grab him but his hand found no purchase on his blood-slicked shoulder and a chasm opened between them, swallowing Ostes into its depths. As he fell, the mystery of it broke into fragments. The warriorchild with his hand transomed to the base of his brother's skull — blood gushing over his wrist — his brother falling, falling, falling — a slivered rib-bone in the boy's hand — a tentacle of blood curling down his chest — the boy now turning towards him, wilful and defiant — his eyes as twin moons, glaring and hateful — raising his bone knife — the knife in Nisi's hand rising to meet it — a terrible rage upon him. Then: the women sweeping past — ferreting out their children — holding them to their bosoms and weeping, as Nisi's own mother had once wept for him.

Nisi sat with his brother until the tent had emptied of the living. The last to depart was the witchwoman. She stood at the flap, watching Nisi take Ostes's head into his lap. The dying man's eyes darted like tadpoles in a shallow pool, his hands, palsied and feeble, shook against his legs, and short, strained breaths issued from between his lips. He did not utter a word. When at last his brother had stilled, Nisi gazed over at her. She bowed her head, touching her right hand upon her brow then dipping it to her belly and bringing it back up so that she could brush her fingers over each of her shoulders.

It was a sign of some sort, Nisi could see that, but he knew not what it meant.

He nodded and she ducked low and slipped out of the tent. Lifting his brother's head from his lap, he set it on the ground and stood. The air again affronted him with its ardour, making him reel and wretch. He bent and spat and found himself peering down at his brother's knife. Wiping his mouth, he fetched it, holding the haft of it in his left hand so that he could run the fingers of his right over the two letters, JL, carved into the foot of the blade.

Can I hold it? he'd asked his brother the first time he'd shown it to him. He was six and his brother twelve. Ostes had just returned from his *pipaamyihtaau* and it was the first moment they'd shared alone. He'd expected his brother to be changed, as young men often were after the first time they'd spent a moon alone in the wild lands surrounding their village, but he was not, just more than ever the same: brazen and arrogant and above all impatient with his brother's endless pestering.

You must never touch it, Ostes had warned. If ever another lays a hand upon it, I must kill him. It is my sacred oath. But you can look at it.

Ostes held the knife delicately between both hands, and Nisi bent over it close enough that his breath fogged on the tempered steel. The blade was almost as long as his forearm and there were serrated teeth along one side. Dried blood spackled the barbs and there was more on the blade, milled to a steely shine.

Nisi asked his brother where he'd got the knife and why was there blood on it and what the letters JL meant.

Ostes waited until Nisi had run out of questions before he'd answered.

There are some secrets that a man must never share, he said, then added, especially with a boy.

Nisi scowled at him, taking his brother's words as teasing, and Ostes laughed.

When we are old men, I will tell you, and a great many things more.

He laughed again and rubbed his hand through Nisi's hair.

And perhaps by then you will have a few secrets of your own to share.

Now, as Nisi held the knife for the first time, he thought of his brother's promise, of the secret unspoken and of all the other things that were forever lost between them.

H e came out of the tent weighted by his brother's body, sagging between his outstretched arms. The moon had fled and the sky was as grey as slate. There was no starmap to guide him — no light at all except from the dying embers in the fire.

The women were gathered again beneath their oak, fussing with their children. They all stopped what they were doing and watched him with eyes like field mice cowering under the shadow of a hawk circling their hole as he walked to the firepit. He lay his brother beside it, then stood, surveying their pitiable lot. None would meet his eyes save the warriorchild, as fierce in his defiance as ever, and Nisi turned to the north, striding away from the camp towards the stand of cedars where they had left their bows and their packs.

He passed without a sound into the forest and the women went back to fussing over their children, pulling out the bones sheathed in their skin and dabbing at the blood that spurted from their wounds with wetted thumbs.

When Nisi returned, he carried an armload of cedar boughs and two bows slung over his shoulder alongside two otter-skin packs. He set the boughs in the firepit, arranging them into a bed upon the ashes, and then built a pyre from the pile of logs foraged by the men he and Ostes had killed. Lifting his brother, he set him on top. He placed Ostes's bow upon his breast and bent to blow into the hot coals. The flames leapt at the dried tinder, quickly engulfing the structure, and Nisi sat cross-legged in front of it. He closed his eyes and slapped his chest softly with the palm of his hand in time to the funerary chant of his people, all the while envisioning his brother upon the netherbridge, proud and resolute, never once looking back as he made his journey towards the light.

D aybreak found Nisi much the same, his hand still moving to the steady pulse of his heart, though the chant had exhausted itself so that no sound parted his lips.

Dawn had brought with it a proliferation of life to the camp. The flies had come first, settling in a petulant haze before the sky was yet bright enough to witness within it wisps of smoke lashing out at the thinning darkness through the frayed canopy of evergreens. The crows came soon after. Some lit upon the roof of the tent, pecking at the seams. The braver ones hopped, frog-like, around its entrance, poking their heads through the flap and squawking to the others of their good fortune but refusing to venture inside. Others preyed upon the dogs, plucking at their jellied eyes and uncoiling their intestines through the slits in their bellies. Vultures paced around the perimeter, red-bonneted and leery, and bestial shrieks from within the forest spoke of a violence yet to come.

The women hoarded over their children, keeping them close to the fire with proffers of food — their breasts and what was left of the pig, and then when those were suckled dry, one of the dogs, skinned and spitted over Ostes's still-simmering body. The other three dogs, the women dragged to the tent. When they opened the flap they were greeted with the drone of a thousand flies. Disturbed from its forage, a creature peered over at them from amidst the dead, its yellowed eyes glaring above a bristled hump of speckled fur, a hiss sounding from between its bared fangs such as no friend of the living would possess.

Retreating in horror, the women took up arms and stood on guard in a circle around their children. The warriorchild paced back and forth between them and Nisi, the blade of his machete propped on his shoulder and his eyes never once wavering from their sentry over the man who had slain his fathers.

Between them, Ostes's blackened skin peeled and split open. His muscles withered and shrank, contracting his arms into raised fists so that he appeared to be fighting some grave underworld foe. His body steamed and spit its juices, sizzling, into the furnace below. The liquefied fat ignited and yellow flames lapped over his body with a sulphurous glow.

It burned all through the afternoon and into the evening. As darkness unravelled over the camp, the wind shifted again. Smoke infected the spaces between trees, and a dense bank of it rolled across the clearing. The women huddled closer to the fire, coughing and rubbing their eyes. Desperate shadows ranged among the dusk-dusted trees fanned against a reddish glow.

Among the howls of wolves and the frantic revelry of carrion feeders fighting within the tent, Nisi began to hear murmurs from amongst the women accompanied by furtive glances in his direction and other signs that they were speaking of him. As he fetched his brother's skeleton from the ashes, he brooded upon what they were saying and upon their future soon to pass, and what his role must come to be in it.

When at last he'd retrieved his brother's skull he set it before him and emptied Ostes's pack onto the ground. The only things in it were a few strips of dried venison, the binoculars, his brother's pipe and the small pouch that contained his store of *kaapii* leaf. He cursed himself for sending his brother on his way without a last puff and packed the pipe full with the green bud. He lit it with the glowing end of a stick, savouring a mouthful of its acrid smoke before propping the pipe between the skull's teeth.

He had just finished filling Ostes's bag with his remains when out of the nightshrill there arose a far-away thrumming. The sound grew into a tremulous vibration that pushed all other thoughts before it — a hum that did not seem human in origin but had no equal in the world beyond men. Nisi listened and absorbed its pulse — a deep and mysterious rumble. The sound hackled the hairs on his arms and he saw that he was not the only one thus moved.

The warriorchild stood erect, his head cocked to the side, and the women cast each other worried glances, listening with nervous devotion as the noise faded, its essence lost now to its own echo.

With its passing, the warriorchild took from the conceal-ment of his loin cloth a small cylinder of bone — a hollowed-out femur perhaps — attached to a length of string. He held one end of the line in his right hand and cast the bone into the air, swinging it above his head in quickening arcs so that it emitted a high-pitched whistling sound.

Nisi was just on the cusp of understanding its import when the witchwoman clutched at the warriorchild's arm. The boy's voice, dislodged from its orbit, lagged to the ground. She chased after it and fetched the bone and gave it a quick jerk. The string snapped from the boy's grasp and she pitched the apparatus into the still-glowing fire.

As the line shrivelled from the heat, Nisi removed the pipe from Ostes's mouth and held the skull up in front of him, peering into its empty eyes as one contemplating his own mortality.

What now, brother? he said.

IV

It was still dark when the boy came out of the house to find his mother sitting in her chair.

Their five hounds lounged on the floor around her and his father stood at the top of the porch steps, puffing on his pipe as if it was the most natural thing in the world, her being there, though she hadn't left her bed for nearly a moon. Her nightgown hung loose and was unbuttoned to her navel so that when the boy looked down at her he blushed at the sight of her exposed breasts. She was barefooted and her toenails were yellow and cracked, her two little toes bent out of sight, her ankles swollen and purple. Sky was licking at her hand and she was leaning back in her chair with her eyes closed, moaning as if nothing could have pleased her more. The boy nudged the dog aside with his foot, telling him to shoo, and she opened her eyes, smiling full-mouthed at her son, her teeth as white as eggshells.

There he is, she said.

Ya shouldna be outta bed, he scolded though he was looking at his father while he spoke.

I'ma feelin better today.

Ya don't look it.

I made it down here by myself, din't I? And when the boy's eyes flashed doubt she looked to her husband.

Tell him.

She was settin there when I come out the barn, so I guess she musta.

I don't care, I ain goin, the boy said.

Nonsense. Is your birthday tomorrow. I made y'a present an everythin. She looked around. Where'd it git to?

I already stowed it in ma pack, her husband answered, nodding to the satchel at the bottom of the stairs, two fishing rods crossed over it.

There ya go. She nodded as if that was the end to the matter and raised her arms out to her son. They were as thin as saplings and trembling.

Now come on over here and give yer ma a kiss afore ya leave.

They crested out over the ridge with the eastern dark fading at their backs, the boy climbing after his father. His hands bore a tenuous grip on the ancient stone as he fissured his way up a crag severing the rock face with a sideways leer. The early morning sky was clear and purple shading to a deep blue at its zenith, the sun known only in the flutter of bats fleeing its advent over the field. From the foot of the cliff, the boy could hear Sky's frantic barks.

Stopping an arm's length from the top, he yelled down at him, Go on around. Go!

Sky cocked his head as if he had a choice in the matter and the moment his master began to climb again he ran up the rocky shale at the cliff's base, his claws struggling to find purchase in the uneven slope, neverminding that it gave way to a sheer wall, some hundred feet steep.

When the boy came over the lip, he found his father sitting on a ledge of granite wheezing and shaking his head, trying to catch his breath and flummoxed by how it fled him.

Thought you'd falln, the man choked out.

Damn near fell asleep, waitin on you.

His father drank heavy from his canteen and held it out to his son. The boy shook his head and turned to the field below, fighting against remembrances of his mother, in years past, standing within the corridor of pines on the far side of the corn patch waving her arms over her head, the boy waving back and watching her as she turned, their pack of hounds billowing around her legs as she started for home.

He heard the clatter of paws bounding up the low rise to the left of them. Blue emerged in one leaping bound overtop the granite shelf and scurried to his master. He'd been named in honour of his grandfather, even though his eyes were chestnut, and while it had been seven years since Sky had sired him he still acted like a pup, lathering his tongue up over the man's face and barking his distemper when he pushed him away.

Below him, Sky was baying and carrying on like he was being left to his demise, and the boy called down to him again but the hound could not be deterred from his dissent.

He ain comin, the boy said at last.

He does this ever damn year.

Never like this.

He's gittin old.

Or maybe he knows betta'n to leave.

They walked away from the ridge, following the spaces between evergreens, not so much a path as a sign that order could exist in the world apart from man's intentions. They travelled always to the south and no words passed between them. Mosquitoes and gnats competed for their blood with deer flies but neither the boy nor his father lifted so much as a hand to ward them off as if they were playing a game of endurance to pass the time.

The heat of the sun pressed upon their backs, though the light that filtered through the canopy was no larger than raindrops. They walked under its oppressive glower until they came to a sunken marshland. The insects here were intolerable and both the man and the boy forsook their game. They scooped handfuls of loamy muck from the shallows, lathering it over their faces and necks, remaking themselves into golems that seemed to have sprouted from the murk. Afterwards, they erased the squelch of their footprints with makeshift brooms made of spruce boughs.

At the southern perimeter of the swamp there was a single strand of fence wire strung between two trees that had outlived all notion of boundaries. The man walked to it and ran his hand along the wire's span, wearing an ochre line into his palm. He laughed and the boy shook his head, waiting for his father to speak, all the while wishing he wouldn't.

I was thinkin bout the time ya brung home that turkey, his father said. Hell of a sight. I ain never laughed so hard.

Now jerking round to face the boy.

It was here ya found it, weren't it?

No, Pa.

Could have sworn . . .

I tol ya a hun'ed times.

Well tell me again.

The boy grit his teeth, whispering a silent prayer to an unnamed god on the topic of salvation.

Ain't but once a year, his father said. Indulge yer ol man.

I come across it on the far side of the beaver pond, the boy started. It was snared in a web of rusted fence wire, the posts long fell to ruin around it. Sky growled at it but wun't come within ten paces, it was so ugly and mean lookin. The first thing that crossed my mind was that I should set it free. But the thought of seein yer face as I led it into the yard gave me another notion, so I set down my bow and took up the length of twine wrapped round my britches and fashioned a lasso. When I approached, it made such a wretched shriek that I stumbled backwards. I tripped and fell and cut my elbow on a sharp stone. Sky started to bayin and chargin at it. I called him off then stood, took up my bow and shot that ugly ol turkey through the neck. It passed all the way through and the turkey sat down with a stunned look. It followed me with one dead eye as I walked past it to retrieve m'arrow. When I returned, its neck was lyin limp beside it. It looked like a snake that had gorged itself and exploded. I hacked off a bough from a cedar tree and rolled that ol bird onto it and dragged it home.

I ain't never laughed so hard as when I seen ya comin into the yard wit it.

I thought ya was goin choke.

I almost did. How old was ya?

Eight.

No, ya was younger. N'older than six.

I's eight.

You say so, his father said and shot him another look. But ya shore as hell weren't no eight.

It was only four summers ago.

And that'd make ya—

Eight.

How old's ya now?

Twelve.

I thought ya was goin on thirteen.

They reached the quarry, just after noon.

The boy stood beneath the white pine clinging tenuously to the quarry's edge and took up the rope tied around its trunk, leaning his weight against it and peering down at the water some fifty feet below. The surface of it was a perfect mirror reflecting sheer walls of grey rock and wisps of clouds against a steel-blue sky, its sheen broken only by the raft floating in the pool's centre.

Don't the years jus slip away, the man thought watching his son. It seems like only yes'erday that ya brung him that first time.

It had been on the eve of the boy's sixth birthday, the same age as he'd been when his grandfather had first brought him.

Can we swim in it? the boy had asked, holding the rope and leaning over the precipice, same as he was doing now.

Later, his father had said, taking his son by the arm.

He drew him to a space between two of the pine's gnarled roots, anchored, it seemed, to the rock itself.

First y'hafta tell me what I jus said.

The boy scrunched his brow and looked from his father to the tree, both towering over him with dubious intent.

Ya said, he answered, this tree is the centre of all things.

Tha's right.

Now can we go fer a swim?

The man had laughed then swept the boy into his arms. For a moment the boy thought he'd meant to run at the quarry and leap, clutching the boy tight to his breast as they fell. Instead, his father had lifted him higher, raising him towards the tree's lowest branch, some seven or eight feet off the ground.

After you've takin a looksee, he said.

The boy pulled himself onto the branch and stood, holding the trunk and staring up through the nettle of branches to where the feathered tufts at the pine's summit seemed to brush against the sky.

Go on, his father urged.

He made his way slowly, resting on the thicker branches, choosing his way with care, circling the tree's girth from arm to arm, pulling himself up by inches, his hands thick with sap and his ascent marked on the back of his neck by a thatchwork of scratches. Only when he'd made it to within reach of the tree's summit did he turn away from the trunk to looksee over the wilderness surrounding him like a vast ocean, casting about to the north, searching for the river where they fished. Intersecting its serpentine weave he saw a narrow channel of trees raised against the low marshes of their birth — a causeway as direct as an arrow's flight interspersed with maples and aspens and beeches, the ground beneath them as black as coal.

When he climbed down from the tree, Sky and his pup sat vigilant beside his father, leant against the pine's base. His straw hat was propped over his face and the boy watched him, thinking that he wasn't really asleep but then kicked at his feet anyway. His father roused, pushed the hat up and blinked, wiping his eyes and stretching his arms, groaning.

So whadya see? he asked.

The river and trees and something else. It was as straight as an arrow's flight and raised up out of the ground. There were trees growing there but the earth beneath them was black.

That'd be the Eleven.

Huh?

Used to have been a road.

139

A road? the boy repeated, trying to place the word. Like'n what they used in the olden days when they'ds wanna take a wander?

Yeah.

Where'ds it go?

I don't know.

Y'ain't never been down it?

Ain't never had a reason.

The boy thought on that.

Well it's gotta go somewhere, he finally said.

His father laughed.

I guess it does.

Taking off his hat, he wiped the sweat off his brow with his sleeve.

Now how's bout that swim?

He set the hat on his son's head, pulling its brim down over his eyes. Sky barked and when the boy lifted the hat his father was gone. A moment later he heard a distant splash. He walked to the edge of the quarry and stared down at his father's head bobbing above the surface of the water.

Ya comin or not? he yelled up at him.

The boy shucked off his foot-leathers and, without a thought, leapt into the breach. The man had never felt so proud.

Ya goin stand there all day? he asked now.

The boy glanced back at him, frowning.

That ol rope ain't more'n a thread.

It's a'right. Been there since I was a boy.

Tha's what I mean.

Water's bound to be cold aryway.

Tain't that.

Shore.

Jus hate to be the one climbin when it snapped.

It'd be a soft landing.

And no way back up.

Speakin of up. His father looked to the tree. That first branch seems a might higher this year.

No, you'ns jus older.

Only feels that way.

Ya comin?

I was kin'a hankerin fer a swim.

Suit yerself.

The boy took two running steps towards the tree, planted his foot on its trunk and thrust himself upwards, shimmying his hands over the rough bark until he'd reached the lowest branch. He pulled himself up and onto it and began to climb. When he came to his perch he looked over the vast expanse. In the distance a black fume of smoke as wide as the horizon blotted out the sky to the south. Lowering himself back down to the lowest branch, he squatted over his father, sitting between the roots of the pine with his hat pushed down over his eyes. Blue lay panting beside him.

Pa?

His father jerked as if awoken from a deep sleep and looked up at the boy like he couldn't reconcile the expression on his son's face with the dream he'd been having.

I thought ya was goin fer a swim, the boy said.

I din't like the look of that rope.

There's somethin ya ought'n see.

What?

Cain't rightly describe it.

Ya playin yer old man?

Only one way to find out.

That the way it's goin be?

Looks it.

Clicking his tongue against his teeth, his father took off his hat and set it on the ground. He took two steps back, drew a deep breath and ran at the tree. He leapt and his foot-leathers scuttered up the trunk, pulling himself even with the boy before he'd grabbed for a handhold. Swinging onto the branch above his son, he peered down at him with a calculated glee. The boy frowned and shook his head.

Ya look like ya was hopin to see yer old man make a fool of hisself.

We ain at the top yet.

The boy clambered past him on the outside, using the spring in the thinned branches to his advantage. He didn't look down until he'd reached his perch, his father but halfway.

Old man, he called to him and when that didn't raise a twitch, he lowered himself to the branch above where his father stood. His hands were set on the same branch and he was peering through bowed arms at the sun's yellowed eye struggling through the fume of smoke on the horizon.

Whadya thinkin? the boy asked.

Is a forest fire.

Well I know that. Whadya think caused it?

I don't know. A lightnin strike, maybe.

It reminds me of somethin. It's like— but he couldn't put into words how it made him feel, seeing the sky sullied so.

Then he recalled a story his father had once read to him.

Mordor, he said. It's like Mordor.

His father's eyes narrowed. He clicked his tongue against his teeth and drew his fingers through his beard.

Whatever it is, ain got nothin to do with us.

They whiled the day away fishing along the rain-swolled river, never losing sight of each other as they trolled their lines towards the fall's thunder. The current was strong and broke in violent tirades against outcroppings of stone forged in defiance against the flood, spewing mist and foam and soaking the boy with a chilled effluence tasting of minerals and algae. On the far side, the river surged over a hillscape of boulders clogged with logs, scoured and sunbleached. Between them, muddy streams washed dense clouds of earth into the river, turning the rapids a reddish-brown.

The boy was shivering and his hands were numb on the rod when he came to the bend in the river before the falls. The thunder here throbbed like the heartbeat of the world. He edged along the shore of a black pool spared the tumult of the rapids by a steepled ledge of granite, crimped and V'd against the bank. Pine needles and dust formed a shifting landscape on the surface of the pool and shadows darted in the sandy-gold fringe at its crux.

The boy cast his line, reeled it back in and cast again. He saw the speckled back of a trout emerge from the water. It lunged at the bait and he gave his rod a tug. The hook caught and he felt the fish bolt for the safety of the fast-flowing stream. It shot into the air, lunging over the granite pier, the boy snapping back hard on the rod. The fish jerked in midflight, plunging back into the water, and he reeled it in until it was a few feet from shore, subdued now so that it hovered just beneath the surface, its languor disproved by the fierce white of its eyes.

I got one, he called to his father, thirty paces down river.

His father looked up at him, fanning his hand at his ear to say he couldn't hear what he'd said, and the boy bent and thrust two fingers into the fish's gills, wrenching it from the water and holding it up. His father yelled something that was also lost to the falls and the boy eased the fish back into the pool. He drew it along the granite slope until he'd reached the bonneted spike that his great-grandfather had pounded into a crack in the rock.

143

Setting his rod on the ground beside it, he wound the line around the spike and, hand over hand, brought the fish within reach. It gave a thrash and he turned away from the splatter of ice-cold droplets.

Here, his father said, holding out a chain of barbed hooks.

The boy took it in his free hand. He clipped one end to the spike, grabbed the fish by the gills, slipping his hook from its mouth, and planted the bottommost hook on the chain through the same hole. When he released the fish, it skewed wildly back and forth at the end of the tether, turning the water cloudy with silt.

The man clapped him on the back and cast his own line into the pool. The boy set to tying another fly and, when he thought his father wasn't looking, chancing furtive glances into the dense foliage behind him.

Maybe he got lost, his father yelled to him after he'd cast a second time.

What?

Sky, he shouted, maybe he got lost.

The boy shook his head and his father's mad grin was clipped by his line jerking. His hands tensed on the reel and his feet slipped downward along the algae-slicked slope towards the pool.

Whoa now!

When they'd caught five fish between them, the man unhitched the chain and led his son through the forest to a field of exposed granite on the northwestern edge of the quarry. It rose past a firepit to a curtain of pines several hundred paces hence, its gradual slope tempered by juniper bushes and stunted spruce trees growing out of the cracks amongst thickets of sumac and raspberry brambles. Pink veins coursed through its grey and quartz deposits in the rock sparkled in the sun.

The man skirted its base until he came to a ridge of raised stone that ran like the spine of a great fish all the way to the other side. There he knelt and lay his hand on it, looking back at his son. The boy was scowling as if there was only so much nonsense he was willing to bear.

Whadya feel? his grandfather had asked the man, then a boy himself, the first time he'd brought him there.

It's warm, the boy had answered.

Tha's because it's alive.

When the boy's eyes flashed doubt, his grandfather had smiled and asked, D'ya feel arythin else?

The boy concentrated on the tips of his fingers but felt nothing other than heat from the sun and the coarseness of the rock.

No.

Then we're safe.

The old man stepped lithely onto the ridge, beckoning the boy to follow.

Safe from what? the boy had asked after they had taken only a few steps.

Achaan.

Wha's that?

The creature upon whose back we tread.

The boy looked across the expanse of pink-hued granite. For a moment he could almost believe that it had once been alive.

It'n made of rock? he asked.

No, but its skin was so thick it might'n well have been. It was as tall as twenty men and so fearsome that, for time beyond memory, it'd kept the ancient ones in caves, scavengin for food by night and hidin by day, until finally the wisest among them discovered a way to defeat the monster. There he stopped and looked to the boy. And how'n ya suppose he done it?

The boy thought on it but could not imagine how a man could kill such a creature.

I don't know. How?

I'll show ya.

He began to slap his hands on his hips, slow and steady, and bade the boy to do the same. When the boy had matched his pace, his grandfather began to sing. At first his voice was just a low murmur, no louder than a stream gurgling over smooth pebbles. Soon it grew into the rush of rapids as the stream turned into a river and rose louder still into the migrant roar of a waterfall. He felt himself being swept along its current, dashed upon its rocks and finally plunging downwards. The moment he was to have hit the crags below, the song ended and the boy was startled from his trance by the sudden quiet.

Ya see, the old man had said, they subdued him with a song.

A song? The boy shook his head, still disbelieving, though he felt its power reverberating within.

Tha's right. Then whispering: So be careful how ya tread upon this earth, for ya do not want to awake Achaan.

As the man now watched his son balancing mindlessly along the ridge, he remembered the terror with which these same words had descended upon the boy when he'd first recounted the story to him. He was six, and a few nights later a storm had swept in from the south. Lightning touched at the thunder in a furious assault upon the dark and it had been impossible to conceive of anything that could have slept through such a crack. The boy had cried out from his bed. His father had rushed to him and carried him back to the room he shared with his mother, the boy muttering that it was comin, he'd seen it within the flash.

Seen what? his mother had asked. What's comin?

Nestled between his parents the boy had regained his courage. He told her about Achaan and how a wise man had subdued it with a song. When he was done his mother had frowned at her husband and he'd hurried to make amends by fetching a glass of milk heated in a tin cup he'd set directly on the dying embers in the stove.

A story to scare children and nothing more, the man saw that now. And also that his son was leaving such things behind and that he had little to offer in their stead.

Rising, he followed the boy up the slope to the firepit ringed by stones that his grandfather had foraged from the river when he himself was but a boy. His son was rearranging the rocks that had become dislodged by the winter rains and Blue was sniffing at the ash. The man hung the string of fish on the branch of a stunted spruce tree and turned, letting the slope carry him back down towards the forest.

I'll fetch us some tinder, he called over his shoulder.

But the boy didn't look up and the man knew that he was thinking about his mother.

After they'd eaten two of the fish and were smoking the others on racks over a fire lushed by cedar boughs, the man smoked a pipe and watched the sky grow dim. When he saw the first star sheering through its gloom, he reached into his satchel and pulled out a package wrapped in linen and tied with twine. He set it in front of his son and the boy stared down at the present as if it might contain some great malevolence.

Yer ma went to a lot of trouble, the man said. Least ya can do is open it.

The boy pulled solemnly at the bow and the linen parted. Inside was a new pair of foot-leathers, same as she'd made him last year, except bigger, and a stick with maple taffy swirled around one end.

Well go on, his father urged, see if they fit.

Slipping off his foot-leathers, the boy tossed them into the fire. He put on the new ones and took up the taffy and sucked on it while he watched his old moccasins curl and blacken.

Ya mind if'n I ave a taste? his father asked. The boy passed the stick over as if he couldn't have cared either way. His father took a lick and handed it back.

Nothin quite like yer ma's maple taffy.

The boy nodded and lay on his back, sucking on the sweetened stick and staring up at the darkening sky, the man watching him and thinking of the last time he'd done so. It had been the year before. He'd been laying down beside his son, recounting one of the stories his grandfather had drawn from what he called the desolate splendor of the world beyond ours — the stars and the constellations. He'd pointed out within the night's thousand-eyed gaze The Bear and The Hunter and told him of how Orion had slain Ursus and had earned the ire of The Great Spirit so that he would never again find a place within her graces. And he'd told him of how, in her wrath, she had sent the coyote to teach man the error of his ways and of how he was forever now at the mercy of this creature's whimsy.

Where'd yer gramps learn to read the stars like that aryhow? the boy had asked when he was done.

From an old Omushkego used to visit his pa when he was a boy. He tol him one time, memory resides in all things. Ya just got to know how to listen.

He taught yer gramps how to listen to the stars?

Tha's what he said.

Did yer gramps ever teach you?

He tried. I never had much of a knack fer it.

Ya think you could teach me?

I don't know, it was such a long time ago. I don't member haffa what he told me.

I'da shore like to learn.

Shoot, his father had said, suddenly sitting up. That reminds me. I almost fergot.

He reached into his satchel and took a small demijohn from his bag. It was pot-bellied and had a short neck with a hoop on it for carrying. It was a quarter full with clear liquid. When he held it up, the firelight bent into streaks of red and yellow over its curve. He jimmied the cork out of its top and sniffed at it.

Damned if it don't smell like ma gramps after all these years, he'd said and leant to the boy so that he could pass the bottle under his nose. The boy startled away from it and sat up rubbing his nose against the sting.

Smells like . . . I don't know.

Ya wun't. It's cornshine.

Wha's that?

Corn that's gone bad and made into a spirit.

Like'n a ghost ya mean?

And an evil one at that.

What'd he do with it?

He drank it.

He drank an evil spirit? Why'n he do that?

Said it chased away the daemons.

Y'ever drink it?

The man shook his head.

Yer ma don't look kindly on men who consort with evil spirits, he'd said, then tilted the bottle back, drinking deeply from its spout. The liquid washed like fire down his throat. When he'd had his taste, he held it out to his son.

Go on, take a drink, he said. Yurra man now.

He remembered how when the boy had taken a gulp from it, his cheeks had puffed out and it looked like he was about to be sick. Then the cornshine had sprayed from between his lips, the drops cascading over the fire, freeing, it seemed, the evil spirits from within so that they reared up in angry furor within the flames. The boy had scuttled backwards and the terror in his eyes had dislodged something deep inside the man, making him laugh like there could be no end to joy in the world.

It seemed so long ago now.

Laying beside his son, he looked up at the desolate splendor, beseeching the stars for a story to ease the boy's pain, but they spoke to him not a word.

H e awoke the next morning, shivering against the morning chill. The fire had died in the night and the boy, he could see, had rekindled it with the drying rack. All that was left of it was blackened ends among the ashes. Blue lay beneath the stunted spruce tree and when his master stood the dog rose from where he lay on a pad of moss. Brittled strands of it clung to the pink of his underbelly.

Where'd he get offta? the man said. The dog cocked his head as if he didn't understand. You know who I'ma talkin bout. The boy.

Blue wheeled round and ran stiff-legged up the rise. At its summit, he turned back to him and barked.

I'ma comin, the man said, his own legs none sprier than the hound's.

When he came astride of Blue, he looked up at the white pine, projected in relief against the smoke-blackened sky beyond. The boy, he could see, sat on its topmost branch, perched as an eagle might. The man whistled between two fingers. The boy turned his way, waving down at him, and the man let gravity pull him down the steep bank. His feet slipped over a wash of crumbled stone, releasing him to the mercy of the slope, hurtling him bottomwards, his hands pinwheeling in deft caricature of the absurdity of it. There was a sharp ridge of stone slanted upwards from a crevice at the base of the pitch — an ankle breaker, his grandfather would have named it. Cursing, he thrust himself up and over. When he landed flat-footed on the level ground beyond, it felt like a spike had been driven into his knees.

Son of a— he said, looking up at the boy, now climbing down from the tree, his back to him so that he seemed not to have witnessed his father's folly.

Ya sleep at all lass night? the man asked as the boy dropped to the ground.

Couldna stop thinkin bout it.

What?

The fire. Pa, ya shoulda seen it. It was like the sun was swallowin the earth.

How's that?

In the dark, the horizon was glowing. East to west. There weren't no end to it.

His eyes were wide and full of wonder and dread so that for a moment he looked to be a child again.

The wind'll shift soon enough, his father said. The fire'll turn back on itself and that'll be the end of it.

And if it don't?

It will.

Howdya know?

It's the way of things.

But—

Don't give it no nevermind. Now come on, it's late. We ought'n be gittin home. Yer ma's like to be worried.

They found her just where they'd left her, sitting in her cedar rail chair, her head tilted against her shoulder, drool spanned between her lips and the collar of her nightgown. Her skin was as grey as ash. Flies circled her and others crawled within the drape of her hair. The dogs were rousing at her feet, jostling against one another with noses raised, whimpering and begging for a touch. The man sidestepped them and knelt at his wife. He took up her hand and held it to his cheek.

Is she— the boy asked from the bottom of the stairs, the word choking in his throat.

His father looked back at him. There were tears on his cheeks. He shook his head.

We never shoulda left her.

Such hate in his eyes that the man had never seen.

He ain't never goin to forgive ya, he thought. He thinks ya hadda choice in the matter. He don't know how she begged ya to go. So she could git on with dyin. And yet here she is, still alive, if'n only by a thread.

Lifting her then, as easy as he would have an armload of kindling, he carried her into the house, through the kitchen and up the stairs. The boy followed them as far as the threshold.

From the barn he could hear the goats bleating, the nannies screaming in protest against the weight of their milk. He turned and padded down the steps.

I'ma comin, he hollered. Goddamnit, I'ma comin!

He hardly left her bedside for the next three days. On the third night of his vigil, she awoke coughing. The boy groped in the dark for her hand and held it tight. She pulled away and leant over the side of the bed, hacking and spitting up. The boy propped himself on his arm and placed his hand on her back. Her nightgown was soaked through with sweat. He rubbed the heel of his palm in gentle circles between her shoulder blades. The knobs of her spine were so sharp they felt like they'd cut through her skin.

There, there, he said. It's a'right. Git it up. You'ns doin good.

Sky roused, rising from the floor. His nails raked against the wood as he padded towards his mistress. He licked at her face and the boy reached over his mother and pushed him away.

Shoo, he said. Go on now.

He heard the dog circle twice at the foot of the bed then lay down, whimpering. The boy recommenced rubbing his mother's back and praying for the coughing to subside.

After a while it did. She lay there gulping air and wheezing, her body convulsing with the force of the attack. The boy reached for the pitcher of water on the bed stand. He poured her a cup and tugged at her sleeve.

Y'ought'n drink somethin.

I won't, she said.

Ya got to.

No.

She lay hunched like some long-dead thing. She did not move nor even breathe. When she'd made her point clear, the boy set the cup beside the pitcher and sat with his legs flat on the floor, his head propped between his hands. He could hear his mother wheezing and Sky whining, and other sounds too: mosquitoes buzzing and battering against the ceiling and the faint swell of music.

He stood and crossed to the upraised window and looked down at his father's workshop. A familiar song leaked out from its open door and slats of light shimmered in the spaces between the boards running along its front wall. The boy frowned and felt Sky nudge his hand. He toyed idly with one of his ears until the dog shook his head and then the boy turned from the window and walked to the bedroom door. When he got there he paused, listening to his mother's rasp. Sky nudged his leg with his nose and the boy opened the door and slipped through. He felt in the dark for the rail around the stairs. It was as cold and lifeless as his mother's hand. He followed it past his own room and down and into the unlit kitchen.

When he came onto the porch, he froze there, leaning against the post and staring at the workshop as if the light and the music coming from within were a form of madness that had stolen his father and would try to steal him as well. He imagined the light was pulling him, that he was powerless against it. He let go of the post and drifted down the steps. His feet found the path and it led him to the workshop's door. He leant against the striated illuminations, the light forming a womb around him, and closed his eyes.

There was a woman's voice set against lightly gilded piano keys. It was the same song his mother always sung while she milked the goats when she thought that no one was around. How often he'd heard it as he'd hidden in the hayloft above the stalls, marvelling at the sound of her voice for it didn't sound at all like his mother when she was at her piano. Again he listened to the words and tried to understand what they were saying but they were foreign to him. The woman was sad, that he could tell, and also that she was trying to pretend that she wasn't — trying so hard it seemed that she might burst from the wanting. It pained the boy that she could want for something so bad and he wished for her to quiet or to stop pretending but she kept at it until the boy thought there was no hope for her at all — that she would die singing this sad song and that the lie would have made her dying all that much the worse.

When the music stopped, he opened his eyes. The light was gone. He heard his father shuffling towards the door and turned and fled back towards the house.

L ater that night, his father found the boy nestled beside his mother, his head resting on her Bible, his thumb suckled in his mouth. He picked him up and carried him across the hall to his bed.

When he returned to his room, his wife was lying on her side. He sat beside her and brushed the hair from her face. Her eyes opened and tears squeezed from their corners. He wiped at one with the pad of his thumb. She clutched at his hand and he longed for her to rub it against her cheek, like she used to, but she pushed it away, pressing it into his lap and rolling away from him. He sat listening to her breathe for a moment then shucked his foot-leathers and lay down beside her.

After a while she shifted against his back. When she spoke her voice was parched and dry, almost unrecognizable.

She said: I'm afeared.

Don't be.

I'ma goin to hell.

Y'ain't.

I know it.

You'ns a good woman.

No.

We couldna ast for betta.

It don't matter.

It should.

But it don't.

She drew in a long staggered breath and exhaled. He could hear a rattle within it, like her teeth had come loose and were knocking against one another, though he knew it was coming from her chest.

And the Levites shall speak with a loud voice, she said, though her own voice was hardly a whisper, and say to all the men of Israel: Cursed is the one who—

He gripped her arm hard enough to stay her tongue.

Hush now, he said, you'll wake the boy.

As if summoned, the boy awoke in the dark.

He awoke from this:

He was five again and standing at the edge of the corn patch. The cacklers were at the height of their frenzy, ravaging the field and remaking the sky into an overreaching void. Lightning forked within their feathered black and there came out of it a sound like rocks fissuring. One of the blue-collared birds dropped at his feet, palsied and rampant in its lust for flight, bedevilled now by gravity and crippled by cindered wings, their hair-thin bones glowing like pine needles cast upon a blaze. A crow set upon it. It had the head of a dog and he recognized it as the one that had come after him at the anthill. He watched it devour the wingless bird, whole as a snake would, and then it turned on him.

He awoke in a cold sweat, his heart pounding. Floorboards creaked and he heard the heavy plod of footsteps descending the stairs.

He sat up and set his feet on the floor. It was cold against his skin. He rubbed his toes together as if he were trying to make a fire between them and then stood and walked to the window. His father was carrying his mother into the workshop. A moment later, speckles of light escaped in a stellar explosion through its open door. Pinpoints of it roved over the ground like stars fallen to earth.

He fell asleep with his head propped against the window-sill listening to the woman sing. He dreamt of the corn patch again except this time there were no birds, there was only the battle-scarred field. There wasn't a soul around and not a sound, nothing at all except the smell of dust turned up by the rain. The sky was clear and blue, and he couldn't think of why that was — the musk of rain so stark, the ground as dry as smoke, the dirt in the field like cinders. Standing there, praying for the rains to come and fearing that they wouldn't, that the time for rain was past, that the farm was already dead, and that he was the only one still holding out hope that there might yet be a little life left in it.

When he opened his eyes, he was back in bed. The drapes were pulled open and a square of sunlight glared at him from the floor. He rose and padded into the hall. The door to his parents' room was open a crack. He pushed at it, holding his breath like he always did, dreading the stink of urine and rotten apples: the smell of his mother.

But this morning the room smelled only of the field. His mother was standing at the open window, looking out. The door thudded against the wall and she turned. Her face didn't look so much like ashes anymore, it looked like wet sand, grey and wrinkled from the surf. She smiled wide, holding her hands out, and he ran to her, burying his face in her breast and hugging her hard enough to make her gasp.

When his father came into the room just after dark, they were lying in bed, his wife curled around his son's back, holding him so tight that it looked like he'd have to break her arms to get them apart.

In the morning, the man carried her to the orchard and set her beside Belle's grave. They took turns with the shovel and neither said a word until the boy dropped back into the hole when it was already above his father's head.

It's deep enough, the man said.

But the boy dug deeper still, filling bucket after bucket until his father repeated, It's deep enough.

The boy looked at his hands, dipped in mud and blistered. He wrapped the bucket's rope around his ankle and let his father pull him up.

Perched over his mother at the edge of the grave, the boy read from her Bible. He read first from Genesis and then a few passages from Leviticus and one from Ezekiel and three Psalms that she had underlined. Then, holding the book up to the wind, he let his mother choose and read an entire page from the book of Deuteronomy. When he'd reached the end he stopped, mid-sentence. He tossed the Bible into the hole and turned his back, weeping as his father rolled her in.

T hat night he slept beside her grave and didn't dream at all. When he awoke he was lying under his father's blanket. He looked to the east and watched the sun laze across the yard, imagining that it consumed all that it touched — devouring the pines and the willow tree and the house and the barn. Finally, it touched upon his foot-leathers, protruding from beneath the quilt, and he held his breath waiting for the light to consume him too.

He arose sometime later.

Sky was lying on the fresh mound of dirt, staring at him with sad eyes, his jowls resting on his crossed paws. The boy stood and relieved his bladder without thought of finding cover. When he was done he coughed up phlegm and spat a globule onto the ground. He searched it for signs of blood, like in his mother's, but it was clear. Hunger gnawed at his belly. He started towards the house. Sky whimpered and when he turned back, the hound was sitting up, his head cocked and one of his ears folded over itself so that he looked the fool.

Ya comin or not? the boy said.

Sky shook the stiff out of his hind legs and walked towards him as if he had all the time in the world. When he'd come astride, the boy grabbed at the dog's ear. Sky dodged away and ran ahead and the boy trailed after him, shaking his head and thinking of where he might have left his bow.

He found it hung on the hook beside the kitchen door where it always was. His quiver was there too and so was his mother's leather satchel. He slung the bow over one shoulder, the satchel over the other and set the quiver inside. He could feel the heat of the stove and walked over to it. The cast-iron pot was on top. He touched the lid. It was hot. He used a cloth hanging on the drying rack to lift it off. Inside the pot there were a dozen eggs and they recalled to him how his mother had cooked up a batch of hardboileds the night before his father had gone off to hunt them wild dogs.

He hadna left us that time, he thought, she wouldna got sick. It damn near kilt her losin that baby. She never really got over it. Now she's dead. It's his fault.

The eggs rattled as the water started to boil and the sound filled him with rage. He snatched up the pot by its wire handle and flung it at the wall.

Goddamn you!

His father was at the beaver dam on the far side of the corn patch. He had Spook hitched to a log jutting from the thatched wattle and daub and was harrying her from behind with his switch. A thin drizzle poured from the dam, muddying the ground at their feet.

The boy strode across the field, not looking at his father again until he'd come to where the ridge sloped at a gentle glide into the field. When he turned back to the dam, a spout flowed from the release. Water drained in creeping lines between the rows of corn and his father stood a few paces from the geyser confabulating with Spook, his hands weaving a story out of the air, the mule braying and swishing her tail as if she'd never heard anything so unlikely. Both had their backs to him so it was only the dogs watching as the boy swatted at a deer fly, waiting for his father to look his way.

A cloud overhead devised a separate world between them — a blotch of shadow that seemed to portend something dire. Sky barked as if he'd sensed it too and the boy's father spun around. He caught sight of his son and waved his hat in a slow arc above his head.

You killed her, the boy yelled. You son of a bitch. You can rot in hell fer all I care. I ain never comin back!

His father was walking towards him now. The boy spat in the dirt then turned his back on him, starting at a jog up the path towards the quarry.

$\underline{V}$

On a hot summer's day they came to a small creek, running fast and clear along the bottom of a gulley. The air was scented with lavender and magnolia and mildewed leaves. Frogsong stilled against their approach and hordes of insects swirled in pestules about their heads.

Gawd, they's bad, Briar said as he shrugged off his pack and knelt at the water. He cupped his hands within its flow and splashed the cold wet up and over his face and neck.

You say it like they's a surprise, Levin said, swishing a cedar bough over his shoulders with the lassitude of a horse's tail and staring up at the hills as if he'd caught the flicker of something on the periphery of his vision but couldn't yet tell if he'd imagined it.

They's gittin worse every year.

They's always plenty bad, far as I recall.

But they's bigger. Hey, Yoke? The skitters is bigger this year, ain't they?

Yoke, lathering handfuls of mud over his bald crown, answered him with a grunt and a wave, his meaning clear to all but Briar.

They's so big, Briar continued unabated, I seen two of them holdin down a crow while a third one fucked it. He let out a startled laugh. Ya hears what I said?

I reckin he's heard ya plentyatimes.

How's that?

Ya tol it afore. Ceptin last time it was a robin and afore that it was a sparrow. I spect next it'll be an eagle.

Tha's what I'm sayin. They's gittin bigger ever damn year.

Lemon and Jude emerged then, stumbling out of the scrub. Their heads were draped with sheaths of rabbit hide to ward off the bugs. Their eyes were dim mirrors, hollow and pained, and their arms batted against their sides like they'd sprung loose from their sockets and were being held up by their sleeves. When they came to the creek, they dropped to their knees and drank straight from the water, lapping at it like they were no better than dogs.

Briar shook his head.

They ain goin to make it, he whispered to Levin.

They'll manage.

If'n it weren't for them we'da been at the lake two days ago.

Maybe.

Maybe, hell.

Levin wiped his chin with the back of his hand and cocked his head towards the east.

You smell that?

Briar raised his nose to the breeze.

Smoke.

They forded the creek and mounted the gulley's slope at a diagonal. The sting of smoke in the air was as sharp as a compass point. They made their way slowly, following Briar's lead, walking bent-legged and low, their gait wearied by even the slightest snap of a twig underfoot. The buzz of mosquitoes and deer flies shortly gave way to a distant splattering. Briar drew them to a large boulder half-buried in the ground and moulded green with moss. They huddled in its shadow and listened.

They's a waterfall up ahead, Levin whispered.

I spect that's where we'll find em.

Reds? Jude asked.

Shush.

If they's a huntin party they's like to have dogs.

I know it, Briar agreed. Lucky we's downwind.

I shore hope they's ain't Crows, Jude said.

They ain't.

Howdya know?

Briar gritted his teeth. Then: I'ma take a wander. Y'alls stay here.

He was gone for a goodly time. When he reappeared he was on the opposite side of the creek. The sun had gone down and the sky's blue was riding waves of red and orange into the west, a lone star poking a hole through its firmament. He was hunkered low and moving through the brush with the pace of a man in flight. His shadow passed them by and Levin sounded the shrill chirrup of a black bird. Briar stopped, searching for its origin. Levin whistled again and he followed its call over a bridge of stones bevelled above the creek's current.

They's Reds a'right, he said when he'd made the cover of the boulder again.

How many? Levin asked.

I only saw two of em.

Tha's all?

And one was a squaw.

They can be as dang'rous as ary.

She's but a girl.

A child?

Briar shook his head.

She had hair down there.

She was naked?

Yeah.

And the other?

A young buck. He was naked too.

What was they doin?

Whadya think?

Ya check for tracks?

Both sides of the creek and atop the falls. There weren't none.

They got a dog?

Not as far as I could tell.

Tain't like Reds. Travellin alone. And this far south.

Whadya thinkin?

It's peculiar.

Din't strike me as such.

Huh?

If'n ya mean it's a trap.

Why'n ya say that?

I don't know.

Ya think it might be?

I done tol ya I din't.

Levin plucked a handful of rust-coloured pine needles from the ground. He ruminated them in his palm and let them go in pindrops, contemplating their realignment as if they were gifted with prescience. After a while he looked up, squint-eyed, into Briar's heated glare.

We'll wait until dark.

N ight fell. Stars radiated the sky and a half moon rose like a great leering eye. They crept from behind the boulder guided by the moon's light and crossed the creek, again taking Briar's lead. He drew them along the gulley's eastern slope. They followed its ridge through cedars twisted and malformed, their roots curled like fingers clutching at the thin wash of topsoil. The drone of water falling in a steady stream grew louder. Soon it dulled knowledge of their own footfalls even to them, and they took confidence in its screen as they made their way up a natural course of stone steps rising to a rim of banded gneiss that formed a horseshoe around the falls.

The water flowed over the drop in a thin veil, lit into flickering strands by the glower of a fire below. Laughter drifted up to them on the orange mist and Briar motioned them down. The party dropped to their bellies and shimmied towards the edge. When they were within an arm's length of it, Briar raised his hand and the others halted. He crawled the last few inches and snuck a peek over the lip. He jerked his head back immediately and crawled backwards until he was once again even with the rest. He pointed at Yoke and to himself, then across the chasm. Levin nodded and the two rose and retreated hunchbacked down the steps.

Shortly after, the laughter stilled and there arose a less tangible noise: a gentle strumming — motes transpired from some deep and lonely place to play amongst the rush of the falls. Jude shuffled forward and felt Levin's hand on his arm. When he looked back at the old man, he was shaking his head, and he drew himself once more away from the precipice. Levin's grasp withdrew and Jude set his head on his hands, listening to the night's serenity gather around him in this strange coupling of sounds.

He dozed and when the music ended the quiet shook him from a dream, forgotten the moment his eyes opened. There was laughter in it. Laughter and ferns and a doe startled into flight. The rest was lost to the vision of Lemon's face inches from his own and the sour rot of his breath. His brother's cheek was plastered to the rock, his eyes closed and his mouth vented and drooling. Mosquitoes fed off his brow. Jude sat up and harried them with his hand. He then set his rabbit hide over Lemon's face and rolled over. Levin was sleeping on his back. Gnats were crawling within the white of his beard. He left them to their forage and crawled to the edge of the cliff.

The fire had dwindled to ribbons of thin, orange flame. In the dark he could not espy much beyond that it had been kindled within a ring of flat stones on a bulge of granite raised up out of a pool of black and turbulent water. At the border of its illumine, a bear was bent over a velvet-furred creature pushed into a recess at the base of the cliff. Its pelt was splayed open and the bear was growling and grunting as it lapped at its guts.

And then there was that laughter again, sudden and shrill.

The bear sat up and the furred creature wriggled out from beneath it with such force that it seemed to pull itself out of its own skin. It stood into the stuttered light and Jude saw that it was a young woman, naked and tittering. Her long dark hair concealed her breasts and her hand hurried to cover the black triangle between her thighs. The bear rose up before her. It spread its arms wide and growled. The woman laughed again and turned and skipped away. The bear then shed his own wrap and Jude saw that it was a young man. He was taller than the woman by a head and gangly. His hair reached the crook of his back and his manhood stood erect, nudging at his belly. He chased her to the lip of the pool and they dove in tandem with pinioned arms. Both were lost to the swirling dark.

Jude fell asleep again listening to the wild ecstasy of their frolic. Nearing dawn he was awoken by Levin shaking his leg. He had his finger to his lips and when he was certain that Jude understood his meaning he jostled Lemon, who sat up, peeling the sheath of rabbit fur from his face and blinking against the light.

There was nothing to see atop the ridge beyond the first strains of dawn prying through the trees. Tiny yellow-winged birds warbled and chirruped, flitting from branch to branch.

Levin duck-waddled to the edge of the cliff, and Jude and Lemon followed him likewise to his perch. They could see now that the water funnelled through a thin gorge, falling from a height of ten men, pooling between the rock wall on their side and a hump of pink granite glittered with quartz on the other. The water frothed white on black, draining through a narrow channel some twenty paces towards the back of the pool then wound serpentine through a rippled span of bedrock and disappeared into a field of boulders.

The lovers lay curled within the bear skin beside the firepit. A miasma of heat shimmered from the ring of river-washed stones. Above it the rock face was formed into striations by grey slabs, its top layers leaning precariously over its bottom like something built by a demented child bent on ruin.

Levin now stood and waved his hands over his head. Looking downstream, Jude caught sight of movement from behind one of the boulders. Briar's head craned out from behind it. He waved back and then ducked out of sight. He reappeared a moment later on its far side, creeping over the peneplain leading upwards into the gorge, Yoke stalking after him. As they came up onto the ledge, the giant drew from the scabbard on his back his machete and swung it in slow arcs in front of him, arousing the blade to its purpose.

The three on the ridge watched as they circled the firepit, watched Briar kneel and lift the flap of the bear's hide exposing the sleeping lovers' entwined feet. Toes twitched in the chill air but elsewise signed no distress and he ran his hand up the woman's leg. She shifted against the touch but still did not awaken and he tried his luck deeper. There was a sudden movement within the bear's stomach. Briar jerked his arm back and stood as the two lovers roused, sitting up from within their wrap. The young man glared with cool disdain even as Yoke pinned the tip of his blade to his chest. The woman had eyes only for Briar. He was saying something and sniffing his finger. He passed it under Yoke's nose, laughing, and the woman sprung to her feet, charging at him with fingers hooked into talons. Briar hit her hard on the mouth with the butt of his knife, sending her reeling up against the rock wall. She came back off it as supple as a cat, blood splayed in tendrils down her chin. She was clutching something in her fist and hurling it before Briar had seen that it was a piece of slate as flat and as smooth as a dinner plate. It missed him by barely a hand's width. So lost was he in his amuse at the woman's folly that it was left to those on the ridge to witness it strike Yoke in the ear. The giant lilted sideways, his hand clutching at his head, blood gushing from between his fingers as the young man rolled onto his feet. He snatched the bow lent against the wall, fit it with an arrow and drew it down on Briar now advancing towards the woman, his knife slung low and his step unfettered by the delight borne upon her face nor the way her eyes sought out her lover about to release his fury, when a sudden thunder rent that moment from the next.

The man flinched and the arrow loosed wild, grazing Briar's arm and spinning him towards his would-be assassin, now sagging to his knees. A red bloom inflorescent on his chest. The bow laggard in his hand. Teetering. Briar stared at him bare-toothed as if the man's plight was a mystery to him. Then Yoke was standing behind him, clutching at the man's hair to keep him upright. He swung his blade at a point just below his jaw. Blood spewed from the gash and Yoke wrested the blade loose and swung again. The man's head came off in his hand and his body toppled, spitting gore through its cavity.

Briar was just turning back to the woman as she came towards him. She clutched at his wrist, steadying his knife and plunging it into her belly. Briar recoiled, staggering back. The blade sluiced from her stomach. Blood bubbled from the slit and over her sex, dripping off the dark curls in droplets. She clutched at the wound and took one step forward before pitching side-ways. Briar shook his head. He said something to Yoke, holding the man's head up so he could look it in the eyes, then stepped to the dying woman. She was choking up blood and muttering in her foreign tongue. He stood over her in silent reproach. When she'd stilled, he nudged her with his foot. She did not move and he turned and looked up at the three on the ridge.

Lemon and Jude were as twin statues — one petrified by horror, the other delight. Between them the old man was still sighting along the barrel of his rifle.

Goddamn Reds, he said.

The three backtracked along the gorge, looking for a way down.

At the bottom of the stone steps, the rock wall tapered and broke into channels of red earth supporting the gnarled frames of cedars. They descended through one of these, balanced on roots spindly and twisted, steadying themselves with the creepvines winding like the threads of a giant spider's web between the trunks. Trickles the colour of rust oozed from the marshy ground.

When they came to the creek, Briar and Yoke were walking towards them. The latter was holding the young man's head by the hair, the young woman slung over his shoulder. Blood the thickness of pine sap drained from the giant's ear and a weal of it trailed down the woman's leg. Briar walked past with his eyes lowered and the old man bent to the creek. There was a sparkle within its current. He reached into it and plucked a piece of quartz from the bed. He squeezed his one eye closed and held it before his other. The stone was dull now in the light. He chucked it back into the water and joined the others watching Yoke trudge up the gulley's far slope — an ogre headed back to the hills with his bride-to-be, Briar scrambling to catch up behind.

Where they takin her? Jude asked when they'd disappeared behind the rise.

Levin sucked at his tooth.

Best not to think about it.

T he man's body lay where it had fallen. Blood seeped from its neck, draining down the slope of the ledge and into the pool where it was swept away by the current. Blue-bodied flies were already buzzing about and the taste of death hung heavy in the air.

Levin stood over the body, clicking his tongue. Lemon stood behind him, dumbstruck by its gore. Jude had spotted the man's instrument propped against the wall. He knelt before it, awed as if he'd happened upon the altar of some powerful and ill-understood god. Its body was hollow and had the outline of a woman. Its neck was long and atop it there was a small square head with six pegs, like ears. Strings of woven hair stretched from each of them and ran its length. Summoning his nerve, he reached out and plucked at one of them. It pinged and he sat back on his haunches trying to reconcile the sound it made with the ones it had made last night.

A'right then, Levin said as if the ping had illuminated a way forward.

He knelt and wedged his hands under the young man's body and rolled it onto its back. Its manhood flopped onto its belly and lay docile against its greyed skin. A fly landed on its shaft. Levin shooed it with a sweep of his hand and took his knife from its sheath.

I'ma goin to need some tinder, he said. And a stick yay long.

He stretched his hands to their limits to demonstrate.

A stick?

Yeah.

What fer?

Jude had stood again but couldn't yet pry his eyes from the instrument.

A spit.

A spit?

He turned, cockeyed, to the old man as if he might have mis-heard.

We's got to make it look like it was Crows that done this.

They foraged along the creek, collecting beaver-felled logs, sun bleached and worn smooth by the current. When their arms were full, they turned back towards the falls, neither of them eager to return.

I don't feel so well, Lemon said.

His legs had the lightness of straw and his head seemed to be floating an arm's length above him. The sun had etched a vein of sweat along his jaw and a drop of it formed a glistening bead beneath his chin. He rested against a boulder and wiped at it with his sleeve.

It's the heat, Jude said.

Tain't the heat. It's—

What?

It weren't nothin like what I drawed on the wall.

Hell's ya talkin bout?

There weren't no glory in it.

Glory?

It's just— I thought—

Ya thought?

I mean— they's jus kids.

They's Reds.

They weren't hurtin nobody.

They's goddamn Reds.

I ain cut out for it, Jude. I ain't.

So what ya wanna do?

I don't know.

Go back to the farm?

No.

Out on our own?

I don know.

Well there ya have it.

Briar came back just before dark.

Gawd, don't that smell good, he said, leaning over the gutted torso spitted and cooking over the fire. He peeled a curl of skin, crispy and black, from its shoulder and stuffed it in his mouth. It crunched between his teeth.

Where's Yoke? Levin asked.

He was sitting with his back against the wall, smoking his pipe. The drift of its tobacco flavoured the simmer of meat.

He's goin be a while yet, Briar answered, unsheathing his knife and cutting himself a strip off the torso's back. He bandied it between his fingers and blew on it before folding it over and eating it whole.

I thah we was out of t'backy, he said, chewing.

We are. It was theirs. They's hid it in a crack in the wall, like they's do.

Whada bout that green t'backy they smoke? Ya find ary that?

No, jus the brown. Ya wanna taste?

I'ma standin here, ain't I?

Levin crooked the pipe at the corner of his mouth and drew from his pocket a small bulb made of leather and held together by a string. He untied it and drew a plug of tobacco from within. He passed it to Briar, retrieving his own pipe from his pocket. Briar packed the bowl with it, then taking a stick from the fire, baited the tobacco with the flame reared at its end. Drawing heavy on the pipe, he looked up at the darkening sky. A raptor circled overhead. Another swooped in on it and the two of them dropped in silent embrace below the treeline.

There wasn't a sound in the world but the rush of the falls and the plink of errant notes from the guitar.

Jude was sitting at the edge of the ledge, dangling his feet in the water and plucking idly at its strings. Lemon sat beside him, prying flakes of pink granite loose and pitching them into the pool. They'd hover there, a moment just beneath the surface — glittering eyes winking at him before the dark swallowed their shine.

Sup's on, boys, Briar called from behind them.

Jude set the guitar down and made to rise. Lemon held him by the arm.

I ain goin to eat him, he whispered.

Then don't.

I ain't.

Shrugging from his grip, Jude stood and Lemon listened to the scuff of his feet on the coarse rock behind.

Ya look like a rib-man, Briar said. Am I right?

Yes, sir.

Man after ma own heart.

After a moment there came a stifled crack.

Gawd tha's hot. Watch yerself, y'all burn yer lips.

Thank ya.

Juicy, ain't it?

Yeah.

Lemon?

I ain hungry.

I can hear yer belly from here. Git on over here, fetch some grub.

I ain hungry.

Jude, tell him how good it is.

I ain never tasted better.

Ain't that the truth.

Gawd, it's good.

The gnash of their teeth and the smack of their lips.

Lemon's stomach clenched and he bent over the pool. He vomited a thin gruel and his stomach clenched again. He retched a second time. When he was done he righted himself, wiping his mouth with the back of his hand. Bile burned down his throat and he could hear Briar laughing.

I don't think he believed ya, he said.

After they'd picked the torso clean, Briar spitted one of the legs and lay back on the rock, looking up at the sky. Wisps as thin as gossamer drifted against the stars.

Anyone ever ast, ya been to paradise, he said, now ya can say ya have. Eh, Levin?

It's right nice. He'd packed himself another pipe and was teasing a flame over the bundled weave of tobacco.

Ain't no skitters and they's a cool breeze. It's goddamn paradise.

Jude was sitting cross-legged before the fire, plucking at the guitar and shaking his head at the discordant sounds it made. Lemon stood behind him at the wall. He had a sharp piece of slate in his hand. He wet the tip of it and drew a circle on a smooth span of granite. Inside it: eyes and a nose. A hollow where a mouth would be. Then a hand clutching the head by a few straggled strands of hair.

The strumming stopped.

Ya cain't be scratchin at the rock here, Jude said.

Lemon spat in his palm, dipped his finger in the sputum and wiped it over the picture.

Lemon.

What?

I tol you, you cain't be doin that.

Why not?

The Reds'll know'd we was here. Ain't that right, Levin?

What?

Lemon's scratchin at the rock.

He cain't.

I told him.

Lemon, ya cain't be scratchin at the rock.

Scratch it out.

Lemon had already finished Yoke's arm and was contemplating the slope of his neck.

Maybe the Crows drawed it, he said.

They wun't.

Howdya know?

There ain't no Crows, Briar said.

Whadya mean? Jude asked.

Shhh.

Someone whistled in the distance, light and whimsical.

Is bout goddamned time, Briar said, sitting up and staring downstream along the creek.

A moment later, Yoke came into the light looking like a daemon come to earth on some mission of devilry. There wasn't an inch of him that hadn't been touched by blood. Two finger-lines on each cheek. A sweep of it over his bald crown. His leathers like an apron worn by a blind butcher. Red so dark under his fingernails they'd turned black.

We saved ya a leg, Briar said.

Yoke grunted and stepped to the fire. Juices frothed out from under the leg's skin, spitting into the fire.

Ya bury her? Levin asked.

Yoke grunted again.

How deep?

He held his hand three feet off the ground.

Crows take the women wit em, Levin said, looking to Jude.

Shore they do, Briar scoffed.

Use em as slaves and such.

That's right kindly of em, Briar said, laying back down with his head pillowed against the rock.

Above him, a grey river flowed past the seam between the trees: a storm bank, washing over the night sky's plenty.

Looks like we's in for some wetter.

T he thunder started just before dawn — an inchoate murmur
infecting their sleep.

Jude awoke feeling a spatter on his cheeks. He'd been
dreaming of rain. He sat up and looked to the sky, though the
damp wasn't coming from there but from the falls. Drops the
size of pinpricks swirled in a funnel over the pool. The smell of
smoke was ripe within it and thunder sounded as mountaintops
crumbling.

He waited for lightning to part the sky's pitch but there was
only the endless dark. Within it now, he could see flits of darker
still: birds flying in a straight line, one after the other. The rock
beneath his hands began to buzz, vibrating up his arms. It felt, all
at once, that it would shake him apart, and he stood. The others
were all standing too, heads craned to the heavens, mouths agape
at the earth's tremble.

That ain't no thunder I ever heard, Briar yelled above the roar.

Sounds like a damn flood, Levin yelled back at him.

What?

A flood!

Levin looked up at the ridge from which the thin curtain
of water fell in pearled strands, expecting the deluge. A slender
form appeared against the charcoaled sky. Legs as thin as reeds
stretched out before it. Its span measured against the treetops.
Soaring above them.

The doe landed on the bed of rippled stone beyond the pool.
Its legs snapped like cattails, its head bowed before it, driven into
the groove, its body rising in pirouette, pinwheeling and dashing
in a violent palsy over the river stones. It came to a rest on its
back, its neck twisted and its head lagging into the creek. Blood
leaked through a dozen patches where its fur had been torn by
the puncture of broken ribs.

The sound was now a world unto itself, deafening beyond the ears of men. Layered within it: the crack of branches and the splinter of trees.

It's a goddamn stampede! Levin hollered.

A desperate bawling rose above the roar and was at once taken over by a frantic shriek.

On top of the ridge two stags fought against a smoky screen, one crashing into the other and the both of them pitching over the edge. They hit the water with a tidal wave such that it washed up over the ledge, knocking Lemon off his feet and sweeping him back towards the pool. Briar grabbed at his arm, holding him fast against the swell and laughing at the terror in the boy's eyes.

Hoo-ee, he squealed as he pulled him to his feet. Now there's somethin worth scratchin on yer wall, boy.

In the pool, the bucks thrashed in a mad frenzy, rallying one over the other. The fury of their hooves clashed as hail upon the rocks.

Watch out! Levin screamed just as another stag careened over the rise. It struck the ledge not more than a pace from where Briar was dragging Lemon towards the safety of the overhang. Spine breaking against the stone, it rolled into the water. One of them in the pool stepped up onto it, pushing it down and lunging up and out. The buck charged straight at Yoke, the giant standing fast in front of the others, bunched in the recess at the cliff's base. The moment before it would have struck, he dodged right and grabbed one of its antlers in both hands and slammed it into the wall. Dislodged rocks pummelled the stag's back. It retreated, shaking all over and snorting at Yoke as he advanced towards it, his blade loosed in his hand. Its hind legs slipped off the ledge and its fronts frenzied at the rock. It went down and the live stag in the pool clambered up and over it.

With a mighty leap, it crested the lip and turned, wheeling away from Yoke. At the edge of the granite hump it leapt again and cleared the rippled span of rock. It wallowed momentarily among the river stones before it found its feet, rearing up now as Yoke had lunged off the ledge and was landing straddle-legged on its back. He gripped two of its antler points like a dowsing rod and there was nothing that could be said or done to testify to the wonder they all felt watching him ride it up the slope, his mad bellows losing ground to the thud of bodies raining from the sky and the rancour of hooves driving the herd before it like thunder.

T he stampede lasted until the dawn's light appeared as a red fringe around the storm bank.

They came out from their refuge, dusted and cramp-legged. The rumble was but an echo rolling through the gorge. Between the tree spires above the falls they could now see that it wasn't clouds that painted the sky black but a column of smoke, billowing in from the south. Tailings leached off it and settled in the gorge, conspiring there with the morning heat to stifle the air and choke the breath out of it. The pool was clotted with the mangled bodies of caribou and deer and elk. Below it, a pack of coyotes skulked along the creek, sniffing at the doe and chancing wary looks at the four men watching them through the smoky effluent.

Go on, Levin hollered, hurling a stone plucked from the hearth after them. Two of the scavengers startled as it clattered over the rocks. The others simply turned and slunk away, disappearing with tails downturned through the foggy mire.

That Yoke shore is a wonder, Briar said.

Tha's one word for it.

Taking the pipe from his pocket, Briar reached into Levin's pocket and drew out the bulb. He packed the bowl and bent to the firepit.

Ya ever seen the like of that stampede? he said rooting through the ash, washed over and sopping so that there wasn't a single spark left to enliven its muck.

Levin shook his head.

Ya think it's Reds drivin em?

They's been known to use fire.

Tha's what I mean.

Never know'd em to hunt this far south.

Maybe they's changed.

Jus as like it was a lightnin strike.

And if it weren't?

Levin scratched at his beard.

They'd be along right present.

If'n they's ain't already.

Both men panned over the top of the rise through eyes red and weltering. The smoke cast the ridge in an otherworldly haze.

We's in a right fix down here if they is, Levin said.

I know it.

We ought'n head back to the river.

They climbed the gulley's slope on its northern side, following the tracks of the stag Yoke had ridden over the top of the ridge. The smoke thickened at its summit and everywhere there was evidence of the herd's rampage — a path of destruction, fifty paces wide, scouring the ground on either side of the gorge. The air reeked of musk and tasted of grit. Dust foundered, borne aloft on the ethereal plain, refusing to settle.

There was a copse of cedar trees on its far side. Levin drew them to it. Shadows swarmed irresolute within the haze beyond, traipsing like thieves, or ghosts, along the periphery of their vision.

Wolves, the old man cursed.

He raised his rifle and sighted on one such form moving with the grace of a predatory bird in flight a foot off the ground, tracking it until it had disappeared back into the smokestream.

They's jus followin the herd, Briar said. Ain't like to bother with us.

You'ns prob'ly right, Levin said though he did not lower his gun nor ease his finger from the trigger.

Unless'n . . .

Unless'n what?

Levin snuck him a cursory glance. Briar was staring rueful at him — his eyes narrow slits, his mouth down-crimped, his hand kneading the crop of the whip hitched to his belt.

Look here, Levin said pulling at the bow slung over Jude's back. The handhold was carved into the shape of a wolf's head. The ones we kilt, they was Wolf clan.

Don even start, Briar said, scowling.

Reds can change.

No, they cain't.

They can change as shore as I'ma standin here in front of ya.

Into wolves? This from Jude.

Into they's spirit critters. But I only ever saw em turn into wolves.

Ya din't, Briar said.

I did. I'da done tol ya afore.

And I believed it as much then as I do now.

Don't matter ya believe it or not. It happened. I saw em. I was with ma uncle and his two boys. We's comin back from the hunt. We'dn seen the smoke through the treetops. When we got home the sett'ment was on fire. Bodies of our kin all strewn o'er the ground. There was a half-dozen of them heathen bastards. It was a scalpin party. They was still collectin their trophies. Ma uncle shot one of em and the dogs lit out after the rest. Changed, the lot of em did, right then, afore our eyes.

Into wolves?

Yeah. Scuttered off into the underbrush. Dogs raisin hell in pursuit.

Horseshit, Briar said.

I saw it.

You's jus tryin to spook us.

I'ma guess'n we's bout to find out.

All we's goin to find out is you'ns a crazy old man.

Briar turned towards the river. He made to take a step when Levin grabbed his arm.

What's that? he said.

Far off a dismal cry.

Sounds like a . . . Levin shook his head, trying to match the sound with some distant recollection.

Ain't nothin but a fawn cryin for its ma, Briar said. Musta got lost in the stampede.

I don't think so.

I'ma tellin ya—

Is a baby, Jude said.

What? This from Levin.

Ya know, like a . . . a baby.

Ya shore?

I heard it plentya times on the farm.

Well, what the hell's a baby doin out here?

Tain't alone, tha's for shore, Briar said.

They all peered towards the east. A shaft of light transposed itself against the smoke making it impossible to see more than a dozen paces.

The crying stopped. There wasn't a sound now in the forest but the creak of pine trees swaying to the breeze. A yelp rent the quiet and out of the vaporous drift there appeared a grey wolf, racing with delirious abandon along the ravaged channel. Its snout bobbed within an inch of the ground and its back legs flailed feebly behind it. There was a felled spruce tree in its path. It tried to leap over it but its hinds couldn't make the jump and slammed into the trunk. It catapulted into the air, did a half somersault and landed on its back, writhing and twisting to right itself. It could not find its feet and dragged itself forward on its belly until it had no more strength for even that. It lay then with its head between its paws, breathing hard, its eyes open and clear, balloons of bloody froth popping against its teeth like soap bubbles.

They's somethin in its gut.

Briar pointed and Levin squinted at it. He could just make a tuft of feathered blue projecting from its side.

It looks like a—

Reds! Levin cried, already sighting his rifle on the figure emerging from the haze. He had long hair draped over the bare skin of his mud-crusted chest. He was carrying a bow with an arrow latched to its string and craning his neck to look back the way he'd come.

Wait, Briar whispered.

The rifle bucked, exploding its charge, and a firewhip tongue lashed out of the end of its barrel.

Ears ringing, the sulphurous sting of powder in their eyes, the four of them watched the man reel and drop to one knee, his bow faltering. He tumbled onto his side, his lips trembling with the stutter of an unknown tongue, the otter-skin bag slung over his shoulder coming undone and releasing what looked to be a human skull from within, his fingers clawing at the earth, scrambling after it.

Damn fool old man. Ya'd like to ave got us all kilt. You and that goddamned rifle.

It was a Red, the old man hissed back at him, reloading the charge and packing it with the thin dowel.

Y'ever know'd one to travel alone? Every Red in haffa day's walka here like to ave heard it and be headin this way.

I din't hear ya gripin yes'aday.

Briar grit his teeth and turned away.

The baby was crying again, its wails growing louder.

Goddamn, Briar cursed. Where the hell's Yoke?

He'da heard the shot.

And is like to be chargin into an ambush.

Briar looked to the west. There wasn't anything to be seen beyond the outline of trees.

Whassa matter? Levin asked as he brought the rifle to bear on the dead man. Yousa kilt a hun'ed of em, ain't that right?

Briar bit his lip. Levin grinned at him and turned to Jude.

Ya know how to use that thing?

Jude looked down at the guitar and then back up at Levin as if he couldn't understand what he'd meant.

The bow, Levin spat at him. On yer back. Damnit, boy!

Levin snatched the guitar and flung it at Lemon. He jerked the bow from Jude's back and drew an arrow from the quiver hung over his shoulder.

It's real easy. Ya hold it like this. See? Now ya fit an arrow on the string. Point. Draw back the string. Release. Ya got it?

Jude nodded and Levin dropped to his belly, worming under the cedar's curtain and sighting along the barrel of his rifle. Briar knelt beside him and pried an eyehole through the cover. Through the mist they could see spots of light flickering like fireflies.

We's in it now, Levin said, closing one eye and tracking a bead on the closest of them.

They came out of the murk in a circle: six women carrying torches, one with both hands buttressed beneath her swollen belly, three of the others with babies harnessed to their chests, one of them fighting off its mother's breast and wailing. Herded between them were three children, all of them bald and ashen grey. The eldest, he couldn't have been older than twelve, brandished a long-bladed knife in each hand, their breadth at comic odds with his stature.

Hot damn, Briar said. They's women and children.

Spoils.

I'd say.

A raidin party.

Yeah.

If it is, they's like to be a heap more Reds.

I know it.

So where they's at?

The oldest of the women was now kneeling at the man, holding his head in her lap and saying something to him, they could not hear what. Her baby's head sagged loose out of its ragged hide pouch, rubbing against the whiskers straggling from the man's chin as the woman bent and kissed him on his forehead. The other women behind her were given over to similar acts of grief, weeping and hugging each other. One had fallen to her knees, sobbing violently, her hands clasped over her mouth, tears spilling over her fingers, her body convulsing, lost to her anguish.

They shore don't act like spoils.

It's peculiar, a'right.

The infant reached up and pulled at the grey-black tassels of the old woman's hair. She drew her breast from its concealment and proffered it to the baby's mouth. When it had latched, she stood and scanned the forest with roving eyes until they'd settled on the cedar tree.

She's looking straight at us.

I see it.

She knows we're here.

What if she does?

If they's spoils, like ya say, she'da like to make some sorta signal.

Briar smacked at a bug drinking off his cheek.

She's bound to think we's a buncha other Reds.

So?

I'ma jus sayin.

They kept on watching her but she neither made a sign nor altered her gaze. The eldest boy had now stopped circling and was staring into the mist. A spot of dark shag appeared within its fog. The wolf, a large black, advanced to within a half-dozen paces of him. It growled and the women snapped from their torments. The ones carrying babies unhitched them and set them on the ground. Turning their backs to the babies they formed a cluster, like herd animals protecting their young. They waved their torches at the wolf, frantic, and the beast lashed its tongue up over its snout, sucked it back in then snarled.

The eldest boy strode towards it, brandishing his knives one against the other. Metal rasped on metal. The old woman grabbed him by the arm, pulling him roughly back and collaring him within the crook of her elbow. The older children were peeking at the wolf through the cracks between their mothers' legs as other malignant shapes alighted in the mist, closing in.

They's in a tight spot, Briar said.

Yeah, Levin agreed.

We's just goin set here.

You'ns got a betta idea?

I'sa got a few.

They's about as good to us dead as they is alive, he said.

Speak fer yaself.

There were now a half-dozen of the beasts prowling round the cluster. The women had pulled together as tight as ferns, their torches dwindling, not a hope before them but their next breath. And still the old woman's gaze had not relieved its sentry upon the cedar tree.

Ah hell, Levin cursed and took aim on the black wolf.

He spat and rested the sight between its ears. His finger brushed the rifle's trigger twice for luck. A long slow breath. He squeezed. The wolf dropped and its pack-mates startled from their rounds. They stared with flattened ears and bristled teeth at the cedar tree as Briar emerged from behind it. He unspooled the whip in his hand and the wolves cocked their heads as if they had nothing to fear from this strange creature, deprived of sense, walking away from reason on a path towards ruin.

When he was ten strides from the closest, Briar snapped the whip. Its lash caught the beast on its snout. The wolf yelped and turned and fled, whimpering with its tail between its legs.

Hurts, don't it, Briar called after it and cracked the whip again. It missed another by a head and the wolf scurried off after the first.

You there, Briar said pointing at a third padding slyly on a wide perimeter.

It stopped and looked at him with its head drooped low, its eyes peering penitent over the bough of its snout.

Yeah, I'ma talkin to you. I'sa got somethin for ya.

He whistled and the wolf cocked its head, watching him advance through silvered slits. When he was within range, Briar's hand jerked on the whip and its shock struck the wolf on its haunch. It reared up, yelping, and fled at a hard run.

Dumbass, Briar said, scanning the forest for another.

The rest of the pack had taken flight and existed only as veiled blurs. Then even those were gone. His gaze fell upon the women. All of them were bedraggled and dirty. Eyes glossed with a painful certitude. Ears deaf to their own children, wailing and clawing at their legs. Staring vacant-eyed at the old man approaching them with a rifle stretched before his shoulder, its muzzle askew, sighting on enemies hitherto unrevealed. There were two young men on his flanks, one holding a flexed bow not unlike the one carried by their redeemer, who had called himself Omushkego and now lay dead before them, the other wearing an idiot grin and cradling a guitar like some shell-shocked minstrel trailing this ragged band into war.

There ary more Reds? Levin said to the old woman.

She stared at him as if he was speaking a foreign tongue. A strand of drool drained from the corner of her mouth and pooled on the boy's head.

Like this'n.

He leant his sight to the dead man.

She shook her head.

Ya shore?

She nodded.

Y'ain't lyin?

She shook her head again.

A'right then.

Levin lowered the rifle and looked to Briar, coiling his whip as he appraised the women scooping their babies into their arms and clutching at the hands of the older ones, drawing them close. Peering out through oily garlands of hair, their eyes darting, skittish from one man to the next. Jude and Lemon with eyes agog as if they were witnessing something from a story recounted to them of better times: a circus or a caravan of gypsies or some similar spectacle beyond the reckoning of simple country folk. Briar circling the huddled mass, wetting his lips with a lecherous tongue. Levin's gaze now settling on the boy clutched to the old woman's breast. Hash-mark scars wept blood over his bare arms and his chest. The knives in his hands quivering as if he could barely contain their intent. The imprint of his skeletal otherself drawn in thin black lines on his face a perfect match to the tyranny of his glare.

Y'all from around here? Levin asked, looking up at the old woman again.

She peered at him squint-eyed.

Yer sett'ment. Where y'all comin from. Is it close?

The old woman shook her head.

We can take ya there.

The old woman shook her head again.

I know ya can spek. I saw ya talkin to the Red afore he died.

She opened her mouth but no words came out.

Go on. Git to it.

Then a shriek.

Levin and the old woman turned to where Briar was grabbing at the youngest woman's hand, jerking her towards him, almost lifting her off her feet.

Well what do we have here? he said.

She clawed at him with her one free hand and he snatched that up too, spinning her around and pulling her back up against him, holding both of her arms by the wrists, criss-crossed over her chest.

You's still a feisty one, that's for shore, Briar said, laughing. But Gawd don't you reek.

Briar, Levin called out. What the hell's ya doin?

Is Henry's daughter, he called back and the old man took two steps sideways so that he could get a better look.

Ya let her go now, ya hear.

I'ma jus take her down to the river, git her warsht up.

He pulled her backwards. She was kicking at him and biting at his arm, and he was whooping glee at her renewed vigour.

The other women had stalled in their amaze and were circling round behind him, their hands to a one fishing for the blades secreted within the folds of their dresses.

Back now, Briar said, forcing the crook of his elbow tight up under the girl's chin. Y'all know what's good for her.

Goddamnit, Levin cursed and turned back to the old woman. I— was all he'd managed before her torch caught him hard on the side of the head, releasing a flourish of sparks.

As he fell, she snatched the rifle from his flailing grasp. She dropped her torch and drew the rifle's stock to her shoulder, bringing its sight to bear on Briar, his surprise giving way to alarm as he found himself enmeshed within the throng of women. He felt a sharp point against his back and another digging into the side of his belly. He looked down at the blade in his gut. It was long and thin — a skinning knife.

He raised his hands, releasing the girl.

The moment she was free, she spun round and brought her foot up hard and square into Briar's groin. He went down groaning, clutching at himself. The woman who'd been holding the knife to his gut bent and took his knife from its sheath then felt along his hip until she'd found his whip.

Drop it, the old woman was saying, the rifle now pointed at Jude.

He released his bow and a sallow-faced woman scurried over and snatched it from the ground. She pulled the quiver from his shoulder and backed to a length of three strides, notching an arrow on the string.

Go on, the old woman said, motioning with the rifle for Jude and Lemon to join the others.

Her voice was stern, unequivocal, and her eyes were afire, alive with malice. A single strand of drool clung to her chin, the only thing left to speak of the dullard she'd appeared. She wiped at it with a shrug of her shoulder and watched as the two young men trod under her mindful glower to where Levin was sitting up, holding the side of his head. Singed hair smouldered between his fingers. Beside him, Briar lay on the ground, his body warped in agony. The other women trailed in ellipse around them, their babies brooked in their arms. The last of them walked stooped over, struggling to keep up, her hands planted beneath the over-ripe bulge in her stomach.

When they reached the old woman, they turned back to face the men. Two now held bows notched with arrows and the others all clutched blades — Briar's and the dead man's and others of a cruder design. The eldest boy paced behind the men, his own knives flexed to their purpose.

Briar strained to sit up and Levin whispered to him, Ya dumb sumbitch. You and that goddamned snake twixt yer legs.

Briar opened his mouth in protest but nothing came out but a pained squeak.

Ya think you'da learnt yer lesson with that squaw.

Pushing himself off the ground, Levin stood on weak knees. He dusted off his pants and touched gingerly at the blisters bubbling over his temple. The old woman and the sallow-faced archer were conferring on some matter pertaining to the bow in her hand, speaking in low tones. Sprung from her deliberations by Levin's move, the old woman levelled the rifle's sight between his eyes and touched her finger to its trigger. One of her front teeth hung over her bottom lip so that she looked not unlike a half-starved cougar might while contemplating a porcupine.

Hold up now, hold up, Levin said, raising his arms. Thisn's all but a misunderstandin. We don't mean ya no harm. Tell her, Briar, you's just playin, right?

Briar had made it to his feet and was standing bent over, trying to find a way of breathing that didn't hurt so much.

Tha's right, he wheezed. I's just playing. I ain mean no harm.

You have my word—

The old woman spat.

That's what I think of your word, she said. Now you listen up and you listen good. He had a sister.

Who?

The man you killed. He was supposed to meet up with her. Her and another. A boy. You know anything about them?

Levin shook his head.

He most likely would have had a bow with a wolf's head on it. Same as the one your boy was carrying.

Levin opened his mouth. No words came out and he shut it again.

That's what I thought.

The sallow-faced woman bent to her ear and whispered something. After a moment the old woman shook her head and turned back to Levin.

My daughter thinks we should kill you for what you've done, the old woman said. But I'm of a mind that you could still be of some use to us.

Yes, ma'am. We's at yer disposal. Ain't that right, boys?

Yes, ma'am, Briar said. Arything ya need.

Arything, added Levin. Alls ya need to do is ast.

Is that right?

Yes, ma'am.

And if I *ast* you to go on over to that tree there, she said motioning with the barrel of the rifle, what would you say to that?

Levin followed the line of her sight and scrutinized the big old ash as if trying to discern some dire intent locked within its bark. When he turned back, a woman with short cropped hair was uncoiling a rope from her pack.

Wait jus a goddamned minute, Levin protested as Briar pushed past him.

Nobody's tyin me to a goddamn tree, he said, glaring at the old woman. You'ns jus goin to have to shoot—

A sharp twang.

The arrow struck him in his right thigh just below the hip. He let out a shriek and clutched at the shaft. Blood pulsed through his fingers. The sallow-faced woman was already notching another onto the string and pointing it at Levin.

Best get to it, the old woman said.

Levin took Briar by the arm and led him, limping and cursing, towards the ash tree. Jude and Lemon trailed behind, casting spurious glances over their shoulders as if their inclusion was some sort of mistake.

Tain't right, Levin said. Leaving us here. Food for the wolves.

It's not the wolves you should be worried about, the old woman said. Now go on, make a ring around it. Good. Now get on your knees. Snuggle up. Nice and close. I said close.

She pushed the barrel of the gun between Levin's shoulder blades, pressing him roughly against the trunk. After a moment, he felt the stiff weave of the rope lashing over his back.

You goddamned bitch, he muttered.

Jude leant towards him and whispered, What she mean? Tain't the wolves we ought'n be worried bout.

But Levin wasn't listening, lost as he was to his vitriol.

You cunt! He was screaming now. Fuckin whore!

The stock of the gun struck the back of his head, mashing his face against the bark.

And put something over this one's mouth while you're at it, the old woman said. I'm about done listening to him.

VI

The herd had veered north along the river.

They kept to the fringe of its rampage, Elsa and Silk and Cherry stooped under the weight of the babies strapped to their backs, Adele heavy with child between them and Wren following close behind, never losing grip on the hands of the two nameless children, one his brother and the other his uncle. All of them walking with feet unclad and blistered, moving in a slow plod — the traipse of smoke set against the southern horizon as sharp as the lash from Reed's whip snapping over the heads of any carrion feeder that dared to cross their path, driving them onwards like cattle.

Nearing dusk, Adele groaned and clutched at her swollen belly. Her legs wobbled and Cherry reached out for her arm. She eased her to the ground and her sisters gathered around. She was breathing hard and her face was flushed and her eyes sutured in pain. Sweat drained from strands of hair plastered to her cheeks.

What is it? Elsa said, kneeling beside her and leaning her weight on the stock of the old man's rifle.

It hurts.

How bad?

Bad.

Like it's coming?

I don't know.

Elsa felt under her dress, probing over the mottled bump for any sign of movement. Her skin was damp and hot to the touch.

Is she having it now? Cherry asked.

No. Not yet.

Then what?

Elsa looked up at her youngest daughter. Once, her cheeks had been as round and smooth and red as her namesake. Such that when she was a baby, Elsa could not keep from kissing them and nibbling at the soft mounds of fat and whispering to her, I just wanna gobble you up, making the child squeal with joy and clutch at her face. Now they were hollow and pale. There was barely enough flesh on them to cover the ridges cutting sharp lines beneath her eyes, and the thought pressed upon Elsa that maybe she wasn't really her daughter anymore at all.

She looked then to the others, their faces likewise ravaged by hunger and deprivation. Each one conjured fretful memories — fleeting instances of joy and sadness, moments of laughter and sorrow — a whole lifetime from a world lost to her now as certainly as the fabric of her own breath draining through her cracked and withered lips.

My daughters were everything to me, Elsa thought. And there wasn't anything I wouldn't have done for them. And now what do I have to offer? Endless flight with death their only release.

She felt a sudden pressure on her hand — a kick — and she turned back to Adele. She'd fallen asleep. Her eyelids flickered and breaths issued from her mouth in stuttered rasps.

They're free, Elsa told herself. That's all that matters. But it seemed to her a lie.

Cherry was saying something. Elsa caught the gist of it and shook her head.

No, she's not dying, she said. She just needs to rest.

There was another kick. Elsa closed her eyes, savouring the feel of the child squirming against her hand and trying to remember the last time she'd felt such a thing and it had filled her with hope rather than the dread troubling her now.

It had been with Wren, she thought.

When Reed had been full with him — her first grandchild — it seemed he had never stopped moving. His mother had joked that he'd be born on the run and they'd have to chase him down to cut the cord, the family laughing and taking turns with their hands on her belly, telling her she was right. Her husband Wilt saying that it felt like she had a jackrabbit inside of her and teasing that if he came out with floppy ears they'd have to have words.

But when he'd been born, he came out limp and grey, lifeless. He was early by more than a moon and, by all rights, shouldn't have lived. Elsa had taken him and held him to her breast. She rubbed his back and whispered into his ear all the names of those who loved him so that he'd know what he'd be missing. All of a sudden he awoke with a strained cry. She handed him over to his mother and Reed took him and set him at her breast. He latched on at once and suckled hard so that they knew he'd be all right.

While he fed, Reed had stroked the soft whisps of his hair, static in the air making the strands cling to her fingers. She bent and kissed the crown of his head and when she looked back at her mother, her eyes were glistening and her flushed face was burning in effigy to joy.

He tried to fly away from me, she'd said.

Elsa sat on the bed. She held her eldest daughter and it had seemed that there was nothing in the world but the faint throb of the heartbeat between them.

After what seemed an eternity, the door to the bedroom opened and Wilt stuck his head in. Elsa could hear the murmur of muted conversation from the kitchen. Everyone in town had heard of the birth and had come to pay their respects and to bring food.

They're asking his name, he'd said.

Elsa turned to her daughter. The tip of Reed's tongue was probing at her lips as if the name was already there and she just needed to speak for it to be so.

Wren, she'd finally said. We'll name him Wren.

A hand now squeezed her shoulder. Elsa startled at the touch and opened her eyes.

It's going to be dark soon, Silk said. We need to keep moving.

Elsa pushed herself up using the barrel of the rifle.

She needs to rest.

We're all tired.

She'll die.

And if we stay here, we're as good as dead. Their dogs will have already picked up our trail by now.

Those men we left. They'll give us a head start. A day, maybe more.

And then what?

If we keep to the river, we'll come to his village. He said we'll be safe there.

He also said it was better than a week on foot.

We'll make it. Her eyes were pleading and desperate. We have to.

Silk turned from her mother and looked back the way they had come. In the gathering dark she could just see the girl, whose name she did not know, crouched on a boulder and peering back down the trail.

We have any food left? Elsa asked.

A little.

See that the children are fed first.

Okay.

Silk started away and Elsa reached out to grab her arm.

We didn't have a choice, she said. Leaving those men like we did. Knowing what's going to happen when *they* catch up to them.

I know, Silk said.

It had to be done.

It's okay. Silk patted her hand and slipped from her grasp. I better see to the children.

Elsa watched her daughter walk away, trying to think of something she could be doing.

Water, she said to herself at last, you need to fetch some water.

She scavenged through their wares and found a bladder made of otter skin in the pack she had taken from the man who had saved them. Its fur was soft and smooth and felt against her fingers unlike anything she thought could exist in a coarse world such as this. As she carried it down to the river's edge, she rubbed it against her cheek and the bristle of its touch revived her skin the same as if it had been the back of a hand, the thick mat of hair over its knuckles caressing the line of her jaw, tickling her, making her titter so that she clutched at it, holding it firm.

She moaned and the impropriety of it ran up her spine like a static shock. She let the bladder fall to her side and peered over the river's grass-fringed bank. The water was a good ten feet below her. Trees as far as she could see had fallen to erosion's steady toll and leaned into the river at sharp angles. She walked to a cedar such sundered and tried to think of another way. She couldn't and so set the rifle against its trunk and climbed onto the fallen tree, laying on her belly and crawling down to within an arm's length of the water. Securing a handhold on a branch, she leant over the trunk and dipped the bladder into the flow. It bucked against her grip and her fingers slipped on its stem so that she was on the verge of losing it. She firmed her grasp and held it under until it was full. It couldn't have weighed more than a couple pounds but it took every ounce of strength she had to draw it back up.

She was tired beyond measure when she'd finally got it onto the tree's trunk and lay her head upon her arm, breathing heavy and coughing against a scratch in the back of her throat. Gathering her strength, she inched herself backward towards land. When she'd come to the limits of her reach, she let go of the branch. She felt herself slipping and frantically clutched at it again, staring down into the swirling depths of the river a few feet below, seeing her face in its dark whorls, mouth open, filling with water, her hands grasping for the surface as the current carried her away.

Help, she cried. Then again: Help.

Her voice didn't seem to her more than a whimper.

She closed her eyes and listened. There was nothing but the steady thrush of the river. Its lullaby carried her into a troubled sleep. A short while later, she was jarred awake by someone calling out to her, Mother, Mother. It seemed a distant echo trailing out of her slumber, for no one had called her that for years.

She'd been dreaming that she was lying in bed and her husband's hand was waxing delicately up her thigh. His skin was rough from the field — as rough as bark. She tittered, clutching at it and pressing it hard to stay its tickle, and then drew it down between her legs. She moaned as his fingers probed into her wet. Then, without warning, they withdrew. She felt the bed heave as her husband's weight departed it.

What is it? she said rolling over.

Her husband was standing at the open window.

I heard something, he said.

Elsa sat up. Dogs bayed in the distance.

It's just Luther's hounds, she said. A damp spot on the sheet felt chill against her leg and she shifted from its reach.

It's not that, it's—

What?

But now she could hear it too. A distant thrumming. Dread crept over her and she pulled the sheet tight to her chest.

There's people out there, her husband said. They're carrying torches. I swear they look like . . . children.

He turned to his wife, his face drawn and pale.

You don't think— he said. That man Deiter found hiding in the woods two months ago? He said something terrible was coming, that we had to run.

He was half-starved to death and delirious.

Nobody would listen.

He was crazy.

He called them . . . Echoes.

And the moment the name had parted his lips, the night went quiet again.

Then there was the voice, Mother, Mother, calling out to her. She'd turned. Silk was standing at their bedroom door, clutching at her cornhusk doll. She couldn't have been older than five. The sight had jarred her awake.

Her head felt light from lying at such a drastic angle and her right arm throbbed from the strain of holding onto the bladder.

205

She lay breathing hard and trying to sort one moment from the other, for it couldn't have happened that way. Silk had been well nigh a woman on the night the Echoes had arrived. Images of what they had done to her family splintered her thoughts into stark flashes and she fought against the memory with the recollection of her husband walking towards Silk on that other night, so long before.

What are you doing out of bed? he'd asked as he pulled a sheet over his nakedness and knelt to her.

I had a bad dream. I want to sleep with you.

Silk had been crying, Elsa could hear it in the way her voice cracked.

Not tonight, he told her, scooping her into his arms. Come on now, I'll tuck you back in.

Mother, Silk called out to her again.

Elsa craned to look back at the shore. Her daughter was standing at the foot of the tree's upraised roots.

What are you doing out there? she asked.

What's it look like? I'm stuck.

Stuck?

That's what I said.

You want me to get the others?

What I want is to never have climbed down on this godforsaken tree.

I can't help you there.

Elsa snorted.

Are you going to help me up or not?

She felt Silk's fingers close around her calf.

I got you.

It doesn't feel like it.

Silk tightened her grip.

You're going to have to let go if you want me to pull you up, she said.

You sure you have me?

I'm sure.

I'm letting go.

Elsa unclenched her hand and inched backwards. The bladder struck on a knot and listed sideways, slipping off the trunk. She fought furiously to keep a hold of it and to stop herself from falling after.

I'm slipping!

I've got you.

Silk's fingers were clamped onto the loose skin below her buttocks, her nails digging into the soft flesh like pincers. The pain gave Elsa the will to pull herself back onto the trunk but no amount of trying could induce the bladder to rise from its pendulum.

Come on now, Silk barked, quit fooling around.

Elsa cast an accusatory glance behind her. Silk's legs were spread between the shore and the trunk, her free hand clutching at the cedar's roots.

Scowling at me won't help you none. Now come on, move it, or else we'll both be getting wet.

Silk dug her fingers deeper into her mother's leg and pulled. Elsa cried out, thrusting herself backwards, and Silk let go, grabbing for her dangling arm. She slid her hand downward along it until she'd reached the bladder and took it by its spout.

I've got it.

Elsa let it go and Silk swung it backwards, pitching it onto the bank. When she turned back to her mother, she was pushing herself backwards with both hands. Silk reached for her shoulder and Elsa shrugged her off. The tips of her toes touched the tree's splayed roots. There was grass beneath her again and she slid her legs off the trunk. When her feet found the ground, she turned herself over and leant her back against the tree, breathing hard and watching Silk retrieve the bladder from within a waist-high patch of scrub at the edge of the herd's rampage. Her daughter's hair hung over her face, strands of it clumped together and mired with tagalongs and burrs — what she would have called a rat's nest when her daughter was young and it seemed there was nothing in the world worse that could have befallen her.

You're hurting me, Silk would protest while Elsa brushed her hair, a hundred strokes every night before she went to bed. Stop. Please.

If you would just sit still.

I can't. It hurts.

It couldn't possibly hurt that much.

That's easy for you to say.

If you'd tie it up like I told you, or let me braid it—

I swear one day I'm going to cut it all off and that'll be the end of it.

You'll do no such thing.

I will.

You have the most beautiful hair I have ever seen. It's why I named you Silk.

I know, mother. You told me a thousand times.

Have I now?

Actually, it's more like a million.

Then you should understand why I won't see it become a rat's nest.

I don't care if it does.

Well I do and I'm your mother. Now quit your bellyaching. We haven't much longer. What are we at?

Ninety-three.

208

That's funny, I'd swear that we'd just passed sixty.

Silk would harrumph and cross her arms, and Elsa would steal a glance at her daughter in the mirror. In the defiance glossing her eyes, she'd swear she could catch a glimpse of her future — of the woman she would become and the man it would take to tame her and the kids they'd have to share their love. One of them a daughter with hair as fine as silk who'd fret and fume whenever her mother brushed it.

You're crying, Silk said now. She was looking at her mother through a worried frown.

Am I? Elsa rubbed at the damp on her cheek with the back of her hand. I was — she shook her head — I, uh, I was thinking of your Omi. We found her stuck up in a tree one time. I ever tell you about that?

Silk nodded.

She was an old woman by then. Frail and with skin so thin you could practically see her bones. She hadn't been out of the house for years. Could hardly walk. Mostly she just sat in her chair in the corner of the kitchen. Then one morning when your Opa awoke, she wasn't in bed. The whole town spent the afternoon trolling the river, looking for a body. We finally found her in that big old oak tree in the back corner of our pasture. I guess it looked the same as one she used to climb when she was a girl. Course it's gone now, struck by lightning. Split it right in two. Gave us wood for nearly two winters. But that was years later.

I remember, Silk said.

Elsa looked up at her, squinting as if she'd forgotten she was there.

I— I was the one that found her, she continued. She was sitting on the lowest branch — must have been ten feet off the ground. Her arm was cradled around the trunk. She was holding on for dear life. Omi, what are you doing up there? I called.

She looked down at me like she couldn't figure out where the voice had come from (she was half-blind by then, so maybe she couldn't). Who's that? she asked. Elsa, I told her. Gregor's girl? That's right. You're my Enkelin. I am. I'm stuck up in a tree, she said as if it was the most natural thing in the world. You are, Omi, I told her. Well, how'd I get up here? she asked. I don't know, I said. You must have flew. I guess I must have. I'll go get help, I told her. I wish you would.

I ran and fetched my father. Him and one of my brothers, Sascha I think it was, climbed up and lowered her to the ground.

Elsa shook her head again, her eyes alight with the memory.

We never did figure out how she got up there.

In the distance a solitary coyote cried its mournful lament. The old woman glanced about the forest, terror eclipsing her features as if, suddenly, she couldn't remember where she was.

You climb a lot of trees when you were a girl? Silk asked.

Elsa scoffed.

I've never climbed a tree in my life.

Then I'm sure we have nothing to worry about.

Elsa lowered a hard look at her daughter, trying to tell if she was being made fun of.

Come on now, Silk said. The others will be wondering where we're at.

There were only scant remains left of the dog they'd cooked — thin strips as tough as belt leather. Silk had given the largest pieces to the three boys and they were still chewing on them when she and Elsa returned. The two younger ones looked up at the encroaching crackle of footsteps, their faces leavened in the descending gloom as if they were expecting someone else.

When the two women emerged into the semidark they frowned and started back at their meal, wrestling with the meat in their teeth like pups fighting over a pig's ear.

Wren sat apart from them, stone-faced and grim. Elsa came to him first, offering up the bladder and running the pads of her fingers over the sharp pricks of hair poking out from his shaved head. When he'd had his fill she took it from him and crouched at the others.

I suppose we'll have to come up with names for you now, she said, looking from one to the other, trying to remember which one she had birthed. It pained her that she could not and she searched about each face for a sign to tell her one way or the other.

I was the first to bring forth a child for them. So it must be the taller one.

But the more she looked at him the more certain she was that he was Reed's, who'd given birth within the same moon.

Six years, she thought. And nine children. A bountiful harvest, in the leanest of times.

Four of them had been girls and the memory of how they'd thrown these to the dogs and the image of one of them walking around with her granddaughter's cord strung between its teeth sent a shudder through her.

The bladder was all but empty when the shorter one passed it back. She proffered him a strained smile and stood. She could hear her baby bawling to her and she walked back to where Cherry was sitting beside Adele. She was holding her sister's hand and brushing the flies from her face, her own child suckling at her breast and quiet for the moment. Silk was lying beside her, her child sprawled, asleep, on her belly.

Elsa scooped up her baby from the dirt and offered him her breast but he wasn't so easily mollified. She did her best to placate him — fussing over him and rocking him in her arms and when he had stilled, forcing her breast to his lips as if these sad, drooping sacks could offer more than a few measly drops. After he'd drained whatever he could, she unlatched him and he started to bawl again.

I ought to call you Squawk, she scolded. That's about all that you're good for.

Her back stiffened against the strain and she set him on the ground. He clutched at her legs, his fingers clawing up the soft flesh of her thighs like he was trying to climb back into her womb.

Cherry, she said. You got any milk to spare?

I got one almost full.

You mind giving him a feed?

You tapped?

Maybe if I was a tree.

Cherry frowned, trying to figure out if she'd said something wrong.

Come on then, pass him over.

I mean when he's done.

He's done now. He's just sucking for sucking.

Cherry unlatched her child with two scissored fingers. The baby awoke groping for her nipple with puckered lips. She stuck her thumb in his mouth and he went back to sleep.

Elsa's child was tugging at her dress and crying, bah, bah. She took one of his hands in hers and led him towards her daughter.

Go on to your sister, she said, she's got plenty of bah, bah.

She bent to her grandson, lifted him and set him on her shoulder. A milk bubble bulged at his mouth and popped. She felt it splatter in minute droplets on her cheeks. When she turned back to Cherry, her child was sucking hungrily at her breast.

He's getting his first tooth.

I can feel it.

If he bites you, give him a pinch, he'll stop.

I'll do no such thing.

It's always worked for me.

Pinch a little baby, Cherry cooed into his ear. However did your mother get so mean?

Elsa watched one of her children feeding another until her shoulder grew numb. She switched her grandson to the other side and looked about for Reed. She was bent over at a tree just off the path, examining something in her hand, she could not tell what. At her approach, Reed craned her head towards her mother and held up a mushroom.

Is this the kind you can eat?

Elsa stooped to look under it. There were black gills running in lines under its cap.

It's a toadstool, she said.

Poisonous?

That's right.

Reed dropped it and wiped its slime off on her sleeve. Her one hand was holding her dress bunched at her belly.

I found some fiddleheads, she said.

I haven't eaten fiddleheads in years.

You want one?

I wouldn't mind.

Reed opened her dress. There were a dozen or so green curls within its hammock. She took one and popped it in her mouth. It was bitter and sweet and she couldn't remember having tasted anything so good.

Mmm, she said. Can I have another?

Take all you like. There's a whole field of them over there.

Elsa took a second, chewing it slowly and sucking the juice from its pulp.

We should fill a bag before we leave.

Reed nodded, though her attention was elsewhere. Elsa followed the line of her gaze to where Wren sat sharpening one of his knives with a stone. Sparks flared off its blade as he ground at the metal but none so much as made a glint upon the dark clouding his face.

You should go to him, Elsa said.

Reed flinched and looked away from her son.

I can't.

You're his mother. He needs you.

Reed shook her head. There was sorrow in her eyes and something else. Hate maybe. It made the old woman smile.

There's the Reed I remember, she thought. Full of venom and bile from the moment womanhood came over her. Envious of her sisters, all of them prettier and smarter, with voices like angels. Reed my little devil and the one I loved the most because of it. But that had all changed, hadn't it? When she met Wilt. Or was that Silk's husband? She was the wild child, wasn't she? Was it Wilt that tamed her? No, Wilt was Wren's father. How could you forget that when you were just thinking about it, couldn't have been more than a moment ago.

If they catch up with us, Reed was saying, I'm not going back. And neither is Wren. I won't make it harder than it already is.

It took a moment for her meaning to sink in.

Reed, Elsa said, reaching out for her daughter's shoulder, but she was already turning and walking away.

I'll fetch a bag for those fiddleheads.

The moon had come out full, hanging low between the trees. It simmered on the water, following them as they trod along the bank — a paper globe cut into ribbons, flapping against the river's current. The only sound was the lap of the river and the whine of mosquitoes.

Midway through the night, the riverbank dipped into a wide ditch where a creek bed fed a flume of water into the main. The ground around its shore was muddied with the stamp of a thousand hooves, and soil leached into the water, turning it into a silty broth. Frogsong trilled in a nebulous thunder and fireflies blinked amongst the trees. Upstream, the body of a deer lay stretched over an altar of stone like an offering to some heathen god. A crow perched on the bone-white prongs of its exposed ribs, pecking at its innards. The stench of its death polluted the air.

Elsa hung back, watching her daughters ford the creek. Reed went first, taking halting steps with arms outstretched to balance against the current, the water frothing at her knees. A few steps in, she stopped and stared into the stream as if she'd seen the shadow of some predatory beast darting just below its surface.

What's the matter? Cherry called up to her.

The bottom's covered with rocks.

I can see that.

It's slippery is all. Adele, it's best if you take my hand.

Adele waded up to her and reached out for her sister's grasping fingers. She locked them in hers and Reed drew her forward, leading her slow and easy through the maze of algae-slicked stones. Cherry and Silk trailed after, both of them hunched under the weight of their children, their legs wobbling among the rocks as they threaded their way towards the far bank.

When they'd reached the shore, Cherry looked back at her mother. Elsa was moving away, treading upstream.

Where you going? Cherry called after her.

To fetch some water, Elsa called back. I'll only be a moment. Be sure to mind the boys while I'm gone.

She cast a furtive glance towards the foot of the channel where the creek funnelled into a narrow chute, flowing deep and fast into the river, so that her meaning was clear. The two youngest boys were leaning into the wake breaking against their chests, their heads bobbing above the swell and their hands raised before them as if they were playing at flight.

Get away from there! Reed yelled. It's not safe. Wren, get them out of there. They're going to get themselves drowned.

She sounded like a mother, and as she continued upstream Elsa smiled as if such had been her design.

The creek ran at a leisurely incline, tracing an ancestral trail pebbled with smooth stones. Elsa's footfalls chastened the frog-song yet did not dull its fervency so that it seemed to be fleeing ahead into some netherland forever beyond her reach. The stench of death grew as she approached the deer's carcass and the crow gazed at her warily. She cupped her mouth in the crook of her arm and hurried past.

A short while later, she came to a waterfall pouring from between the trestled roots of a spruce tree perched atop a crumbling granite ledge. She refilled the bladder under its flow and thought of herself hanging onto that cedar suspended over the river, whimpering, Help, help, like a child strayed into some mischief that had turned foul.

Damned old fool, she muttered to herself.

Water spurted from the bladder's spout. She stoppered it and leant against the rock wall, too tired to take another step. Cushions of moss padded her tailbone and her child felt like a dead thing on her back.

She was crying again.

A cup of tea. A thought from a distant past when that was all that she needed to set her world to right. She followed its will towards its end. There's a pot in that old man's bag. And a tin cup, the same as the four hanging in the kitchen on hooks above the sink.

You'll need a fire, she told herself, stemming the urge to inventory her cupboards and her larder, to walk through her house again, to seek out her bed, to lie down, to go to sleep, to never wake up. A pot, a fire, water and—

She shook her head trying to shake loose the missing ingredient but it eluded her.

Closing her eyes, she listened to the frogsong rolling down upon her from higher ground. A thousand voices beseeching her, it seemed, but to what end she could not say. Then their chatter dulled again, fleeing back upstream.

She opened her eyes to an endless void that seemed to have swallowed her into its fold. Her sight came back to her slowly, bleeding in from the edges of her periphery, filling in the dark with a manifold of shapes — of rocks and the twisted bodies of trees, of a great serpent slithering by towards the limits of her vision. A shadow materialized, moving along a felled tree suspended over the creek. It gave her a start and she held her breath, watching it prowl over the log. When it reached the first spindled branches, it stood on its hind legs.

It's just the girl, she thought.

A firefly flit past her face. The girl swatted at it and dropped from the tree, vanishing.

Look at how she moves. Like a cat that's been kicked too many times. As if every sound meant to do her harm. We'll all become like that before this is over, I suppose.

Elsa chewed on her lip and shook her head.

No, she told herself. I won't let it. I won't.

The frogsong was rolling back over her. She pushed herself off the rock and hurried back towards the river. A solitary thought bubbled up within her trying to still the race of her heart.

Camomile, it said. You can't make tea without camomile.

J ust as the sun was rising through the trees, the trail dead-
ended at a low marshy area where the river had swolled from
its banks, taking on the breadth of a lake. Streamers of mist
lazed from its surface. Ducks and geese bobbed among them,
and there were blue herons hunting in the cattails that prolif-
erated from the shore, and birds of prey circling above, and the
splash of trout lunging spasmodically from the black water. The
remnants of the herd could be seen grazing along its banks.

Glorying in the sight, Elsa stood holding her breath and
waiting for the sun's warmth to light upon her face. A noise rose
sharply from somewhere behind her. A wolf yelping, or maybe a
scream. She turned back to her daughters. They were as statues,
standing and staring back the way they had come. The babies
were asleep and there was no sound at all now but the shrill
chatter of crickets and bullfrogs.

She walked to Silk and leaned to her ear.

You hear that? she whispered.

Sounded like a scream.

The girl?

Maybe.

When was the last time you saw her? Silk asked.

When we crossed that creek.

You saw her?

I told you I did.

What do you think?

I guess someone should go check on her.

I'll do it, Reed said, unslinging the bow from her shoulder.

Be careful.

Fitting an arrow on the bow's string, Reed started back down
the path. The others watched her until her shadow had been consumed by the dark.

A sudden skirmish in the water turned Elsa back to the lake. A heron dipped low over the water near the shore.

Something's coming, she thought. And on the heels of that: The rifle!

She glanced about as if its absence was but a trick of the light.

You damn fool old woman. You would have lost your own head too, if it wasn't attached.

Footsteps now, hurrying towards them.

Silk took a line on their advance with the arrow notched to her bow. A thin wedge broke out of the gloom. Within it, Elsa could see Reed's familiar lank.

There's no sign of her, Reed said when she'd come astride of them again. She was breathing hard and her cheeks were as fish gills. She couldn't seem to catch her breath and bent over, drawing great gulps of air and coughing up spittle.

You weren't gone very long, Silk said to her.

I heard something, Reed choked out.

What?

Reed cleared her throat and spat and looked to her mother.

You still got that rifle?

Elsa shook her head.

We ought to find cover, Cherry said.

What was it you heard? Elsa asked.

A chicken.

A chicken?

Clucking.

Elsa chewed her lip.

We really ought to find cover.

Elsa glanced about trying to sort which way to go. Her eyes settled on the three boys. They'd found a patch of prickle bushes primed with hard green berries just off the path and were stuffing the unripe buds into their mouths. An old impulse had her bristling forward and crying out, Stop that! You're going to make yourselves sick.

She had almost closed the distance between them when she heard the twang of a bow loosing its arrow. She swung around and caught sight of a man rising out of the water at the lake's edge. He was as big as a grizzly on its hinds and naked save for a strip of tattered leather over his loins. The emerging sun shone in pearled beads off the water dripping from his bald head. He was holding a machete in his hand, its blade sluicing out of the water as if there were no end to its reach. An arrow projected from his shoulder and a few feet away Reed was fumbling another from the quiver on her back.

She'd got it onto the string and was just raising it when the man swung his blade. It struck the bow just above her hand, severing it in two. Reed flung the bottom half at the man even as she drew out the knife scabbarded in the leather sheath at her waist. She threw herself forward, slashing out at the man's stomach. His hand batted it away and his other shot out, grabbing her by the throat. She flailed wildly, hacking at the arm lifting her off the ground, cutting deep gouges into its flesh.

Elsa had her knife out too and was rushing towards them when a voice rang out from behind her.

Yoke, it said. Tha's enough.

The giant released his grip.

Reed fell to her knees, coughing and choking and clutching at her throat, and Elsa spun back to the path. The old man was standing there, cradling the rifle in his arms and chewing on a stem of grass with the leisure of a farmer conducting business over a fence. Beside him, the pock-faced man held the girl in front of him. His left hand was clamped over her mouth and the other clamped hard to her breast. The two younger men were cowering behind.

Elsa looked from one to the other then to the rifle.

I wun't do that, if I was you, the old man said, looking past her. Like to jus make him mad.

Elsa turned to the giant standing as stiff as a tree and staring over at Silk, her fingers quivering on the arrow notched in her bow — his expression quizzical, like a child who'd caught his parents up to no good.

Silk, Elsa pleaded.

Silk frowned but lowered the bow.

The old man now clicking his tongue and appraising the lot of them with a look of wilful petulance. His gaze passed from the old woman, over Silk and Cherry clutching Adele's hand and then swung wide so that it fell upon the three boys. The two nameless ones were staring with open-mouthed awe at the giant. The smallest one took a step forward as if summoned by the memory of his fathers and Wren reached out, grabbing him by the arm and pulling him back.

The old man bit the end off the grass sprig, spat it out and chewed on the fresh stem, sucking at its juice. Finally, he took it from his mouth, pitched it into the scrub and looked back at the two younger men behind him.

What you waitin on? he said. Fetch their weapons. Go on, git to it.

The two men moved to the task, skulking with lowered eyes among the women, taking from Silk her bow and the pock-faced man's whip from Reed and knives from all of them. When the taller one came to Wren, the boy flexed his blades at his side and stared at him with such fiery hate that the young man took a step back.

Ain't you somethin, the pock-faced man said, laughing. Scared of a little boy.

He had retrieved his whip from the shorter one and was unfurling its lash onto the ground.

Your goin wanna step aside, Lemon, he said and drew his arm back.

Reed lunged between him and her son. She grabbed the boy's hands and wrested the blades from them and then wrapped him in her arms, pulling the boy's head to her bosom and stroking the back of his head.

Elsa watched the scene like it had all been preordained or was merely a play of shadows against a wall. Her mouth parted to permit her tongue to touch at the cleft on her top lip. Her hands kneading her dress in religious fervour. Her eyes glazed and dim. Watching now the pock-faced man slinging his whip over his shoulder. A strip of cedar bark was tied around a square of moss over the wound on his leg. The fingers on his left hand were threaded tight through the girl's strawberry hair, pulling her onto the balls of her feet. He slid an arrow from the quiver draped over the young man's shoulder with his free hand, his gaze never once leaving Reed.

You'ns the one that shot me, he said. That right?

Reed looked back at him as if she had been slapped. As the pock-faced man limped towards her, dragging the girl on her heels, she detached herself from Wren and stepped in front of him. When he was less than a pace from her, the pock-faced man halted. He ran the tip of the arrow up the curve of her neck and probed it beneath the drape of her hair, lifting the veil covering her face.

It's you'n a'right.

He trailed the arrow back down her neck and over her breast and across her belly, letting it linger a moment at her sex. Licking his lips, he dipped the arrow back and thrust it forward into the soft flesh of her thigh. Her body stiffened and she gritted her teeth but did not make a sound. Wren came out from behind her with fists raised. His mother grabbed his arm and squeezed it hard enough that the boy dropped to his knees. The pock-faced man twisted the arrow deeper, but still Reed wouldn't give voice to her pain.

Cherry though was screaming to wake the dead and so was her child. Elsa hadn't the will to look their way and felt their passing like a chill wind off the lake — listening to her daughter crying out and hearing the beat of her fists on the giant's back as he carried her off to some dismal end. The pock-faced man now dragging the girl after, her feet kicking at the track-worn earth trying to keep herself from lagging at the end of his arm.

And then the old man was striding towards Elsa, carrying the rope coiled at his side.

You and me got to have words, he said.

Yet he did not speak at all as he tied her hands behind her back and a noose around her neck and strung her from an elm tree's branch. He heaved on the rope until she was standing on the tips of her toes, then tied it off on a root and stood back to appraise his handiwork.

Elsa twisted against the cord. The rough fibres of it creaked and felt like thorns against her throat.

I'll wager that guitar of yers against ma knife that she don't make it to dusk, the old man said.

Elsa could not see to whom he was talking and whomever it was did not reply.

From somewhere behind her she could hear Silk's baby and her own crying out. Try as she might she could not turn herself far enough to catch sight of them, her world reduced to the lake and the trees on its far shore and the sky, blotted with soot and murky. The sun had come out full and its paled globe shimmered on the water. As it crept towards the west, she thought about her Omi stuck up in that tree, and of her husband stroking her thighs, wishing she could remember his face though it had been lost to her years ago, and of Wren coughing to life, and of fighting with Silk as she brushed her hair, a hundred strokes each night.

And when these thoughts failed her she hummed old hymns, whispering to herself between the verses, One more breath. That's all, old girl. Just one more breath.

I n the late afternoon, the sun dappled through the elm tree's leaves and a spot of it lit on her cheek. She could not feel its warmth but its glare squinted her eyes.

You're still alive yet, she thought, though it was hardly a comfort.

She could feel nothing below her neck. It was as if her body had died and the mortis had set in, turning her as stiff as a plank. She couldn't feel anything at all except the rope sawing at her throat and a fly padding delicately over her forehead.

Go on now, she hissed at it. You'll have me soon enough. Go on. Shoo. Leave me alone.

But it would not.

T owards evening a fire crackled and a short while later there was the simmer of meat cooking and then voices.

Give one of the legs to the boys, the old man said. They can share it.

What about the womenfolk?

What about em?

They's got to eat too, ain't they?

You'ns gone soft in the head?

Huh?

Do I have to spell it out.

Whadya mean?

Just do like I told ya.

Elsa closed her eyes. When she opened them again the sky was dark and the lake was dark too. The only light she could see was the fire's glow at the edge of her vision and another orangish spark pulsating before her. Acrid smoke from the old man's pipe tickled her nose.

Somewhere close, a baby cried — it was Squawk, she was sure of it. She listened to his furor thinking she'd never heard a sweeter sound.

Then there were footsteps stumbling through the brush behind her.

That you, Briar? the old man called out.

Hell you think it is?

You shore were takin yer time about it.

I got lost.

Lost?

It's dark.

What the hell happened to yer head?

I fell.

You fell?

I tol ya, it's dark.

Where's the girl?

Back in yonder woods.

Ya bury her?

Yeah. Three feet down, like ya tol me.

And yer knife too.

Shoot, I musta— I musta dropped it when I fell.

Let me see yer hands.

Why'n ya wanna see my hands?

Just give em here.

No.

Ain't a speck of dirt on em, I'da bet.

So I warsht em. Went for a goddamned swim in the lake, ya hafta know.

I thought maybe ya'd found a shovel.

Hell ya talkin bout?

It was the girl done that to ya, wad'n it?

I tol ya, I fell.

And if you'da tol me you was a horse, I wun't believe that neither.

You watch yer tongue, old man.

Hit ya over the head with, what was it? A rock? A stick? Looks like a rock.

Quit pokin at me.

She hit ya over the head with a rock then she stole yer knife.

Tha's not how it happened.

What was it then, a stick?

No.

So it was a rock.

I tol ya it weren't.

Cherry, Elsa thought. They're talking about Cherry. But wasn't it the giant who took her? No, it was the pock-faced man. He was the one. And now she's got away.

The rope was pulling tight against her neck. She couldn't breathe. The voices were now only whispers.

Hold up, now, the one was saying.

What?

226

Tha's the green t'backy you'ns smokin.

Is it?

Ya know goddamned well it is. Wheredya git it?

It was in that there Red's bag. Along with a pile of bones.

A pile of bones?

Yeah.

They's odd creatures a'right.

Ya don't hafta tell me.

Come on, now, pass it over.

Shore thing. Here ya go. Set yerself down, have a puff. And don't ya worry bout that girl. She won't git far. We'll fetch her in the mornin.

Elsa could feel her heart's beat slowing in her chest. It was but a murmur now, fading.

Run, Cherry, she thought, run.

VII

He'd been at the quarry for two days when the wind shifted. He'd awoken in the late afternoon reclined beneath the pine, Sky's head resting in his lap. Grey flakes swirled above the quarry like ashes stoked from a fire. When he climbed to his perch, the smoke stain was bent towards him — a black wave that seemed on the verge of washing the forest under its menace.

Nearing dusk, the wind shifted again. It lifted the ash from the canopy below him so that it looked to be taking away the forest itself, bit by bit. The sunset was the reddest he'd ever seen — enflamed as if the sky itself had caught fire. Its hue tapered with the dark, settling once again into a fringe on the horizon. He sat and watched it all night. When the coming dawn had diminished its glower, he climbed back down.

Sky lumbered up from his spot and nuzzled his hand. The boy knelt at him, running his fingers through the greying folds of skin loose around the dog's neck. Ash from his fur dusted the boy's hand.

I'ma thinkin we ought'n git a closer look at it. Howdya feel about that?

The dog let out a sharp bark as if he were thinking the same thing.

Jus let me grab a quick nap, the boy said, settling into the space between the tree's veined roots, then we'll go. I promise.

When he awoke he was hungry and went down to the river to fish. He caught a couple of speckleds and took them to Achaan's Back and cooked them over the firepit. By the time he was done eating it was getting dark again and he returned to the pine. He climbed onto his perch and sat with his back against the trunk. Placing his thumb on the tip of his nose he measured the distance to the fire between it and his forefinger. He couldn't tell if it was any closer than the last time he'd done so.

Only one way to find out, he told himself.

Git to it then.

If only the river ran to the south, we'd be able to follow that, and fish in the meantime.

There's plentya game in the forest. It's not like'n you'da starve.

Ya should have brought Pa's compass.

The Eleven'll lead ya home if'n tha's what you'ns worried about.

I ain't.

Then do it.

We'll go in the morning.

But in the morning when he climbed down from the tree, he was tired and his legs were numb from sitting for so long. Sky was curled up on the soft patch of moss between the pine's roots. He wedged in beside him and the dog peered up at him with eager eyes.

We'll go tomorrow, the boy said scratching the dog behind his ears. I promise.

Sky set his head down in his lap and the boy pulled the brim of his hat down over his eyes.

In the early afternoon he was startled awake by three sharp barks. He lifted his hat and looked over at the dog standing at the edge of the quarry. He was wagging his tail so hard that it looked like he might shake it off.

Wha's got into ya? the boy asked kneeling beside him.

The dog whimpered and batted his snout up against the boy's chin. His tongue lashed out and lapped at his face.

Ya smell somethin? That it?

Sky barked again.

You say so.

O n the far side of the quarry the granite sloped on a steady decline. To the south it dropped off to make way for the Eleven and to the east and the north it descended into the dark web of the forest. Sky walked ahead of him sniffing at the air and walking with the wary gait of a fox that had smelt its first hound. Every few steps he turned back to the boy and his master urged him on with a sweep of his hand, telling him, Go on.

In this way they came to the treeline. Beyond it, the subtle grade gave way to stone steps covered with moss. They switch-backed down them, winding between cedar trees and rocks phosphorescent with green lichen until they'd reached level ground. The air smelled wet and mildewed and sundrench parched the forest floor into splinters of light and dark. Faded yellow leaves littered the ground, windswept, the boy knew, from a field ringed with beeches and maples and birch. He could hear the dim hiss made by the falls, overlaid with the scutter of squirrels and the chatter of chickadees calling out their namesake. The field he could see as a bright patch through the cedars.

At its outset, the trees opened up onto to a wide swath of ferns filling an inlet on the southern edge of the glade. Sunlight bandied about its canopy and its leaves rustled against a breeze carrying within it a faint taste of the river.

Coming upon it like that it seemed to the boy as if he had arrived at a cove on the outskirts of a small green lake. He swished his hand through the ferns, peering over their surface as he would have while contemplating a swim in untested waters. He'd just taken his first step into them when a doe shot up from within the folia. He froze, watching it bound into the field, zig-zagging through the timothy grass and vanishing through a copse of birch trees on its far side.

That what ya smelt? the boy said, looking down at Sky.

The dog licked his hand and his master swung his gaze past a barn on the far side of the field, settling it on the old wreck of a house partly concealed behind an oak tree that had long since been split in two by lightning.

He'd been here once before. He was nine and the spring had been in full bloom. The ground between the cedars was filled with an endless wash of streams lapping at the maze of root clusters over which his father and he had balanced. They'd made a game of trying to see which of them could traverse the flood without soaking their foot-leathers, the boy laughing at his father when he'd lost his balance, teetering and clutching at a low hanging branch to steady himself, skipping past him and calling over his shoulder, Cheater! Sky and Blue bounding through the water, one splashing after the other in tight whirls — not a care in the world between any of them.

When they'd come to the ferns, his father had stopped and looked to his son with wide-eyed glee. He'd put his finger to his mouth and made a great show of tiptoeing through their spread. Every few steps he turned back to his son, his finger tapping at his mouth so that it seemed to the boy that his father must have been leading him towards something dire.

What it was, though, was just the old fallen-down house and the barn, the latter's roof caved in on one end and ivy wound up through its boards so that it looked to the boy like the ground was trying to drag it under.

It's where yer ma's from, his father said while they stood at the edge of the field.

Whadya mean? the boy asked, I thought—

She lived here with her grandpa till she was, oh, about yer age. The old man — his name was Pike if I recollect — died and she came to live with us. Happiest day of ma life, I tell ya.

Beaming, his father ruffled his hand through the boy's hair. The boy frowned and shook his head and his father's smile turned dour as if he knew what was troubling his son.

Then forcing a smile again he said: Come on now, I'll show ya round.

They followed a deer path threaded through the glade all the way to the house. His father circled it, peering in its windows and entreating his son to do the same, the boy dissolute as he went through the motions so that he saw nothing but his own grim reflection in the dirtied windowpanes and, when there were only gaping holes, chastened glimpses of chairs submerged in holes rotted through floorboards and crumbling plaster walls and dark corners.

When he led him towards the barn, the boy refused to follow his father through the bramble of thimbleberries to where the door hung half off its hinges.

Git over here, his father had called. I got a surprise for ya. Come on now.

The boy wouldn't budge an inch and finally his father gave up. Watching him trudge back, the boy had thought, I was awake, Pa. Ya thought I was sleeping but I weren't. I was awake.

His thoughts churning over a night when the winter rains had turned to hail and the rat-a-tat-tat of it assaulting the roof's metal had driven him out of his bed. The terrible clatter had made him think that Achaan must have awoken at last and was raining his vengeance in stones cast down upon the earth. He'd rushed to his door and swung it open, in flight towards his parents' room. Just before he'd reached it, he'd heard his mother's voice raised shrill against the clatter.

Stop it, she'd said. I tol ya I ain doin that no more.

The ferocity with which she spoke stalled the boy. He'd stood shivering from the cold and the fright. Hearing his father's voice, but a whisper so that he could not make out what it said, he'd crept to their door and placed his ear against the wood.

I'm yer sister, his mother had said. Is wrong.

Then from his father: Tain't.

It is. The Book says so.

Go forth an multiply, the Book says that too.

But not wit yer sister.

What about when we're gone? He'll be alone.

Oh yer doin it fer him, are ya? his mother answered, her voice rising towards hysteria. It's lust, tha's all it is. The devil's got in ya. I can see it in yer eyes.

I love you. Can ya see that too?

I'm tired.

I love you.

Go to sleep.

Goddamnit, woman.

Leave me alone!

And then he'd heard his father's feet tromping towards the

236

door. He'd run back to his room, flinging himself into his bed and hiding under his blanket, listening as the thud of his father's footsteps on the stairs was lost to the rat-a-tat-tat of hailstones upon the roof.

The night all but forgotten until, months later, his father had led him through the same patch of ferns that he stood before now, telling him that he was taking him to see where his ma had been born, remembering only then what it was she had said: I'm yer sister. Certain then that his father had known he'd heard her say it and had brought him here to conceal his shame.

And then recalling his father's words: What about when we're gone? He'll be all alone.

The terrible certainty of it descending on the boy as he watched his father threading his way back through the briar.

I ought never ave been born! he'd screamed, turning and fleeing for home.

He hadn't been back since, and seeing the house again, anger welled in his chest as it had then. Weeping for his mother and hating his father — for leaving her when he was five and for letting her die and for telling him that lie all those years ago, the thoughts all jumbled into one so that it seemed to the boy that it was the lie that had killed her — he strode into the ferns.

I'll burn that house to the ground, he thought, as if such a petty act could erase the past.

A flicker of movement on his peripheral stalled him. He looked up and saw that there was someone standing beside the oak staring out at the birch trees through which the deer had taken flight.

Whoever it was had reddish hair hanging in frayed tassels halfway down her back and was wearing a crude dress made from animal hide.

Is a girl, he thought, blinking as if he wasn't sure if she was real, as if she was a momentary delusion conjured to soothe his rage that even now he could feel relenting, seeing at once that she was still there, leaning against the tree's trunk.

Sky barked and she turned his way. The boy ducked low, hiding among the ferns. The dog lashed his tongue over his cheek, his mouth pulled wide in a goofy grin and his tongue lolling askew over his jowls, expectant, like he was waiting on his master's gratitude for the gift he'd bestowed upon him. After a few long-drawn breaths the boy poked his head above the canopy and looked to the oak tree again.

She was gone.

H e took the long way around, circling behind the barn, telling himself, Best not to spook her — his only experience with this sort of thing being on the hunt, though his father had read him plenty of stories that might have remarked to him on the proper decorum for such occasions. Still, he could not reconcile himself to their verity, no word in any of them speaking to how he felt now: a deathly sort of stillness becalming him such as he'd only ever felt in that moment when he'd drawn the arrow back on its twine, in that instant before release, the twang of the bow string making his heart skip a beat then coming back to him full force as he saw his prey startle and flee. Such was his state that when he came to the corner of the barn he could not bring himself, at first, to peer around it, worried that she would see him and run.

He took a moment to banish the thought. When he'd settled his mind, he took a deep breath and stuck his head around the corner. He sighted on her immediately. She was standing in front of a frayed cord hanging from the oak's lowest branch. She was batting the rope with an open hand and the boy would have given anything to know what she was thinking just then for the way she stood — in rapt to the motion of the rope's lazy arc — told him that it must have spoken to her of something deep within. At last the rope swung to a standstill and she turned and walked towards the house.

The oak's severed half had come down on the porch, crushing it on one side. The foundation had given way beneath and the roof leaned at a steep pitch, the walls cracked near the end and the window frames splintered and empty but for a few shards. The doorway was also vacant, the stairs at its foot long disintegrated into pulp. She took the frame in her hands, pulled herself up onto its stoop and stood a moment balancing on the threshold, peering into the dark interior. She must have seen something beyond ruin for after a moment she stepped inside, padding delicately over the slanted floor, clutching at the door frame until she'd come to the limit of her reach then skipping forward.

She reappeared a short while later at a window on the second floor, pulling the moth-eaten drapes aside, peering down into the yard and then departing again.

He watched the house all through the day waiting for her to reappear and measuring her absence by the sun's slow decline.

She's got to come out sometime, he told himself when it had reached the treetops.

And then what?

I guess ya ought'n go talk to her.

What I'ma goin say?

I don't know.

Well ya betta think of somethin.

He heard a crackle from behind. Sky emerged from the forest carrying a grouse between his teeth. He set it down at the boy's feet, wagging his tail. The boy's stomach whined and he tried to think of the last time he'd eaten.

She's bound to be jus as hungry as you are, he thought, looking back at the house.

Ya ought'n start a fire. Cook up that bird. When she smells it roastin—

Yeah, he spoke aloud, nodding and standing up straight like it was an end to the matter and not just its begin.

He stowed the bird in his mother's satchel and picked among the buckthorn trees crowding the barn until he'd gathered an armload of tinder. He carried it southward, towards the field. The sun wasn't but the flicker of a campfire beyond the treeline. Shadows ranged long over the house, looming large in its greyed sentry. He was just approaching the oak tree when Sky stopped ahead of him. The dog cocked his head to one side, listening for a moment. His jowls pulled tight against his teeth and he growled. The boy stared into the gathering dusk. Something was there, he could see its shadow moving against the dim speckles of blue light cast through the trees at the western perimeter of the yard, beyond which he knew lay the falls.

Sky growled again.

The shadow stilled and the boy crouched down beside the dog. He held him with his free arm curled over his back, the palm of his hand pressed tight against his chest and whispered into his ear, Hush now.

The tall grass didn't afford much cover. While the boy was contemplating that and trying to find movement again within the folds of the shadow-laced yard, there came a sharp whistle. Sky's ears perked. The boy clutched him tighter and listened but could not hear anything beyond the whine of cicadas.

The tinder was cramping his arm and he bent and set it down without making a sound. He lifted his other arm from its compress around the dog and ran his hand up along Sky's rump, pushing him down. The dog flattened and the boy whispered, Stay.

He duck walked away from him in a slow creep towards the oak tree. He was breathing hard and his heart was hammering against his rib cage when at last he came to its splintered trunk. Lying on his belly, he shimmied up under its fallen half and peered through the dense weave of branches and scrub nettled beneath it.

A figure appeared, walking towards the house. The boy could hardly see enough of it through his blind to form a clear picture beyond knowing that it was a man, bearded and with a sash wound tight around his head. Limping, that was the impression he got, as if each step was taken in agony. The boy pressed his face to the ground and held his breath against the race of his heart.

Well shoot, he thought, y'ought'n have known she weren't alone.

Like'n it's her father.

Shoot.

Now whadya goin do?

Ya ought'n tell Pa.

And if they move on afore ya git back?

Then tain't yer concern.

A faint cry then, a bird maybe, calling from some far off nest, protesting this intrusion upon its territory. He waited for it to trail off but instead it rose into a seamless wail growing louder with each passing breath.

That ain't no bird I ever heard.

He raised his head ever so slightly. The man was staring back the way he'd come and the boy saw two other forms moving towards him. The one in the lead walked with a peculiar gait, hunched over and stiff, like his father when he was playing at being old. He was carrying something in his hand. Long and thin. A rifle maybe. The one following on his heels was short and stout and was carrying a curved stick. As they came abreast of the first man, the boy could see that it was a bow and that its owner wasn't much older than he was.

The first man was kneeling beneath the porch's stoop. The others bent, squinting at whatever it was he saw there, and then the old man righted himself, pointing towards the rear of the house. The man carrying the bow nodded and set off around back. The other two talked for a while, the younger shaking his head and looking up at the house's empty windows. Finally he said just loud enough for the boy to hear, If she ain't already heard all that crying, she shore as hell goin to hear me walking on all that glass strewed o'er the floor. Then, his voice rising so that anyone in the house would have had to have been dead not to hear it: We ought'n just burn her out!

The old man nodding when, all at a sudden, a frantic yell called out from around back.

I see her, it said. She's comin outta the winda!

The younger man, shaking his head and stomping off around the corner of the house, called back, Don't you touch her now. She's mine. Ya hear me? She's mine!

The older one leant his rifle against the house and took a pipe from his pocket. He clamped it between his teeth and searched about another pocket for something else. Finally, he pulled forth a small bundle. He opened its string, reached into its fold and brought out a clump pinched between his fingers. He packed it into his pipe and felt about his pockets again, probably looking for his flint.

The others' voices came reeling back to the boy.

If you'da kept yer mouth shut fer a breath longer, the one was saying, she'da been on the ground and we'da had her.

Ya tol me to yell, I saw arythin. That's what I did. I saw her comin out the winda and I yelled. Ain my fault she climbed back in.

The two of them rounded the corner just as the old man struck a spark into his pipe.

Dim son of a— the bearded one started and then looked over his shoulder.

Where the hell ya goin?

I—

I tol ya to stay around back. Go on now, git.

The other slunk back to his post and the younger bearded man strode past the older, yelling back towards the river, Yoke, git yer ass up here.

He grabbed onto the door frame with both hands. He tried to pull himself up but his wounded leg seemed to have other ideas.

I thah ya was goin burn her out, the old man said.

You stay outta this.

Hopping up, the bearded man set his knee on the stoop and pulled himself into the doorway, his wounded leg trailing stiff as a plank after him.

The old man shrugged.

Don't say I din't warn ya.

He leant back against the house, puffing on the pipe with the idle conviction of a man trying to keep himself from falling asleep.

The boy could now see other shapes emerging from the trees. A mountain's range worth of blotted peaks shuffling out of the dark, the tallest of them standing a head and shoulders above the rest. The crying grew louder as they approached and was soon joined by the clatter of things being thrown around inside the house and the man shouting, Goddamned, sumbitch!

Footsteps crunched in rapid acceleration over broken glass and then the girl's shrouded form appeared in midflight, leaping through the door. The old man struck out with his hand and caught one of her feet, sending her sprawling. She did a half-circle in mid-air and landed hard on her back. Rolling onto her front with the grace of a cat, she shot forward just as a crack, like a rifle shot, rang out. The girl's feet sprang out from under her, toppling her hard onto her rear.

In the dark, the boy could not see what had happened to her, just that she was lying on her back, writhing and clutching at her throat not more than two or three paces from where he lay, his hands planted flat on the ground and his arms tensed as if he was getting ready to pounce. So close that when she thrashed her head his way she couldn't help but see two whitish globes staring back at her through the drape of branches, her own eyes widened and her lips parting, though nothing came out of them but a strangled gasp.

What'd she hit ya with this time? the old man was saying. Was it a fry pan? We shore could use a fry pan it was.

The bearded man was circling around to her feet, keeping the whip taught in his hand, its lash-end wrapped around the girl's throat.

Git up, he said, giving her foot a stiff kick.

She rolled onto her front and the bearded man jerked the whip backwards, dragging her up onto her knees.

Careful now, the old man said. She's like to still got yer knife.

The bearded man took a step back, tightening the grip on the tether and craning his head towards the newcomers.

Yoke, he called out, pass me yer blade. If'n I'ma goin do this, I'ma goin do it right.

A figure departed the morass of huddled shapes gathered at a distance, so large that it seemed they'd trained a grizzly bear to walk on its hinds. As he approached, the man drew from behind his back a thick wedge of sharpened steel such as the boy's father used to clear brush, except bigger by half. He strode past the old man, suddenly stilled by the turn of events, his only movement being the gnash of his teeth as he chewed on the stem of his pipe. The giant offered up his blade and the bearded man tested its heft by swinging it in a slow pendulum at his side.

The girl was but a statue now — her body rigid, the tendons in her neck buttressed against the lash of leather, her face ballooned against its hold, not a single breath issuing from between her pursed lips.

The night went suddenly chill for the boy and there wasn't a sound to distract him from the terrible plod of his heart, counting towards the ruin he saw spelt out in the girl's fevered eyes, cast down upon him, a single tear squeezing out from the corner of one, tracing a thin rivulet over her dirt-mired cheek.

The bearded man cinched the whip in one hand and raised the blade over his head with the other. He looked, skittish, towards the old man and the old man nodded, the boy could see it in the way the pipe's orange spark dipped before him.

Ya brought this on yerself, the bearded man said.

His hand quivered as if it wasn't up to the task its owner had set for it and in that instant the boy was up on his knees as quick as if he'd been spring-loaded, stringing an arrow on his bow and loosing it. The arrow struck the bearded man just below his shoulder, its shaft burrowing halfway to its feathers. He let out a stifled yelp, dropping the machete and stumbling backwards. The girl, wrenched along with him, found herself suddenly on her feet again. She spun, snatching at a length of antler tucked into the cord wrapped around her waist. The blade came out of its sheath with stealthful liquidity but it wasn't long enough in the boy's sight to divine its scope before the girl had made the distance between her and the man and was plunging it haft deep into his chest. His body jerked and he muttered, Goddamn, blood bubbling over his lips as he toppled sideways. The lash around the girl's throat dragged her down on top of him.

There's someone there, the old man screamed. Behind the tree!

But no one seemed to have heard him, or if they did, none of them seemed to care. The giant staring in mute disbelief at his friend and the girl frantically unwinding the lash from her neck and rolling off the bearded man only to have the giant's hand clamp around her throat the moment she was free. He dragged her up, raising her onto the tips of her toes, rage spilling out of him in a bestial roar. The others beyond him reduced to a blank canvas upon which the girl's fate was being drawn. The boy fumbling for another arrow, the quiver dislodged somehow and draped low over his back so that it seemed an eternity before his fingers latched onto one. Drawing it out and threading it on the string and raising the bow in unison with the old man raising his rifle, an act, it would seem to him later, he must have divined from some prescient corner of his mind — his gaze so fixed on the girl's madly thrashing legs and the palsied twitch of her hands that he couldn't possibly have seen it then — for the moment he'd let the arrow fly he threw himself sideways. An explosion splintered the branch under which he'd lain and a whoosh of air swept past him carrying the stink of sulphur.

His ears ringing, the taste of blood in his mouth, his arms groped for the ground suddenly unsure of which way was down. Something sharp pressed against his cheek — a fallen branch or the crown of a thistle. He felt Sky's tail brushing his shoulder as the dog leapt over him, darting through the scrub, a snarl trailing in his wake such as the boy never would have imagined he could have made.

Sitting up now, time moving to the slow plod of his heart, reaching out for the oak's trunk, pulling himself up.

A frantic scream drew him out from behind the tree.

Sky was on top of the old man, sprawled on his back, the

dog's teeth tearing at his arm, the old man wailing, Call him off, goddamnit. Call him off!

They seemed a world away to the boy though, removed to some dark and remote corner. Only the giant seemed real. Towering above him, close enough to touch, his eyes downcast, sad and confused, flumes of blood spewing from the holes on either side of his neck through which the arrow had passed. Now a subtle downward hitch to his shoulders as if his legs were giving out by degrees. Steadying himself and raising his arm. Reaching out for the boy even as he lilted sideways. His mouth gaping, a bubble forming at his lips, popping the moment he spoke.

Oke, he sputtered and then fell.

His body seemed to deflate with its passing, making no sound beyond a gentle thud as it hit the ground. Only then did the world beyond his come back into clear focus.

The old man was screaming a long and continuous agony, his words lost to the tyranny of his pain. Sky relentless, his teeth gnashing at his arm, hanging at an odd angle as if it was just tendons holding it together. The others gathered around them, watching from within the cover of dark, heads lowered as if in prayer. The girl on all fours, coughing up phlegm, her whole body heaving, trying to find its breath. The bearded man on his back beside her, his fingers plucking at the knife in his chest as one might at a splinter, their fretful movements slowing, his arm dropping away, coming to a rest against his chin.

Then a hand was touching the boy's arm. He jerked, startled, and looked to the woman standing beside him, her face gaunt and her arms as thin as reeds. She was leaning on a stick, bent at the top like a cane.

Call him off, she said.

He looked at her as if he didn't understand.

Your dog. Call him off.

The boy turned and whistled through the gap in his teeth. Sky swung his head round and his body followed it in a quick lope towards his master. When he'd come to within a few paces he slowed, his head hung low, expecting to be punished for what he'd done. He circled the boy wide, coming up behind him and brushing his snout against his master's hand, then trotted past on a direct line for the girl. She was still on her knees, gasping for air. The dog daubed his nose against her cheek, licked at it and turned back to the boy, beaming.

The girl was looking at him too, an expression on her face that he'd never seen before, almost like his mother gloryin in the day but wide-eyed and fierce. It made his stomach clench and blood rush to his cheeks. He turned away, suddenly struck shy.

The old man's screams had turned shrill and delirious. His whole body was shaking to it as he clutched at his arm, severed just below his elbow, the errant part resting on his belly attached by no more than a thin strip of skin, blood spurting out from the sharply fractured bone. A deathly quiet fell over him as he looked up at the woman appearing at his side. She was carrying the giant's blade and paused a moment staring down at the old man as if there was something unspoken between them or she wasn't yet ready to end his pain.

Go on, he finally said. Do it.

She did.

Raising the blade and bringing it down straight upon the man's mouth, splitting his head in two and then turning her back on him as if it hadn't meant more to her than another log for the fire. The boy stunned beyond words, turning away even though the gore of the thing was drowned by the dark, hearing that strange cry again and a voice raised in alarm.

Don't, it said. Please. I'ma glad he's dead. I am. Glad they's all dead. They's evil. Please. Wait. Don't. I ain't never shoulda left the farm. The voice then breaking into blubbering sobs.

The gaunt-faced woman touched his arm again. When he looked to her she was staring at him through eyes as gentle as his mother's. Another face bobbled beside hers, pinched and bawling, its tiny mouth chewing at its tiny hand.

It's a baby, he thought, turning the word over in his mind like it was a prized toy he'd lost and now held again.

You alone? the woman said.

The boy nodded and then reconsidered.

There's my pa.

Where's he?

Home.

And where's that?

Not far.

You'll take us?

The boy nodded again, never once taking his eyes off the child on her back.

A baby, he thought. Magine that.

This here's our corn, the boy said as he led them across the field.

The moon had come out full, lighting up the rows as clear as any sun.

Pa always saves haffa it for seed. We'da have to be starvin down to our last breath fore he'da let us eat the seed. Seed corn is sacred, tha's what he says. And up ahead there, tha's the path. One way leads to the farm, the other down to the river where we swim. I'll take ya some time.

He hadn't stopped talking since they'd come to the quarry, the drama of the night's events dulled by the familiarity of the granite field. Telling them about the perch atop the white pine — Ya can pract'ly see to the end of the world from up there, he'd said pointing it out — and then, leading them downwards past his grandfather's firepit, about swimming in the quarry and Achaan, about cornshine and the pool below the falls in which they fished. And when they'd reached the swamp, about the turkey he'd shot through the neck, just like he had the giant. Then, drafting a single breath of air, he'd told them about how Sky had saved him from a wild dog when he was five, and that led to how his father had gone off to hunt the ones that had got away, and then to how his mother had taken ill fighting the cacklers.

He hadn't thought about it for years and the remembrance came into his mind afresh, invigorated by the passage of time. And in the telling he found the grudge he bore his father for leaving him and his mother all those years ago crumbling to dust, seeing now that if he hadn't have left, this memory of her wouldn't reside inside him like it did. When they came, at last, to the ridge overlooking their field he was just getting to the part about how the thunderheads had come roiling out of the west.

If the rains come I'ma done fer, Ma says to me.

I knew it was true but I told her I'da build her a tent. She squeezed ma hand again, driving a sharp nail into it so I'd listen.

I'ma done fer, y'understand, she said. Ain't no two ways about it. If the rains come I won make it and you'll be on yer own until yer pa gits back. Ya need to set yer mind to that. Look at me.

But I wouldna or couldna and I stared up at the clouds boiling angry over top of us. Raindrops fell on ma cheeks as fine and as sharp as needle points.

You can do it, she said. I know ya can.

Then lightnin was flarin from within the great black mass

overhead and the both of us waited for the thunder. The lightnin flashed again. It lit a fringe around the cloud and there wasn't a sound in the world at all except Ma's laboured breaths. I reached for the tooth in ma pocket, diggin pass ma knife and ma magnifying glass and findin nothin there but a small hole.

Pa ain't never comin back, I cried. He ain't!

He heard the women sniffling behind him as if it was foregone that his mother had died on that day and not eight years later. The sound of their grief trailing after him as he made his way along the cliff's edge hastened the story towards its end. He was just stepping onto flat ground when he got to the part where his father had returned.

It's Ma! I yelled to him and in the next moment, Pa was kneelin at her, wedgin his hands under her back and liftin. Her body convulsed against his and she let out a pained sob.

And never, the boy said, turning to face the others, have I heard a more joyful sound.

The moonlight cast a ghostly pallor about their faces. In that moment, they looked to the boy like spirits summoned from the afterlife to bear witness to his tale and now brought back to life by its message of hope. The women were smiling and wiping tears from their cheeks, holding the younger ones to their breasts with crooked arms, the three of them gazing up at the boy with curious looks as if they'd never heard anything so strange, the two men they'd spared standing among them, the shorter one kicking at the dirt with downcast eyes, the taller one with downcast eyes as well but flickering as if he was working out some deeper mystery to it.

Only the girl was absent from their fold.

The boy scoured the forest behind them but could not find her within its shade. Someone coughed and he turned back to the others, all of them beseeching him with grateful smiles.

He wheeled around and started towards the corn patch.

Come on, he said. We're almost there. Wait'll ya see the look on Pa's face. Won he be surprised.

H e could hear the hounds baying the moment he stepped through the break in the pines. They were coming across the pasture, parting its weeds with a dim rustle. Sky rubbed anxiously against his hand and the boy said, Go on then.

The dog took off like a shot, disappearing into the tall grass as his master plucked one of its stalks. He set it between his teeth, chewing on its shoot, and looked to the house and barn, their forms stark against the night sky. The only light he could see beyond the moon and the stars were the white rails leaking between the boards of his father's workshop. He thought he could detect the faint strains of music creeping up through the cricketsong but it was drowned out by the hounds' fevered medley.

Their yips and yelps quieted the moment before they broke free from the pasture's cover — a mass of wagging tails and flopping ears breaking apart as they swirled around the women and children, sniffing at hands and wending through legs and pushing their snouts up into the must hidden under the hems of ragworn dresses. The two youngest boys greeted them with wide grins and dipped their faces low to accept sloppy licks, but the women, to a one, stood stock-still under the assault, fear carving their faces into grave masks.

It's okay, the boy said. They's jus saying howdo.

And when that didn't ease their fright, he swatted after the brood, telling them, Go on, you'ns had yer fun. Go on now. Shoo.

The dogs, to a one, paying him no heed, barking and snarling at one another, making a game of which could play the biggest fool.

Blue came last, bounding up behind the boy and ducking between his legs, almost knocking him off his feet.

Ya missed me? the boy said scratching him behind his ears.

The clownish peel to the dog's lips made the boy laugh and he turned back to the workshop. It was dark, he now saw, but he could just make out a speck of orange flickering where their gate would have been.

Best git a move on, he said more to himself than to the others. Pa's like to be wonderin what all the fuss's about.

He traced the amber glow from his father's pipe in a straight line across the field. The dogs had awoken the animals in the barn. The goats sounded their siren call in frantic bleats, and he could hear Spook braying to wake the dead.

Pa, the boy called out. We's got comp'ny!

His father stared back at him as if he couldn't understand what his son had meant.

Comp'ny?

And they's got babies.

Babies?

They were close enough now for him to see the truth of what the boy had said. He tapped the bowl of his pipe against a fence post, shaking his head, his lips curling into a question mark. His face was leaner than his son remembered, his beard whiter, so that it seemed he'd turned into an old man since he'd last seen him. His eyes were red and rheumy and rimmed with dark folds. It looked like he hadn't slept in a week. Finding him like that, the boy felt a deep shame for leaving him and met his gaze with a clipped smile as he skirted past, making his way towards the house.

They's half-starved, he called over his shoulder. I'ma goin light a fire. Why'nt ya git one of them to fetch some eggs?

H e fried up some onions with a spoonful of the congealed goat's fat they kept in a tin on the shelf above the stove. The smell of them simmering had his stomach in knots. While he stirred them with a wooden spoon he watched his father bouncing one of the babies in his arms and blowing wet kisses against the nape of his neck. The child squealed and slapped at his face and the man laughed.

He shore is a feisty one, he said, looking to the women sitting at the table.

One of them was nursing her own baby and another was leant back in the chair with her eyes closed and her legs spread wide, holding fast to the bulge pressing out from under her dress. The thinnest of the three was staring back at the man like she couldn't believe there was a place left for such joy in the world.

Wha's his name? the man asked.

The thin one opened her mouth and then shook her head as if she didn't know what to say.

He hasn't got one, the woman sitting beside her said.

Ain got a name?

Gregor, the thin woman said all of sudden. His name's Gregor.

The man lifted the child up and looked him in the eyes.

Gregor, he said. Tha's a fine name.

And this here's Sascha, the other added, unlatching her baby and slinging him over her shoulder, patting his back.

The man then looked over at the three boys sitting against

the kitchen's southmost wall. Sky and Blue were draped over the laps of the two youngest while the oldest sat between them with his eyes closed. All of them bore fine skeletal lines inked into their skin so that, in the soft glow emanating from the candles perched at intervals along the kitchen's high shelf, they looked as much like ghouls as boys.

He opened his mouth but couldn't think of what he might say to give voice to the alarm he felt looking upon them. Then the door was swinging open and the shorter of the young men swept through it carrying a basket filled to the brim with eggs.

Gawd, ya should have warned me about that rooster, he said, his voice a shade too loud for the confines of the room. He's right mean. Damn near took out one a ma eyes.

He offered up his cheek to the boy and the boy nodded seeing the thin scratch running along the side of his face.

Ya gotta carry a stick wit ya, the boy said.

That the trick?

He won't come near ya, ya carryin a stick.

I'll member that for next time.

How many eggs ya git?

Gawd, I don't know. I cain't count that high. A lot.

Give em here.

He did and the boy set to cracking them into the pan.

Arything else ya need?

Ya mind fetchin some water?

Ya got a bucket?

It's there by the door.

I see it.

The well's just round the side of the house. Ya goin want to pump it a few times to git ridda the grit.

As he was taking the bucket from its hook the other young man came in carrying an armload of firewood.

Jus set that by the fire, the boy told him.

The young man nodded gravely and walked past the table, his eyes lowered, shamefaced, it seemed, in the presence of the women.

Just then Gregor gave out a loud squawk.

What was that? the man asked, peering at the child with a scrunched up nose.

He's just hungry, the woman with the baby said. Give him here, I still got one full.

The man stepped to her. She set her child on the floor at her feet and took up Gregor. The man bent to all fours and butted the one she'd called Sascha in the belly with his nose. The child stared at him, lips a-tremble as if he was about to cry. The man growled loud and deep, bearing his teeth and the child let out a startled laugh then turned to flee. The man made to pursue when he felt something sticky against his hand. He raised it up and saw that it was smeared with blood. He traced it back to a stream dribbling down the thin woman's leg. When he looked up at her, she was staring at him with a queer expression.

The man's face reddened.

My wife, he said, stammering, she had some pads she made. I'll git ya some.

Pardon? the woman said.

For yer . . . I mean . . . she called it her moonly.

Her— the woman started.

She shook her head and looked down at her leg.

It's not that. I was hurt.

Hurt?

Yeah.

How bad?

Bad.

The man rubbed at his whiskers with the back of a knuckle.

Ya mind I ave a look?

I'd be much obliged if you did.

He shuffled on his knees towards her and reached out for her dress. As he lifted its hem, the sour smell of her sex made him pause.

Ya wearin drawers?

What?

Under yer dress.

No.

I can fetch ya some.

You said you had a wife.

The man nodded.

Then I probably don't have anything you haven't seen before.

The man laughed.

You'ns prob'ly right bout that.

Go on, the woman said. I don't mind.

The man lifted her dress ever so slightly then rolled it up to where the skin was bruised in a wide circle around a festering sore.

It looks bad a'right, he said, lowering her dress and looking up at her again.

The way her eyes were shining made him blush. He reached for the table and pulled himself to his feet.

How'd it happen?

I was stabbed.

Stabbed?

By one of the men your boy saved us from.

My boy— the man swung his head towards his son stirring up the eggs.

If he'd heard what she'd said, he made no sign of it.

He saved ya?

He did.

The man ran his fingernails through his beard and then remembered himself.

Yer wound, he said. We need to warsh it, else it'll git—

Infected.

It's like to be already.

I know.

I got somethin fix ya right up.

Your grandpa's cornshine? the woman said.

Yeah. Then looking at her sideways: Howdya know about that?

Your son.

That right?

He's hardly stopped talking since we met.

And again the man gazed over at his son as if there could be no end to his surprise. After a moment, he turned back to the woman.

I'll fetch that cornshine.

I'd be much obliged.

I wun't be but a moment.

I'll be here.

Good.

W hen he was done serving the others, the boy brought the pan onto the porch. All the while he'd been cooking he'd imagined the girl was there, sitting in his mother's chair, waiting for him, but there was only the satchel where he'd left it, hung by its strap over the chair's back. Sky padded out and touched the wet of his nose against his hand. From the kitchen, he could hear the scrape of forks and knives and joyful squawks from the babies and then his father's voice, There we go. Good as rain. So now how's bout ya tell me how it was ma boy come to save ya's all.

The boy weeded among the dogs sprawled over the floor. At

the porch's edge, he stood picking idly at the yellow curds of scrambled egg and peering out into the dark, trying to recollect when it was that he'd last seen her.

It was up by the quarry. You was jus leadin them past the firepit, tellin them about how yer gramps'd gathered the stones from the riverbed and carted them up one by one when he was n'older than three. You'd looked back to make shore the others were followin ya and ya'd seen her standin atop the ridge, silhouetted against the night's splendor.

Thinking about it now, his breath hitched just like it had then.

But was that the last time? he asked himself, searching his remembrance for another sighting.

The pregnant woman had groaned and clutched her belly, and the thin woman had touched her shoulder and asked, You all right?

She'd nodded and then the thin one had turned to you and asked again how far it was.

We'll be there well afore dawn, you'd said. It's jus through here.

Leading them past Grandpa's firepit, the stories had taken hold and they'd blotted out the memory of anything else until he was coming onto the field.

He returned to the chair and set the pan on its seat. He took up his mother's satchel, still weighted with the grouse, and slung it over his shoulder. He could hear the thin woman's voice, low and serious, telling how the old man, whom she called Levin, had strung her mother from a tree.

He left her there to die, she said, her voice halting and pained. He— he made us watch. We— we— her voice stuttering then breaking down. She was sobbing now and so were the others, and his father was saying, It's okay— Ya don't— the fury of their grief beyond the salve of mere words.

The boy hurried down the steps. He crossed the yard and skirted the garden until he'd come to the cherry tree. Its limbs were heavy with fruit. He picked one and popped it in his mouth, chewing it slowly. It wasn't quite ripe and its sour dried his cheeks. He spit out the pit and picked a handful, stuffed them into the satchel, then picked four more handfuls and turned back to the garden, trying to think what else he might take with him.

His father's voice sounded from the porch.

Y'ain never seen nothin like this, it said, loud and boisterous. Come on. Bring the young'uns too. They ain seen nothin like this neither.

His father was leading the injured woman across the yard. He was holding a tallow candle in his hand, his other guarding its flame against the breeze, his eyes fixed on the way the light danced in shadows about her face. The others came after, the two women carrying the babies followed by the three boys and the two young men.

It's jus in here, his father said, reaching the workshop. He swung its door open. Let me light the lantern. There ya go, now. Come on in. Don't be shy.

The boy turned his back on them and climbed through the fence. Sky burrowed under the lowest rung and ran to catch up. As he trod across the pasture, the sad song rose against the whine of crickets — his mother's voice, calling out to him from beyond the grave, chasing him across the field.

VIII

H ere now he comes to Achaan's Back with racing heart. The dawn was fast approaching and as he made his way up the rise he could feel the past day's heat radiating in waves from the stone, leeching through his foot-leathers. Crows squawked their mad refrain in the distance and in the northwestern sky he could see larger birds, vultures maybe, circling above the trees.

Whadya goin do if she ain't here? he asked himself.

Sky'll find her. Won't ya, boy?

But the dog was already bounding ahead, his snout lowered to the rock, leading the boy to the top of the ridge overlooking the quarry. He spotted her right away, sitting on the white pine's perch, her legs dangling below, her bare feet swinging against the breeze. Sky barked and the feet jerked upward. The girl stood and pressed herself against the far side of the pine's trunk, hiding herself from view. The boy waited for her to reappear and when she did — her face probing warily out from behind the tree — he waved his hand over his head.

After a moment she waved back and the boy smiled as if it couldn't have happened any other way.

H e tindered a fire. When it was going strong, he plucked the grouse and dressed it. By the time he'd spitted the bird, the fire was down to embers. He layered it with the charcoal he'd saved from the remnants of the last and set the bird to roast on a spit a hand's width above the heat. When the skin on its underside had turned to gold, he gave it a half turn and stood.

The sun had come out full and Sky had retreated to the shade under the stunted spruce tree. He'd fallen asleep and as the boy trod past him, he thought about how he should be tired too and yet had never felt more awake.

At the top of the rise, he saw that the girl's legs had resumed their dangle.

Whadya reckin she's lookin fer? he asked himself.

Muss be somethin.

But what?

Only one way to find out.

Git to it then.

He skittered down the steep slope beyond the ridge, carrying its speed at a run towards the tree. He climbed towards the perch haltingly, stopping at almost every branch to look up at her feet. The soles of them were black with dirt. Spots of blue winked at him between the curl of her toes. At last he came to the branch just below hers. He took two sideways steps out along his own and draped his hands over the one above. As he stared through his arms at the smoke-cloud fuming on the southern horizon, he chanced fleeting glimpses up at the girl. At her patchworn dress flowing over the curves of her body, its sheen unmolested except by two small bumps where her breasts pressed against the hide. At the weals of purpled flesh swelling her throat so that it was almost even with the nub of her chin. At the orange-tinged hair hung in garlands over her cheek, her nose slightly askew, its nub marked with a delicate notch, her mouth down-crimped and solemn.

Whadya lookin fer? he asked when it seemed she'd never turn his way.

She did not move and the boy went back to staring at the smoke.

Is somethin ain it?

He glanced up at the girl again but she was as still as ever.

Pa reckins it was a lightnin strike.

This time when he looked up she was shaking her head.

It weren't, she said.

Howdya know?

The girl bit her lip and went back to watching the smoke, the boy watching her. He heard her stomach whine.

Ya hungry? he asked.

She seemed to feel the weight of his gaze and shifted.

I brought some cherries. Ya want some?

I wun't mind.

He drew out a handful from his pocket and passed them up to her. One tumbled from between her fingers and dropped, spinning stem over stem. She stared after it, her face taut with alarm.

Don't worry about that'n, I got a whole bagful.

Nodding, she teased her finger among the red balls in her palm. She chose the reddest of the bunch and popped it into her mouth. She chewed it slowly and spit out the pit.

They's good, she said, eating another.

They ain't quite ripe yet. They's a bit sour.

They's still good.

I got a grouse spit o'er the fire too.

Wha's that?

Y'ain't never hearda grouse afore?

I'da tell ya I did.

Is a bird. Kin'a like a chicken.

I shore like chicken.

I ought'n go check on it. It'll almost be done.

He crouched, about to climb back down, and then looked back up at the girl.

I could bring it up to ya.

If'n it's all the same, she said, I'da rather come down.

S he ate the grouse, holding it like a cob of corn. Sky had awoken from his slumber and had lain down beside her at the firepit. One of his ears lay flopped over her leg, twitching at a fly crawling over the veins on its underside.

It shore is good, she said. Ya shore ya don't want some?

The boy shook his head.

I could spare ya a leg.

I'ma'right.

Shore is good.

She picked the bird clean, then threw what was left in the fire and licked her fingers.

The boy had stood and was looking down the rise, towards home.

We ought'n be gittin back, he said.

Ya fixin to leave?

I din't tell my pa where I was goin. He'll be worried, is all.

Ya can leave ary time you want.

She glared at him with narrowed eyes and the boy looked down at his feet, kicking at the grit spread over the granite.

I could stay. If'n you are.

I am.

Okay. Then looking up at her again: Ya still hungry?

I could eat some more of them cherries.

I'll fetch ya the bag.

Walking to the stunted spruce, he unhitched his mother's satchel from the branch where he'd hung it.

Eat all ya want, he said, setting the satchel beside her.

She reached into it and took one out. She clamped it between her teeth and yanked off the stem, sucking the fruit into her mouth. It made a popping noise.

I could catch us a couple a trout for supper, the boy said as she chewed on it. Ya know what trout are?

They's fish. Everyone knows that.

They's plenty in the river. Mostly speckled. They's some rainbow but mostly they's speckled. Ya like fish?

Shore, she said eating another cherry.

Ah shoot, the boy said, frowning. I done forgot, I ain got ma fishin rod.

Tha's okay. I'da prefer another one of— whatdya call it?

Grouse?

Yeah. I'da shore prefer another one of them.

T hey spent the morning hunting in the field beyond the ferns. You shore are hell with that bow, the girl said with amaze when he'd shot the first bird before it had barely made two flaps out of the tall grass.

Pa says I could knock off a grasshopper's wing at fifty paces wit ma eyes closed.

That's what he says?

Yeah.

Y'ever try?

The boy spat.

Shoot, tha'd jus be a waste of an arrow.

Sky brought the grouse back and set it at his feet. The boy plucked the arrow from it and set the bird in the satchel.

One time I killed two birds with one shot, he said.

Ya never.

I did. When Sky brung it back, he was carrying the shaft of the arrow in his teeth. There was a bird on either side. I ain't never laughed so hard.

Yer lyin.

I ain't.

He tried to keep a straight face but couldn't stop his lips from curling.

I knew it, ya is.

I'ma goin to one day though.

The girl cocked her head sideways at him.

I'da bet you are.

She watched him shoot another grouse. While Sky was fetching it she walked over to a honeysuckle bush at the edge of the field and squatted behind it. The boy was just stowing the bird in the satchel as she came back across the field tucking a stem holding three of the pink-belled flowers into the hair above her ear. He watched her until she glanced his way then averted his eyes, settling his gaze on the barn.

Hey, ya wanna see somethin? he called to her.

What?

Is a surprise.

What kinna surprise?

I don't know. It'll be a surprise to me too.

They took the long way to reach the barn door, circling the briar patch and coming to it as if on the sly. It hung half off its hinges and when he reached out for its handle the door broke off altogether and fell inward. Swatting at the dust billowed in its wake, he peered in the doorway, the girl crowding against him.

Y'ever seen arything like that?

She shook her head.

Whatever it was sat on the straw-matted floor in the space between the two lofts. It was covered with a fine layer of dust and sprigs of hay and looked at first glance to be some sort of giant metal insect — a beetle maybe — its pale green shell concealing its wings.

What is it? the girl asked.

I reckin is what ma pa calls an . . . automobile.

An automobile?

Yeah. He read to me all about em.

Wha's it fer?

In olden times people used to drive em whenever they wanna'd to take a wander.

Drive em?

Ya know, like a . . . a wagon.

With horses?

The boy shook his head.

It din't need no horses. It had what they calls an engine. It could turn water into fire. Infernal combustion, tha's what ma pa said. It made so it could pull itself.

The girl stared at it for a while.

Them's tire's ain't they? she finally said, pointing at the black circles flattened underneath.

They's called wheels, far as I know.

We had one of them hung from a rope, like the one on that

tree out yonder. Ma pa called it a tire swing. I used to push ma little brother on it. Is a tire a'right.

You say so.

I always wondered where it'd come from.

Well, now ya know.

The girl stretched her arms over her head and yawned. He cast her a hurried glance as if the sight was too bright for him to bear for more than a second. She caught him looking and smiled. His cheeks flushed and he lowered his eyes. When he looked back up, the girl was stifling another yawn with her hand.

They's a bed up in that ol house, she said. I think I might have a lie down.

G awd, what a mess.

She was walking amongst the three bodies arrayed in front of the house, shaking her head and tsking at what they'd become. They were in a most sorrowful state — their bellies torn open, their guts trailing into the grass like loose threads, their eyes empty holes.

The critters been at em all night.

The crows had scattered at their approach and now sat perched in restless vigil along the roof of the porch and crowded the fallen tree's branches, all of them squawking their ire.

The boy stood at a distance, watching as she stopped at the younger of the bearded men. She placed her bare foot on his chest and wrapped both hands around the handle of the knife stuck there. She pulled hard and the ease with which it slid out caught her off guard, stumbling her backwards. Recovering, she bent, wiped the blade on the man's shirt and then held it up to the sun's glint.

Tha's a good knife, she said.

It your'n?

She shook her head.

It'n his. I jus took it from him. That old man's got one jus as good.

I already got a knife.

Never hurts to have another.

Yer right there.

It's on his belt.

The boy took a tentative step towards him.

Go on, he ain goin bite.

Trying not to look past the old man's chin where his head had fallen away, he bent at his waist and lifted his shirt. The knife beneath it had a yellowed hilt of antler. He undid the belt's buckle, slid the sheath along until it was free and then stood and drew the knife out. He ran his finger along its sharp.

Tha's a good knife, he said.

I tol ya.

It's not a bad belt neither.

Go on, take it then.

I think I jus might.

Unhitching the belt, he looped it around his waist. There wasn't a notch within a hand's width of making it tight. He took it off and slung it over his shoulder. When he looked back up the girl was pulling herself onto the porch's stoop.

She took one step into the house then stopped and craned her head back towards the boy.

Y'ain tired? she said.

I'ma bout ready to fall over.

Well they's plentya room in that bed for two.

The porch opened into a hallway leading past two doorways, one on either side. Splays of dirty light coming from each lit warped floorboards and a hole five paces across where the wood had rotted through. From within its dark: the splash of something thrashing about in water — a rat maybe or a snake. The musk of mould thickened the air.

To the left of the hall, stairs rose to the second floor. The steps creaked underfoot as the girl mounted them.

This'n where ma ma used to live, the boy said, following after her.

Tha right?

She left when she was but a girl.

And whyn's that?

Her pa'd died.

Her pa ya say?

Yeah. Why?

Is jus there's a woman settin up in a rocking chair in the room where the bed is.

Dead?

She ain nothin but a pile of bones.

Then how'dya know it was a she?

She's wearin a dress. She's right in there. Come on in and see fer yerself.

They'd reached the top of the stairs and the girl was walking through the open doorway across the hall. The boy held up and the girl called back at him, Ain that a thang, scared of a pile of bones.

He willed his legs forward and into the room. There was a double-wide bed against the far wall, its mattress covered with a patchwork quilt, a dresser layered with dust and mouse turds beside it. Otherwise the room was barren except for a rocking chair in front of its lone window. A shawl was draped over its back so that all the boy could see of its occupant was the bony shape of an arm projected from between two of its spokes.

Gawd, the girl was saying as she stretched out over one half of the bed, feels like is been years since I slept offa the ground.

The boy approached the bed from the other side.

Ya slept in here the other day, din't ya?

She turned to him with a curious expression.

You was watchin me? she said.

I saw ya go in the house is all.

Well, I guess it was lucky for me ya did.

She rolled over so that her back was facing him.

You jus goin stand there?

The boy set the satchel and his bow and quiver on the floor then lay down beside her with his hands folded over his stomach. Straw from the mattress poked at his back through the blanket. He shifted restlessly against its prickle, listening to her breathe. He did not think he would sleep but after a while he did. When he awoke it was still bright and the girl was curled up against him, her head pillowed on his arm and her one hand draped over his chest, her hair tickling at his nose. She smelled faintly of honeysuckle. He held his breath, savouring the scent, and then exhaled slowly, trying not to disturb her.

He awoke again sometime later.

The light parsing through the window was a shade duller and the girl had her back turned away from him. Her body shook and he could hear her sobbing.

You'ns okay? he said sitting up.

She did not answer and he reached out and touched her shoulder. Her body went stiff.

Don't, she said.

Wha's wrong?

Jus leave me alone!

S ky was laying in the shade beneath the porch's stoop when the boy came onto it. The crunch of glass underfoot roused him and he raised his snout. The boy dropped down beside him and knelt to scratch him behind the ears.

How bout we try fer nother grouse? he said.

He stood and made off towards the field.

Come on then.

The dog looked after him but would not be lured from his sentry.

Suit yerself.

He zigzagged through the field, finding nothing but grass-hoppers and the rustle of something in the grass that might have been a hare. He shot at it. The arrow didn't find anything but dirt and after he'd retrieved it he returned to the house by way of the honeysuckle bush. He paused there and plucked one of the bells. He squished it between his fingers and pressed its scent into his nose, thinking of how his mother would sometimes rub flower petals behind her ears and on her wrists, wondering if maybe the girl had done the same.

Having the two of them in one thought like that, it recalled to him how, even before she'd got sick, his mother would some-times lay in bed crying too. Once she'd stayed there most of the day and when he'd asked his father what was wrong with her he'd said, Ain nothing wrong. Is jus the way they is.

Who?

Women, son. They hold all their sadness in their hearts until they cain't hold onto it no more and then it all comes gushing out at once. She'll be okay once it gets out.

She's had a rough go of it, the boy thought walking back towards the house. Jus give her time, she'll come round again.

And sure enough, when he came around the corner of the house, she was kneeling beside Sky, letting him lick at her cheek. The dog barked and she looked up. Her eyes were still red but she was smiling, in her shy way. She stood, smoothing out her dress and tilting her head towards the sky, her hand visored against the sun's glare, just like his mother used to do.

Gawd it's hot, she said.

We could go for a swim.

I wun't say no.

He led her to the quarry's edge. Standing within the pine's shade they peered down at the sky's blue reflected in the water's mirror.

How we a'pposed to git down there? she asked.

Howdya think?

The girl thought about it for a moment.

Then how's we a'possed to git back up?

See that ol rope?

He pointed to the one tied around the tree's trunk.

It don't look strong enough to hold an ant.

Is a'right.

Whyn't we just swim in the river?

Hell, that ain no fun, the boy said, shucking his foot-leathers.

He peeled off his tunic and stripped from his pants. Taking one step back, he pinched his nose between his thumb and fore-finger and then catapulted himself into the breach. When he came up out of the water, he backstroked away from the rock's face, watching the girl slip off her dress. She folded it into a square and set it on the ground. As she stood, the boy could see her sex dark against the white of her skin and two small pinkish dots marking her breasts.

She called something down to him that he couldn't make out and he yelled back up at her, What?

Turn around!

The boy flipped onto his front, his back to the quarry's wall.

After a moment he heard her screaming and craned to look over his shoulder. Her arms were waving frantically over her head as she dropped. She hit the water with a terrific splash and came up a few seconds later, coughing and wiping the hair out of her eyes.

I shore ain goin to do that again, she said. Thought ma legs was about to come up through ma neck.

Ya got to point yer toes.

Now ya tell me.

The girl swam past with a light and easy stroke and the boy set off after her. He reached out, grabbing at her foot and she shot him a fierce look.

Cut it out.

Weren't me, the boy said.

It were too.

Musta been Ol Clawtooth.

Clawtooth?

He's lives in a cave at the bottom of the quarry. Pa said he's a Muskie.

Wha's that?

A fish. A big'un with razor teeth.

There ain no such a thing.

There is. Pa reckins he musta got trapped here by a flood happened when he was a boy.

The girl kicked a splash of water back at him and the boy closed his eyes against its spray. When he opened them again she was a good three or four lengths away. He chased after her but she was too fast. She was ten lengths ahead of him by the time she'd reached the raft, ducking down under the water and coming up a moment later on the other side. The boy dove under, kicking hard and running his fingers along the raft's centre beam as he passed beneath it. On the far side, he saw her toes dangling just above the surface. He opened his mouth, about to have a go at them, then thought better of it. Twisting onto his back, he thrust his hands up, grabbing hold of the top edge of the raft and pulling himself out of the water with the guile of an otter.

The girl was lying on her belly, water beading off the subtle curve of her spine. He sat beside her, slicking his hair back and shaking its wet off with a flick of his hand.

You shore are hell in water, he said.

Use'n to be I lived by a lake.

That right?

Couldna hardly see the other side from the shore. Every spring since I can member, I'da swim across it. When I'd git to the other side, I'da swim back. My pa thought I was crazy.

Sounds it.

He kicked idly at the water and looked down at the girl's toes.

Where's he at now?

Who?

Yer pa.

Kilt, she said then groaned. Gawd, I keep fergittin.

About yer pa?

No, what I got inside.

Whadya mean?

A baby.

How's that?

Ya don't know where babies come from?

He blushed.

Course I do, I mean—

I gotta roll over.

I ain goin to stop ya.

Close yer eyes. Go on.

He did.

They're closed.

He could hear her turning over.

You can lay down now, she said.

The boy lowered himself onto his back.

Can I open ma eyes?

As long as ya keep em to yerself.

I will.

You betta.

The boy opened his eyes. The sun was directly above him. He turned from its glare so that he was facing the girl.

Wha'd I tell ya?

I cain't see nothin but yer face and I already seen that plentya times.

The boy smiled, trying to draw her into his good mood but her expression scrunched as if she'd felt a sudden pain. Out of the corner of his vision he could just see her arm crimp as she brought her hand to her belly.

Ya really got a baby in there? he asked.

Give me yer hand, ya don't believe me.

He held it out to her. She took it and drew it down and placed it firmly over the slight bulge in her stomach.

Ya feel it?

I don't feel nothin.

Well, tain't moving yet.

In the next moment he felt himself inflating against his belly. He sat up, covering his shame with a cupped hand.

When he looked back at the girl, she was rolling her eyes.

Gawd, she said, put that thang away.

I n the early evening, they cooked the grouse and after they'd eaten, they sat by the fire and the boy told her the story of Achaan.

Ya reckin tha's true? she asked when he was done.

As true as any story, I reckin.

Dya know any more?

Stories?

Yeah.

A few.

I'da shore like to hear another.

He told her a few of the ones his father had told him and then, as the first pinpricks of light were poking through the sky's blue, he lay on his back and told her a new one, about a girl who, long ago, had gone swimming amongst the stars and had lost her way.

You jus made that up, she said.

I din't. If ya look real hard ya can still see her tryin to swim home. Look, there she is now.

That's jus a fallin star. A seen a hun'ed of them.

Tain't. It's her.

Ya cain't swim in the sky.

Shore ya can. The sky's jus a big ol lake.

Wheredya hear that?

Everybody knows. The sky's made of water. Wheredya think the rains come from?

She laughed a staccato burst, sharp and shrill.

Tha's jus silly, she said. Rain comes from clouds.

H e'd gone to forage for more tinder. He was on his way back, dragging a cedar bough up the slope under light of a full moon. The girl was standing at the top of the ridge and

Sky was standing at attention beside her. He heard the dog growl and dropped the branch by the firepit, taking his time as he climbed the rise though his legs were urging him towards haste. When he reached them, the hair was bristling along Sky's back. He growled again and the boy peered out into the forest's dark beyond the Eleven.

A quarter the distance to the red fringe on the horizon, an orange patch simmered within the trees and there were distant specks of light, like ants on fire, marching in a line away from it.

Whadya reckin that is? he said.

It's them.

Who's that?

Them's that comin.

They watched the specks draw closer. When they'd almost made it to the Eleven the girl asked, How many arrows ya got?

A dozen, maybe.

Best go fetch em.

He found his bow and quiver beside the firepit. Slinging them over his shoulder, he chased her down the northeastern slope and into the forest.

Ya wan tell me what's goin on? he said when they'd reached the ferns.

She did not look back and the boy stopped, watching the thrust of her shadow as she plunged into the field.

He caught up to her at the oak tree, this time grabbing her arm and spinning her around. The smell of rotting meat from the three bodies had turned the air foul.

Who's comin?

She pulled against his grip, her head turning, her eyes sweeping past the house, straining towards the bank of trees hiding the river.

Is it the one's kilt yer pa?

She nodded.

What they mean to do when they git here?

Whadya think?

We ought'n warn the others.

There ain't time.

Shore there is.

Go on then, if ya want.

Shaking his head, kicking at the dirt, the stench of death twisting his belly.

When he looked up again, she'd turned back to the trees on the far side of the yard and he turned too. A distant thrumming rose against the cricketsong. Sky growled and his ears flattened against his neck.

Wha's that? the boy whispered.

Shhh.

They listened. The thrumming grew louder and a lone speck of light appeared, flickering through the trees.

Stay here, she said starting off towards it.

Wait.

He moved to pursue.

Ya want to live, she called back at him, ya'll stay there.

What about you?

I'ma be fine, if'n ya just do like I tol ya.

He watched the shadows swallow her and watched the light stutter to a halt beyond the trees and start again, moving up through the evergreens.

The thrumming rose in a thunderous swell and the girl stopped, maybe twenty paces from the treeline. The boy could now see that the speck of light was coming from a torch. It wove in and amongst the pillared trunks of jack pines and brushed against the low hanging branches of other firs, the dried needles flaring against their touch, sending sudden showers of sparks scattering skywards. When the torchbearer came into the clearing, whoever it was paused — to what end the boy could not fathom beyond the sudden acceleration of his heart.

Beneath the flames' wild glow he could see that the person holding the torch had a shaved scalp and elsewise was pale and thin and shorter than him by a head. Beside him were two others. Barely enough light shone upon these for him to discern anything except that they were smaller still and that they were holding each other's hands.

They's children, he thought, unsure of what to make of that.

The thrumming faded and was lost again to the cricketsong.

Now the girl was striding forward, waving her hand above her head as if in welcome.

Hey there, she called. Her voice was buoyant and joyful — a tone unlike any he had heard from her before, though it had about it a practiced air, like a daughter imitating her mother.

Why'n you'ns jus kids, she said coming astride of them. What y'alls doin out here alone? These woods is dangerous. Where's yer parents? Ya lost? Whassa matter, can't ya spek?

He could see the children's heads swivelling, the younger ones turning to the older, the older one turning to look behind him.

Ya look half-starved, the girl said. Come on up to the house, we'll fetch ya somethin to eat.

She was reaching out to take the closest by the arm when at the perimeter of the torch's illumine there appeared a blotch of dark shag, moving swiftly towards her. She took a step back and the creature slowed. The boy could see that it was a dog. It was almost as tall as she was to the shoulder and covered with black fur threaded with lengths of white — sunbleached sticks maybe, or bones, that rattled at its approach. Its snout extended, sniffing at her neck. The boy's heart skipped a beat as the nub of its nose brushed against her cheek. Its lips pulled back, emitting a low growl that the boy could feel in the hackles rising along the back of his neck.

Sky let out a snarl and the boy reached for him but he was already away.

Sky! he cried out, threading an arrow onto his bow as he chased after him.

He saw the black dog tear out from behind the girl, its ears flattened against its crown, its body hunkered low, the rattle of bones sounding a death knell as it loped towards Sky. The boy took a running bead on it and released but the arrow went wide. He was just notching another when he saw a second dog surging past the girl. She spun round, tracking it, and swung down, the blade in her hand glinting orange in the torchlight. She struck it on its rear and it skewed wildly away from her, though the blow hardly slowed its pursuit. And then there was another dog emerging out of the boy's periphery, racing on a hard line towards Sky. The boy took aim and fired just as it leapt. It was too dark to see if his mark was true. He watched, breathless, as the dog tackled the hound, Sky yelping as he was devoured into its tumble. Then the other was soaring over the two of them, charging hell-bent on the boy.

Not a moment left to breathe, nor to think about Sky, lying maybe dead on the ground. Not a moment but to find the black well wallowed in one side of the dog's head and to feel the arrow's wind against his arm as he released. Now diving sideways, the thing barrelling full bore into him, knocking him off his feet. The world spinning upside down. The wind wrenching from his chest as he landed on his back. Gasping. His hands empty, his bow gone. Rolling onto his belly and clawing at the ground as if he were in danger of falling off it. Shaking his head. A pain in his chest. He couldn't breathe. Pushing up onto his knees he flailed out wildly, groping for his bow. One of his hands felt its curve and he snatched it up and drew the arrow from the dead dog's eye.

Sky, he gasped as he fit it on the bow. He saw his hound's head pop up above the scrub and then heard the wounded dog snarling.

Watch out, he yelled, they's still another.

He started forward, his steps measured, his breaths coming back to him as a stuttered wheeze. He cast a fevered glance at the girl. She was now holding the torch and the boy was at a loss to explain what she was doing. The older boy was nowhere to be seen and she was advancing on the two youngers, her knife raised above her head. Within the torch's glow he could see they were still holding hands and looking up at the girl.

Were their faces marked with the same terror that had seized his heart?

He could not tell.

No! he screamed as she drove the blade down into the top of the closest child's head. The boy saw his body stiffen, saw his hand fall away from the other's, saw the spurt of blood as she drew the knife out, saw his little body sag.

He was running now, screaming, No!, as if words could still hold any power in a world such as this.

No. Stop!

She slashed at the last child and caught him in the neck. A smile opened up beneath his chin and his head leaned back same as if it had been on a hinge. As he toppled the girl turned back to the boy, the torchlight dancing about her face and glinting in her eyes, making her look crazed. The knife dropped from her hand and she turned, walking slow and deliberate into the woods.

The boy could hear Sky barking, faint, like something he was remembering from a dream, growing louder now, drawing him towards wakefulness. Turning, two rows of teeth burst out, snapping at him from the grass. He reeled backwards and then Sky was there chomping down hard on the creature's foreleg.

The black dog swung its head round, biting at Sky's ear, and the boy released the arrow. It struck just above the nape of its neck. The animal died without a sound and the boy retrieved his arrow then turned towards the forest, finding the speck of light within its fold almost immediately.

He charged off towards it, Sky sprinting ahead. The dog had just made the treeline when the boy heard the girl scream. Sky darted under a cedar tree and the boy pushed his legs faster. The bodies of the three boys lay in a line on the ground. In the dark, they might just as well have been sleeping. He leapt over them and plunged into the forest. Branches lashed against his face. He closed his eyes against their sting and swept his hand in front of him. When he was clear, his eyes opened to a blur of light not ten paces away.

The torch lay on the ground and within its glow the sight of something outside of his reckoning. It was huge beyond the limits of man though it stood erect and had a man's legs and arms and head. It was naked to the waist, and wore what, at first glance, appeared to be a suit of bones. Its face was similarly adorned, though the bones there were clearly pierced through its flesh. Its bald scalp was painted red. If his father had stood there in his place he might have called it a ghoul though his mother most surely would have named it daemon. Whatever it was, it held the girl with one hand clamped around her arm while its other hand was raised, fending off Sky, the dog's jaws latched onto its forearm. It lifted the dog off the ground and with a snap of its arm flung it, caterwauling into the pitch. The boy shot the thing through the eye. It staggered back and disappeared into the dark.

What the hell was that? he said, threading another arrow in the bow.

The girl was bending for the torch. She looked up and her eyes flared.

Behind you!

The boy spun. Another of the daemons was striding towards him, a barbed shaft of steel raised above its head. The boy startled backwards, raising the bow. His feet gave out from under him, toppling him onto his rear, his finger jarring loose from the string, releasing the arrow. He saw its feathered tuft disappear just above the daemon's shoulder. He tried to scuttle backwards but he was wedged between the roots that had tripped him up, not that a few inches would have done him any good. The thing was already upon him, the blade in its hand devouring the space between.

Ma! the boy cried out.

Was he calling to her in the afterlife so that she would be there to greet him? Or did something deep inside merely conjure her name so that she would be the last thought on his mind when he met his end? Or maybe it was just that he was still a boy, scared beyond all pretence of being a man.

He'd never be able say beyond that he'd cried out, Ma!, and that her face had appeared before him, the evening sun setting on her cheeks, the faintest impression of a smile parting her lips, her eyes closed and her head thrown back against the cedar rail chair — glorin in the day.

Ma! he cried out as the blade came down.

In the next instant Sky was leaping and clamping onto the daemon's arm. The blade veered left, gnashing into the hard tangle of roots, and the boy felt Sky's nails digging into his legs as he scrambled to keep hold of the thing's wrist. Its other hand seized the dog by the scruff and jerked him backwards, tearing his teeth from its arm in a welter of blood and swinging the hound as if he were as light as a pillow. The dog's body buckled against a tree with a pinched yelp and the crack of bones.

The boy screamed, Sky!, and reached for his quiver, drawing out an arrow, lacing it and firing. It struck the thing in its ear, mottled into the ghastly approximation of a mouth by a half-dozen teeth. The thing bolted upright, swatting at the shaft like it was a fly, took two stuttered steps sideways and fell. The boy was already on his feet, aiming at a shadow merging into the shape of a man, shooting at it and stringing another arrow and loosing that too.

He fired another and another and another.

When he reached for his quiver and found it empty he took the arrow from the daemon's ear, shot that and then strode forward stripping arrows from the bodies of the dead, fanned in a circle around where the girl stood, holding the torch aloft, the flames fanning against her ecstasy, searing her face into a mask, delirious with glee.

Finally, the shadows ceased in their transformations, becoming again the trunks of trees and the nettle of branches and low-lying shrubs, the interweave of grapevines between. He held his last arrow in guard against anything yet to come. He was drenched in sweat and blood. There was the sting of salt in his eyes. Tendrils of snot clung to his lips. Gasping through palsied breaths and waiting for any sign of movement, but there was none beyond a subtle hitch to the light evanescent behind him. He wiped his mouth on his sleeve and turned to where she had once stood. There was only the torch lying on the ground.

The fire was spreading to the surrounding leaves and the boy ran to it, picking it up and stamping out the flames it had left behind. When they were but sparks, he held up the torch, scouring the dark for any sign of where she had gone.

A faint whimper called to him and he looked to where Sky lay halfways bent around the base of the Jack pine, his chest heaving. He tried to raise his head when his master approached but couldn't manage more than to roll his eyes up at the boy as he knelt. Wedging the torch into the tree's roots, he slid his hands underneath Sky's haunches, pried him from the ground and stood. The dog drooped between his arms like a bag half-filled with sand.

He let out one last whine and then went still.

Oh, Sky.

D awn found him sitting under the spruce tree beside his grandfather's firepit with Sky's head in his lap.

With the sun creeping into their haven of shade, the boy eased out from under his dog and set Sky's head on the cushion of moss.

He spent the morning trolling along the river looking for her tracks and finding only those of the ones he had slain. He came back to the quarry just as the sun had reached its peak. He checked the perch and then walked down the slope to the spruce tree. Sky was as he'd left him, though he seemed flatter than he remembered and a shade greyer. His eyes were open, their globes clouded and rolled upwards so that the boy could not tell of their blue.

Crouching beside him, he took up one of his ears. He flopped it backwards over the dog's eyes and ran his hand along the loose folds of skin billowed over his neck. He felt warm and gave off a faint scent of decay. Blue-hooded flies scattered at his touch. He stood again.

What say we git ya outta the sun, ol boy?

L ate in the afternoon, the boy broke through the corridor of pines. Sky was slumped over his shoulder, his whole body aching under his weight. Grasshoppers battered his legs and the bleat of goats sounded from under the pasture's shade tree. All the boy could see of the herd was Spook staring back at him, her tail swishing against the flies. After a hundred or so paces, the anthill appeared like some ancient ruin turning to sand. He set Sky down beside it and stood, stretching the strain out of his back and watching the ants.

A shadow passed over him and he craned his head towards the sky. Two vultures circled in patient loops against its blue.

He walked to the fence and climbed over, traversing his mother's garden until he came to the side of his father's workshop where a shovel hung from a peg on the wall. He could hear the faint strains of music from within and his father's voice, muffled, humming to its melody.

He listened until the song had ended then took up the spade and walked back into the field. He had just pitched its blade into the ground for the first time when the brood of hounds found him. They did not make a sound as they swirled about, tails low, each one getting in a touch and then sniffing around Sky's body and finally settling into the tall grass, panting against the heat. Blue alone whimpered, nosing his father's cheek. He licked at a spot on Sky's belly where one of his ribs had punctured the skin then looked up at the boy with confused eyes as if there was some other truth beyond the smell of death and the taste of blood in his mouth.

The boy dug to his waist. When there wasn't room enough in the hole to raise the shovel anymore, he discarded it and dug with his hands. Blisters stung against the sand, the grains filling pockets in the weltering skin.

Sometime later he heard a woman's voice calling out, Sup's on!

It sounded just like his mother and for a moment he thought he must have imagined it before he remembered that there were other women here now.

He dug on until he could no longer bend his fingers and then climbed out of the hole. He pushed Sky in and reached for the shovel. His hands ached such that he could not grip it and resorted to using his feet to push the red and orange sand from the pile into the grave. When he was done he crouched at the grave's edge, his head lowered, thinking of his father when he'd buried Blue, all those years before.

He was the only damn dog I ever knew et apples, he'd said. Eat himself sick if you'da let him. Who ever heard of a dog that et apples?

It had seemed to the boy then, as it did now, the perfect thing to say and he searched his memory for something to give birth to words of equal merit.

Finally he just said, You was a good dog, Sky. I couldna ast for betta. His voice breaking at the end, tears surprising him and tracing cold lines down his cheeks.

He stayed crouched in vigil there until he felt the first prick of a mosquito on his neck. The sun was just setting. The vultures had departed but there was a red dot flittering above the barn. He studied it, thinking it looked familiar and trying to figure out why that was.

Why, it's yer ol kite, he told himself at last.

I haven't seen that in years.

The red dot swooped towards him, growing larger — a red diamond with a train of smaller diamonds trailing behind. It caught a downdraft, diving towards the field, its string drifting loose, and vanished into the tall grass. A moment later, the three boys appeared climbing up onto the fence. The line was attached to an old fishing rod and the youngest boy was winding its handle. The string grew taut and he jerked at it but the kite was stuck fast.

Hold up, hold up, the boy yelled to him as he strode towards it. Ya'll wreck it.

He followed the string to where the kite was mired in a thistle patch. He lifted it gently and held it up over his head.

Reel it in, he called out.

The tallest of the three made to reach for the rod but the youngest boy wouldn't let it go. It looked like there was going to be a fight over it and the boy called out, Well one of ya reel it in. Ma arms are gittin tired.

The older one relented and the younger began winding the handle. The string sprung loose from the field grass and the boy followed it in inches all the way to the fence. When he got there, the eldest was staring at him with narrowed eyes, his ghoulish mask making the boy turn away. He handed the kite to the one holding the rod. The youngest boy jumped down off the rail and took off at a gleeful run, the two older ones chasing after him. The kite bounced in furious tumult along the ground just out of their reach.

The dogs wormed under the fence and all of them except Blue joined the pursuit. He waited for the boy to climb to his side and then set off at a light canter towards the house.

The taller of the young men was scratching something into the workshop's door. As he passed him by, the boy saw it was a ring of stick figures, holding hands and staring up at a globe cut into squares, the space between them bespeckled into what looked like a child's drawing of a starry night.

The other young man was sitting cross-legged on the porch plucking at the top string of his guitar, bending it with his finger and cocking his head at the way the tone changed, then plucking the string again.

The boy's father sat in the cedar rail chair beside him, the thin woman nestled in his lap. He was whispering something in her ear and she was giggling and slapping him on his arm.

You're the devil alright, the boy heard her say as he came to the porch. I knew it the first time I saw you.

Blue padded up the stairs and brushed his nose against his master's hand. The boy's father looked up and saw his son standing there at the bottom of the steps.

He was filthy beyond remembrance. His hands like they'd been dipped in dirt, channels traced in the mud of his face that could only have come from tears, blood spackled over his clothes.

Yer back, the man said.

I am.

Ya hungry?

The boy nodded. His father's hand was resting on the woman's belly, his fingers tapping gently against the warp of one of his mother's dresses. He couldn't take his eyes off of it.

Adele had her baby lass night, his father said. Reed here and Silk made a right feast to celebrate. We din't hardly put a dent in haffa it.

I'll fetch him a plate.

The woman pushed herself up and took her cane from where it was hooked over the back of the chair. The boy's father reached after her hand and she let her fingers trail through his as she hobbled into the kitchen.

I'ma git warsht up, the boy said, starting for the well.

There'll be a plate waitin on ya.

Good.

When he'd reached the well, he primed the lever. When the water was flowing fast and clear, he drank deeply from its spout then filled the bucket they kept there and submerged his hands in it. The cold came as a relief to their sore. He held them there until he felt the day's heat leach the chill from the water and stripped to his naturals. He doused himself with the bucket, filled another and doused himself with that too.

He heard the woman, the one his father had called Reed,

hollering, Time for bed. Come on now. Don't make me tell you twice.

As he walked back to the porch pulling on his shirt, the three boys were running towards the house, the eldest of them carrying the kite wedged under his arm and chewing on a knot tangled in its string. They skirted past Reed standing at the top of the steps, leaning on her cane and holding a plate above their bustle. It was loaded with a quarter chicken and potatoes and squash and carrots, two chunks of cornbread balanced on top, gravy smothering all of it. His father was standing beside her. When the boys had passed into the kitchen, she lowered the plate and the man plucked a piece of loose skin from the drumstick. Reed slapped his hand, chiding him softly as the boy mounted the steps.

There's more if you want it, Reed said handing the plate over.

This'ns plenty.

Just give me a holler if it's not.

Turning to the man, she offered him a clipped smile and walked into the house. The man watched after her until she was at the stairs, herding the kids towards bed. He then took his pipe from his pocket and packed it with tobacco from the pouch on his belt. Striking a flint to it, he drew heavy and turned to his son. He'd hardly touched his plate.

Whyn't ya sit down? the man said. Ya look bout fixed to fall over.

The boy nodded and shuffled past. He sat in the cedar rail chair and stared down at his food as if he couldn't fathom what he was supposed to do with it. Finally he picked a carrot from the edge and bit into it, chewing it to mush.

Reed's one helluva cook, ain she?

It's good a'right.

Ya don't eat all of it, she goin be mighty sore.

I'll try.

Ya best.

The dogs padded up the steps and settled on the porch. The man counted them off and turned towards the yard as if he was expecting another.

Where's Sky? he said.

Dead.

The boy was swallowing a piece of chicken and it got caught in his throat. He coughed.

Tha's too bad. He was a good dog. Ya couldna ast for betta.

I tol him.

Ya bury him over by that anthill?

I did.

Ya always said ya would.

The man smoked and watched his son eat. When there was nothing but ash left in the pipe, he made to put it away, reconsidered and packed it again. His son was just finishing his plate, sopping up the last of the gravy with a few crumbs of cornbread.

Reed tol me bout that girl, he said when the boy was licking his fingers. Figured ya'd set out to find her.

I did.

So where's she at?

The boy told him. His father interrupted the telling but once, when the boy had come to the part about how the girl had killed the children.

Gawd, I— But he couldn't think of what to say to make sense out of it.

They looked jus like the three I brought back, the boy said.

The children?

They was markt up the same.

That right?

The boy nodded.

Ya reckin there might be more?

I'da bet the devil on it.

The man stared out into the yard, puffing on his pipe.

Their tongues, he said after a while and shook his head.

Whatta bout em?

They's cut out. Hard to believe . . . Who coulda done such a thing?

I guess you'da haffta ave seen em.

And you did?

The boy nodded.

Well go on, then.

When the boy had finished telling the rest, his father's pipe had long gone out.

Ya kilt em all, the man said. Jus like that?

Weren't no other choice.

The man looked down at his son but found he could not meet the boy's eyes.

And then she jus lit out?

I don't understand it.

His father nodded like maybe he did.

You goin after her?

Whadya think?

You'll need a dog. I reckin Spark's got the best nose of the bunch.

Blue, the boy said.

His father chewed his lip and snuck a rueful glance at his son out of the corner of his eye.

He's in the house. I'll have a spek with him. You need arythin else?

We got ary hardboileds? the boy said.

I reckin we got a few. I'll fetch em for ya.

The man turned and walked to the door. Just inside the

threshold he stopped and turned back again. The boy was standing up from the chair.

I ain't leavin without them eggs, he said, if'n tha's what yer thinkin.

The man smiled and walked into the kitchen.

As the boy waited for him to return, he watched the young man scratching at the workshop. The barn door clattered shut and the other walked over. He stood behind him shaking his head and the boy turned to the thermometer hung from the porch's post. The nail had dipped just below thirty. He was pinging it when his father came back with the eggs hammocked in his shirt. Blue was padding along behind him.

I had a spek with him. He said he'd go wit ya. As long as ya bring him back.

The boy bent and scratched the dog behind the ears and let him lick his face.

I shun't be more'n a few days, he said. A week at the most.

Whadya want to do with these eggs?

I had ma's old satchel. He looked around. I must ave left it up at the anthill. Give em here then, they's plenty room in ma pockets.

He passed them over and the boy fed them into his pants.

There arythin else ya need?

Y'already ast.

I guess I did.

A strained cry rang out and the man turned towards the one he'd called Adele. She was at the door, cradling her newborn in a quilt. When the man set eyes upon her, he smiled and strode towards them.

Well, there she is, he said leaning over and blowing air at the baby's face, crinkling her nose and stemming her cry. Elsa, you shore is a beauty.

I want to show her the light, Adele said.

Go on out then. I'll be with ya presently.

The house emptied behind her, Silk coming first, cradling her own baby, then the three boys and finally Reed.

Where's Gregor? the man asked her.

He's down for the night. I'm going to let him sleep.

Reed reached out and ran her fingers down the man's arm, trailing them over his hand and casting the boy a shy look as she passed.

I'll see ya in a moment.

He watched her limp across the yard. When she came to the workshop door, the taller of the young men was holding it open and the others were threading past. Reed entered last, pausing a moment to look over her shoulder at the boy and his father.

She's waitin on ya, the boy said.

The man started down the stairs and stopped.

You could join us.

I ought'n git a move on.

Won't be but an hour.

She's out there all alone.

A'right then.

Come on, Blue.

The boy started across the yard. The dog made to follow then stopped and looked to his master.

Go on, the man told him.

Blue hurried to catch up, settling into a slow trot as he came alongside. When they'd reached the pasture gate the boy looked back at the porch but it was empty.

A noise rose above the whine of cicadas. It sounded almost like a distant thrumming and the boy held his breath, listening. After a moment, it broke into the low rumble of thunder.

Maybe, he thought as he stepped into the field, the rains is jus come early this year.

with thanks to

dave, for the idea
jack, for lunch
   &
nick, for his kitchen table

and to

john, stephen, clifford, luke
nicholas, justin, michael
david, erin, emily, laura
susan, jennifer, crissy, jenna
wayland, louis, masoud, sahar
mom, rod, guy, ellen, drake
and, of course, mr. king.